Making the Play

By T. J. Kline

Hidden Falls
Making the Play

Healing Harts Novels
Heart's Desire
Taking Heart
Close to Heart
Wild at Heart
Change of Heart

Rodeo Novels
Rodeo Queen
The Cowboy and the Angel
Learning the Ropes
Runaway Cowboy

Making the Play

A HIDDEN FALLS NOVEL

T. J. KLINE

AVONIMPULSE
An Imprint of HarperCollins*Publishers*

Excerpt from *This Earl is on Fire* copyright © 2016 by Vivienne Lorret.
Excerpt from *Torch* copyright © 2016 by Karen Erickson.
Excerpt from *Hero of Mine* copyright © 2016 by Codi Gary.

EPub Edition SEPTEMBER 2016 ISBN: 9780062651808
Print Edition ISBN: 9780062651815

Avon, Avon Impulse, and the Avon Impulse logo are trademarks of HarperCollins Publishers.

10 9 8 7 6 5 4 3 2 1

For the man who makes me smile and reminds me that there are always second chances. I love you.

Chapter One

BETHANY MILLS WANTED to give in to the normally angelic cherub face in front of her that was now scrunched in anger. "Because we aren't playing football at recess today. I already explained that to you."

Like most six-year-olds, her son, James, was prone to throw temper tantrums when he didn't get his way. Unlike other kids his age, James would refuse to say anything verbally. Instead, his fingers flew in a blur of American Sign Language, letting her know just how angry he was at her explanation. Although he was perfectly capable of speaking, thanks to the cochlear implants her ex-husband's medical insurance had provided before James' first birthday, Bethany's son continued to fall back on signing when he was angry. She understood it was due to the fact that he stuttered and had a hard time pronouncing his words when he was emotional, but she was trying to teach him to continue to use both. Life wasn't easy and, in spite of what many saw as a disability, she couldn't allow her son to take the path of least resistance. It was a painful truth she'd been forced to face early on when her husband ran out on both of them twelve months after James' diagnosis at two months old, just before serving her with divorce papers.

Life as a single mother was hard enough. Life as a single mother at twenty to a child with a disability and no child support would have been impossible if not for her parents' stepping in and allowing her to move back in until she could finish college and earn her teaching degree.

"Not today, James," she reiterated. "The other kids are playing T-ball. You should go ask if you can play too."

She watched as her son pursed his lips and balled his fists before stomping across the playground to pout near the swings. Bethany sighed loudly, knowing this was something every child went through, that every *parent* went through, but wondering if it would ever get easier. She couldn't give in to James' demand but she couldn't stand the thought of her son being angry at her all day either. Not to mention, it would only cause trouble when they returned to the classroom after recess. There were definite drawbacks to being her son's kindergarten teacher.

She traced his steps to the swings, trying not to smile when she saw him turn his back on her as he continued to peek over his shoulder to see if she would come to him. Bethany squatted down beside him, her peasant skirt billowing around her, and waited for him to turn and face her.

"James, if you go play ball with the other kids, we'll go to the park after school today." She signed as she spoke. His blue eyes sparkled at the thought but he paused.

"Ice cream too?" This time he spoke and she let the smile curve her lips. *The little stinker thought he was conning her.*

"Yes, I think we can get ice cream too, but only if you are able to read all your sight words for Ms. Julie."

At least, she prayed that's what her teacher's aide had planned for the kids today. Julie was indispensable in her classroom after lunch, when most of the kids were hyper beyond belief, and she hoped they weren't going to have to change the lesson plans again today to accommodate the kids' activity level. Bethany couldn't help but wonder if her students' parents were feeding their kids straight sugar for lunch.

James pursed his lips and looked toward the sky. It was his "thinking" look and it never failed to make her want to hug him. Before she could, he threw his arms around her neck and ran off to meet up with the group of kids playing on the open lawn. Bethany stood and sighed again just as James stopped to get her attention.

I want chocolate, he signed.

She nodded and signed her approval as he spun on his heel and hurried toward the other kids. Her baby was growing up far too quickly for her liking.

She heard the quiet chuckle from behind her as Steven Carter, the other kindergarten teacher at Hidden Falls Elementary walked toward her. "I don't know how you do it," he said with a shake of his head.

"Do what?"

"Teach him just like the other kids."

Bethany felt herself bristle. She'd dealt with people singling James out because of his disability for years. It never failed to make the mama bear in her rise to the surface. "I'll have you know, James is just as bright as any *normal* child, Mr. Carter. In fact, he's already reading at a second-grade level. Just because he has implants to help him hear doesn't make him stupid."

The other teacher took a step back, his eyes widening. "Uh, that's not what I meant," he said, holding his hands up in front of him. "I just meant that it's hard enough to keep twenty kids under control in the classroom and keep my mind on what I'm teaching without trying to sign at the same time."

"Oh!" Bethany felt the blush rise up her neck and cheeks at the way she'd immediately become defensive. "I'm sorry, I just . . ."

"No, I shouldn't have said it that way." He moved to stand at her side, slipping his hands into the pockets of his slacks and watched the kids play on the field. "Truce?"

She ducked her head, embarrassed to have jumped to conclusions. "Yes. I *am* sorry though. I have a tendency to be a bit overprotective."

He shot her a sideways glance. "And I have a tendency to speak before I think," he admitted. "Maybe I could make it up to you over coffee?" He cleared his throat nervously. "Or dinner?"

Bethany felt blindsided. She hadn't expected him to ask her out. She'd heard several of the other women talking about the new teacher in the break room, swooning over his tall, lean physique and stormy gray eyes, but she thought it strange to want to date someone you worked with. What if it didn't go well? What if it did? It was just too much drama either way for the workplace, especially when that workplace was as an elementary school in a town as small as Hidden Falls.

"Ah, I really appreciate the offer, Mr. Carter," she said, trying not to seem too callous. "But I don't think it would be a good idea."

She'd been out of the dating pool so long, the refusal slid easily from her lips without her having to struggle with what to say. It wasn't that she hadn't been asked out. She had, far too many times for her liking, but she wasn't about to introduce another man into her life, or James' life, only to be abandoned again. Her son would be forced to deal with enough adversity in his future. She didn't see the need to add an emotional tie to someone who wasn't likely to stick around. It was better that James knew her unconditional reassurance than suffer the added sting of rejection if that was something she had any control over. He'd been hurt enough. They *both* had.

"IS THIS REALLY what you dragged me out to the park for? To be your official stopwatch?" Jackson complained, rolling his eyes at his oldest brother. "You know Dad is going to jump all in my shit if he finds out I'm here with you instead of finishing that fence in the north pasture."

"It's barely one o'clock and I'm only doing some

sprints. When we get back, I'll help you with the fence until sundown, deal?"

Grant McQuaid glared at his brother, the youngest of the six of them. The last thing he needed right now were any more arguments. His father had already been more than willing to give his two cents about Grant's plans to return to professional football. He didn't care how many people tried to convince him to the contrary, he was going to be the guy who proved the doctors wrong. He couldn't be finished at thirty. He *wouldn't* be.

"Fine," Jackson agreed with a sigh. "You ready or what?" Jackson rolled his eyes as Grant swung his arms in large circles, loosening up. Grant then kicked his heels toward his butt before making a few quick tuck jumps into the air. Tired of waiting, Jackson said, "Any day, bro."

Grant ignored him. Just because he felt great didn't mean he was about to let his brother's impatience risk an injury. He jerked a knee toward his chest, lifting the opposite arm, mimicking the movement of a sprint before repeating it several times on the other side. Moving into position, he bounced in place to warm his joints then settled himself and looked out over the grass to where he'd marked a spot with an orange cone.

"Are you ready, now?" His brother laughed, shaking his head.

Grant knew his brothers didn't understand the seriousness with which he took his workouts, but they didn't have to. He did. This was business. This was his job and he worked harder than any other running back in professional football. He had to if he wanted to see another season.

Grant took a deep breath and relaxed the tension he felt building in his shoulders, knowing it would only slow him. One focus—this forty-yard sprint. One goal—faster than his best time, 4.54 seconds. He took a deep breath, relaxing his face.

"Ready."

"And . . . Go!" Jackson yelled.

Grant pushed off, letting his back leg propel him forward, his arms pumping as the breeze blew from behind. He felt his limbs stretch and flex, his feet pounding against the grass, the cleats digging into the soft earth. And then he was at the cone, making a sharp right turn. He slowed to a jog before stopping and looking back at Jackson.

"Five point zero seven," he called.

"Damn it!"

That was never going to be good enough. There were too many younger men trying to take his place, too many uninjured players without big contracts willing to do it for less money. He jogged back to the starting spot and settled himself into position.

"Again," he called, ignoring his brother's frown.

"Are you s—"

"Again," Grant insisted, not even letting Jackson question his decision.

Grant repeated the sprint seven more times but couldn't get under a five-second run. As much as it frustrated him, continuing would just break down his body and make him more prone to re-injury. It was better to come back out in a couple of days and try again. Until then, they might as well have some fun before heading back to the ranch. The fence could wait for another thirty minutes.

Grant did a few ballistic stretches and picked up the football he'd brought along with him, tossing it toward Jackson, knowing his brother wouldn't turn down a quick game.

"How's that arm of yours?"

Jackson shrugged. "I guess that depends on your point of reference. I'm no Miles."

He meant Aaron Miles, the starting quarterback for the Mustangs and the guy who'd rallied the team, taking them to the playoffs last year. The same game where Grant had sustained his last concussion, the one that might have ended his career. He crushed the thought before it sank in. He was *going* to play this season, there was no room for doubt.

"Let's see what you've got." He jogged down field from Jackson, effortlessly catching the ball. Grant had been a decent receiver in high school but his size had made the transition to running back a no-brainer in college.

The two of them played catch for the a few hours while Grant tried to ignore the people beginning to crowd under several of the shade trees nearby, watching. It wasn't unusual to see at training camp but here, in his hometown, he hated being a spectacle. He couldn't walk down the street without someone pointing, staring or asking for an autograph. Here he just wanted to be Grant, not Grant McQuaid, starting running back for the Memphis Mustangs.

"Last one," Jackson called, lobbing the ball down the field for a Hail Mary pass.

Grant went long, sprinting to make the catch. He was damned if he was going to look like a fool with this many people watching. It wasn't until the last second he heard the child's yell and the woman's voice calling for him to "Look out!"

"I've got it!" the boy yelled as he reached into the sky, a broad grin plastered across his face.

Grant glanced away from the ball in time to see the little boy run directly into his path.

BETHANY COULDN'T WATCH. She'd looked away from James for two seconds to find a napkin in her purse to wipe away the ice cream dripping over his hands, and the next thing she knew, she was chasing after him as he ran directly into the path of the two men playing catch. She should have known better than to believe James would sit still when someone was playing football.

The man who'd gone out for the pass barely flinched before he leapt over her son's head as if he was no more than a small hurdle, clearing James' outstretched hands by at least six inches.

Holy crap!

James might be small for his age but that was incredible, to say the least. A few of the other spectators agreed and began to applaud as the man caught the ball and jogged back toward James, tossing it to him gently as he came close. She watched him go to one knee in front of

James and place a massive hand on his shoulder. She tried to fight down the overprotective instinct rising up in her. He obviously wasn't going to hurt James after he'd just, miraculously, avoiding crashing into him. She caught up to where the pair chatted like old friends.

"I'm so sorry." She gasped for breath, cursing the sandals she'd worn and her lack of aerobic exercise since moving to town. "I looked away and he'd taken off." She squatted down to James and grasped his shoulders. "What in the world were you thinking? You could have been hurt, badly. If this man hadn't seen you—"

"It's no problem, ma'am. He's just keeping me on my toes and prepared for anything." He smiled at James and gave him a wink before turning his deep chocolate brown gaze on her.

He rose slowly, unfolding his tall frame to tower above her, leaving her eye level with his bared, sweaty chest. Bethany felt her mouth go dry, unable to speak, even if she was able to get her brain functioning again, which it didn't seem inclined to do. The second man jogged over to them, laughing.

"Where've you been hiding those moves, Grant? Because I haven't seen that on the field in a long time."

His friend tossed him his t-shirt and he slipped it over his head before glaring at his partner, then turning back toward her. "I'm Grant McQuaid and this is my brother Jackson. Jackson, meet James and . . ." He let his words trail off expectantly.

"Oh, I'm Bethany," she filled in. At least with his shirt on again, she could breathe.

"Bethany," he repeated, as if testing the name on his lips. "That's pretty."

"You're on the Memphis Mustangs," James announced, excitedly. "Mom, he plays football for Grandpa's team." He set the football Grant had handed him at his feet and signed to her, his hands moving with lightning speed.

As soon as James pointed it out, she realized this was Grant McQuaid, star running back of the Mustangs and James' favorite player. Both men watched them curiously and she could read the questions in their faces. She signed to James to wait and let her speak for a moment before turning back to the pair of too-attractive men still standing in front of her.

"Mom?" Grant asked, arching a brow.

His brother laughed. "What were you, twelve, when you had him?"

Bethany crossed her arms over her chest defensively. She had always looked young for her age but if this was an attempt at starting a conversation, this guy sucked at it. "Not that it's any of your business but I was twenty."

"Sorry, you just don't look much older than twenty now."

Jackson nudged his brother but Grant glared at him and looked back at James. "When did he get his C.I.?"

She tipped her head to one side, surprised he knew anything about cochlear implants, let alone the abbreviation for them. "When he was an infant."

"I guess that explains why he can speak so clearly." Grant nodded. "So why go through the extra work to teach him to sign too?"

While she was touched by his acknowledgment of the hard work she and James had put in on his speech, she arched a brow, wondering what made this man feel he had the right to question the choices she'd made for her son. Just because he was some sort of star didn't make him entitled to answers about her parenting decisions. Before she could answer, Grant awkwardly signed *hello* and introduced himself to James in ASL. James face lit up with excitement.

"He knows how to sign, Mom," he whispered loudly.

"Yes," she agreed. "And he can hear you too."

James giggled at her and introduced himself to Grant in sign language. The irritation she'd felt a moment ago disappeared as her son's boyish laughter filled her ears. She had no idea how Grant knew ASL, or why, but neither mattered right now.

Thank you, she mouthed to him, her heart swelling with gratitude at the fact that Grant had gone out of his way to meet James on common ground.

Grant grinned. "I haven't had anyone to sign to in a long time."

Bethany ruffled James' hair before returning Grant's smile. "I admit I'm impressed you know any. Not many people do."

He shrugged. "I used to be better when I was volunteering at the children's hospital back in Memphis. I've gotten rusty."

"We can help," James chimed in. "Right, Mom?"

"Oh, um . . ."

James wasn't about to be deterred. "And you could teach me to be better at football."

Bethany felt the panic rising up in her. So far, she'd been able to confine her son's love of football to a safe, controlled version of catch with her. She knew it meant the world to him to meet his favorite player and, from the look of pleasure on his face, Grant McQuaid enjoyed spending time with his fans, but he couldn't possibly understand the precautions she needed to take with her son, especially where contact sports might be concerned.

"James, I'm sure Mr. McQuaid doesn't have time for that. He's an important part of the team. He'll be in training again soon and it takes a long time to learn to sign, remember?"

"Actually—" Grant began.

"We should probably get going," Jackson muttered to his brother, jerking his head toward the parking lot. "Gotta get a fence fixed. It was nice to meet you, Bethany. You too, James. Maybe next time we come out here, you can come play ball with us."

James immediately looked up at his mother. "Can I?"

"We'll see," she answered, humoring him as Jackson left the three of them and headed toward the parking lot. The two men were just being polite and didn't really mean it, but James was still too young to understand that.

"Yay!" James scrunched up his face, looking up, and a bright smile spread as he got an idea. "Then you could come to my house for dinner and call my Grandpa and tell him I played football with you."

A blush covered Bethany's cheeks. Her son didn't realize he was practically setting her up on a date. "James, I don't—"

Grant dropped his head back and laughed out loud. It was a warm, relaxed sound that reminded her of the afternoons she'd hung out in sweats, watching football with her Dad, or nights curled up with James, watching him sleep. Inviting, homey, comforting.

"Little man, you're on." Grant winked at her son. "I'll make you a deal. If you promise to help me practice my sign language, I'll take you guys out for pizza tonight. Your Grandpa can join us."

He turned his gaze toward Bethany, jerking her back to reality. He looked like he was waiting for her agreement, as if the idea that she might turn him down wasn't even an option. She stared at him, unsure where to begin—by flat out turning him down because of his assumption that she wouldn't or being honest and explaining she'd chosen not to date until James was older.

James broke in, filling in the moment of uncomfortable silence. "Grandpa doesn't live here. He lives at my old house in Tennessee."

The note of sadness in her son's voice made Bethany's heart ache and her throat close. He might have acclimated well to their move last summer but she knew he missed living with his Grandparents. It had been a big adjustment for the child to go from doting grandparents giving him attention twenty-four hours a day to only the two of them. For a child who had few close relationships he could trust in, tearing him away from two people who loved him had devastated her.

"Oh, I see." Grant squatted back to James' level. "Well, then we'll call him after we eat. What do you say?"

"Can we, Mom?" James clasped his hands together and turned his angel face up to hers, the way he did whenever he wanted something badly. "Please?"

"Yes, please?" Grant copied her son comically, but she didn't miss the way his eyes darkened, or the arrogant wink he gave her.

He obviously thought he could turn that deep brown gaze on her and charm her. He might be able to use his good looks and celebrity status to get his way with other women but, unfortunately for him, the only eyes that charmed her were her son's deep blue ones. She wasn't about to fawn over this man simply because he knew a little sign language and smiled at her.

"I don't think it's a good idea."

Grant's brow immediately furrowed and he looked back at James. She reached for her son's hand, forcing him to drop the football.

"We really need to get going. It was nice to meet you, Mr. McQuaid."

Even as she pulled James back toward the trees, she could feel him tugging against her hand, turning to look behind him. It wasn't fair for this man to use her son's hero worship to finagle a date and, while it hadn't been the first time a man tried, it still pissed her off that anyone would use a child that way, let alone hers.

James planted his feet and stopped. "Mom, please. Do you know who that is? He plays football for—"

She turned around and knelt down. "Baby, I know who he is, but I have some things to get ready for school tomorrow."

She was lying through her teeth, something she rarely did to James, but she couldn't explain to him why they couldn't go out for pizza. How was she supposed to tell a six-year-old that his hero was far too good-looking, that he made her stomach flutter in ways she hadn't remembered it ever twisting and twirling or that he had what her mother fondly called "bedroom eyes?" Just because she didn't date, didn't mean her libido was dead.

But since she couldn't say any of that to James, it was far easier to tell a little white lie.

Glancing up, she saw Grant jogging the short distance to catch up to them. "Bethany, look, I think you got the wrong impression." James' eyes swung toward Grant as he reached them and immediately lit up. Grant pressed the football into his small hands. "Would you hang on to this for me, big guy?"

"Yes," James answered, completely serious as he watched Grant move closer to her.

"I don't want you to think I go around asking pretty women and their sons out to dinner at the park all the time." Bethany tightened her jaw and crossed her arms, refusing to admit that was exactly what she suspected. He flashed her a smile. "As a matter of fact, I've never done this before."

She found that hard to believe. "While I appreciate the offer, Mr. McQuaid, I don't date."

"What's a date?" James asked. Bethany cursed the fact that they were even having this conversation around James and ignored her son's question.

Grant stood and shrugged. "Who said anything about a date? This will just be two guys talking about football in sign language, right, James?" Grant held his hand out for James to give him a low-five and her son obliged.

Bethany was having a hard time looking away from Grant's dark eyes and the entreaty she could see there. When she looked down at James, the pleading blue was even harder to deny. She knew how much this opportunity to spend time with his hero meant to James, regardless of how cocky Grant might be, but she didn't like the way he was going about this. Regardless, she could feel herself caving.

She took a step closer, moving between Grant and James so her son couldn't see her face or read her lips. "I'm sorry, Mr. McQuaid, but my son isn't some kind of toy for you to use to get a date." She pressed a finger to his chest. "No one is going to use him as an easy target."

"Whoa, wait a minute—" He took a step backward. "Now, I *know* we got off to a bad start." He looked at James, peeking at him from behind her skirt, then back at her. "Look, it's obvious James is a fan and I really was just looking for a way to hang out with him for a bit. It had nothing to do with you."

She arched a brow in disdain. "Right, because all football players enjoy hanging out with six-year-olds."

His eyes slid over her slowly, taking in every inch and she cursed the way her body responded, feeling heat travel the length of her spine into her legs. "Okay, maybe not *nothing* but not what you think either. I really *could* use the refresher with signing. I wasn't trying to use your kid to get a date. I swear." His eyes softened as he held up his last finger. "Pinkie promise?"

"Seriously?" What kind of man even *said* that out loud? "How old are you?"

"Pinkie promise," James interrupted, moving beside her and raising his hand to hook fingers with Grant.

Bethany sighed, realizing she'd just been overruled by her six-year-old. "Fine, but not dinner." Grant nodded and James mimicked the movement seriously. "Tomorrow after school. We'll come *if* he gets his homework done."

Grant grew serious with James and let his fingers move. "You hear that?" *Do your work so we can play football tomorrow,* he signed. "I'm looking forward to playing ball with you . . ."

He stood up and stared down at her. "I really am, you know."

She wanted to ask him why, to find out exactly what his intentions were. There had to be something in this for him, some good press at the very least, but he took off before she could speak. Bethany watched as he jogged across the field to meet up with his brother in the parking lot, trying not to appreciate the way the muscles down his back and legs rippled under his clothing with the movement. She felt her stomach twist and somersault like a gymnast, something it hadn't done since she'd started dating Matthew in high school. Grant McQuaid was definitely a fine male specimen, maybe enough so that she should rethink her no-dating policy.

What in the world was she thinking? She'd made the rule to protect James from getting hurt. The last person she needed to date was a professional football player who was only home for vacation, especially as cocky as this one seemed. James didn't need that kind of emotional upheaval in his life. But she couldn't help wondering if she was more worried about James or herself.

Chapter Two

"YOU'RE REALLY GOING to meet up with them again?" Jackson asked as he drove them back to the ranch.

"Sure, why not?"

Grant wasn't actually sure what possessed him to ask Bethany and James to join him the next day, other than the fact that he'd been completely taken in by the kid. Not only was he fearless enough to go after the football when Jackson threw it, but Grant had never met a kid that young who recognized him and knew his name. The kid's Grandfather must be one hell of a Mustangs fan. He made a mental note to get his address to have some Mustangs gear sent his way.

The kid's absolute joy at the thought of having dinner with him had been infectious. Of course, it didn't hurt that his mother was gorgeous, even in her near-panicked state. However, Bethany hadn't seemed impressed in the slightest by his status as a player, unlike her son. Most of the beautiful women who hung around the locker rooms and bars couldn't wait to nab a "player." In fact, she'd seemed dubious of him and, at times, rather antagonistic. Although it was pretty adorable to see her jump to James' defense. The look of surprise in her big, dark eyes when he began signing to James had made every second he'd spent learning sign language worth it. Regardless of how cute she was, she seemed like a damn good mom and, if the kid was any indicator, she had to be pretty amazing.

"I didn't know you knew sign language." Jackson cast him a questioning glance. "Surprised me a little."

"Yeah, learned a few years ago while I was in Memphis."

It was one of the many things Grant loved about the Mustangs' team. The owner was big into giving back to the community, something he enjoyed doing. Each and every one of the players took part in several charity events each year, and over the past eight years since he'd been drafted, he'd been able to work with different charities— raising money for homeless shelters, building houses for low income families, visiting hospitals—but his favorite, by far, had been working with special needs kids.

The first time he returned home from the children's hospital, he'd stayed awake all night. They'd left him completely energized. Seeing the kids in the hospital coping and thriving, facing circumstances that would bring most adults to their knees in fear, had been inspiring. He'd gone back every day after practice, just to visit and play games with them. Over the next few months, he'd learned American Sign Language from a private tutor just so he could spend time in the children's hospital, conversing with several of the young patients who'd received cochlear implants, letting them laugh at his antics and pitiful ASL techniques.

Seeing the joy in the faces of kids who faced struggles he couldn't even imagine had made him feel like he had a purpose outside of football. He'd heard the melancholy in James' voice when he mentioned his Grandfather and found himself wanting to see the kid's face light up with that smile again. While it might have just been home-sickness for his Grandparents, Grant got the feeling that there was more to it. He wasn't just a kid looking to connect with his sports hero, there was a loneliness that seemed to come off him in waves, in spite of his happy-go-lucky attitude.

Maybe if he ended up not returning to football, he could find a way to work with kids like James. At least then the last ten years of fame would have some benefit rather than being a millstone dragging him down.

Don't even go there.

He couldn't let his mind stray toward some of the more negative predictions he'd read about himself online just this morning. Sports commentators were already speculating about the extent of his injuries and what it would mean for the team to lose him. He wasn't about to buy into their prophecies. He *had* to come back. It was as simple as that.

"Did you forget you promised to help me with the fence?" Jackson's voice was a welcome distraction from the turn his thoughts had taken.

"We can finish that tonight."

"Uh, nope. You haven't seen it. It's going to take a few days."

"Great." Grant rolled his eyes. "Because I was kinda hoping that if things went well at the park tomorrow, I'd ask them out for pizza after." Grant didn't want to bail on his brother but he couldn't mend fences and go out to dinner. He was sure Jackson would have done the same. "Come on, Jackson, you saw that kid."

Jackson chuckled. "He was a pretty cool kid. And, no fear."

"Right?"

"But didn't she already shoot you down once?"

Grant shrugged. "Never hurts to ask again."

Jackson sighed but Grant knew he was less irritated than he was pretending to be. "Go. I didn't really expect you to help anyway. But I'm not going to be the one to tell Mom you won't be there for dinner. You can face that firing squad alone."

"Please." Grant waved his brother off. "All I have to do is tell her I have a date and she'll start begging me to hurry up and make her a grandmother already."

"Well, you're the oldest and it's not like you're getting any younger, bro."

"At least I have a prospect," Grant taunted.

"Sure you do," he said with a laugh. "Most of the time you were talking to her, that woman looked like she'd rather scratch your eyes out than let you kiss her. I don't see any kids coming out of this date."

"Yeah? Well, it's the rest of the time that matters," he replied with a chuckle.

In spite of the teasing note in his voice, Jackson wasn't wrong. For all her civility, Bethany had seemed annoyed at the prospect of dinner with him, even if it was just pizza. He'd barely gotten her to agree to them hanging out at the park. It wasn't a reaction he was used to getting. Most of the time, women were lining up for his attention. Not that he expected women to fawn over him—hell, they lined up for any pro football player. Regardless of the fact that he was one of the "old guys" on the team now and most women wanted the up and coming stars, even the longtime veterans weren't lacking for dates.

You're not on the team at all now, he reminded himself.

Funny how every subject seemed to return to his undecided future. Grant didn't want to think about his pending retirement right now. It hadn't been announced yet, wouldn't be until after he was given a final evaluation just before their pre-season workouts began. He had two weeks left to prove to his doctors that he was healthy enough to return.

"So, are you wanting to hang out with the kid or his Mom?" Jackson pressed. "I mean the kid was cute but his mom—whoa!" Grant looked at his brother and arched a brow in question. "What?" Jackson asked. "She's hot."

"Mom would kick your ass if she heard you call a woman 'hot.'" Grant shook his head. "But, yeah, she was pretty."

Pretty didn't even begin to describe Bethany. She was beautiful . . . and prickly. She'd been as friendly as a porcupine with a cactus up its butt. "Know anything about her?"

His brother shrugged as they pulled off the main road onto their family ranch. "I've never even seen her before but it's not like I get into town that often. Dad keeps me pretty busy at the ranch since all of you decided to take off and leave Jefferson and me behind. The only time I get into town is when I hit the feed store."

Grant wanted to deny his brother's jab. As the oldest of seven kids, he'd jumped at the chance to play college ball and get as far from the family ranch as possible. He didn't hate the ranch, but he didn't want to be stuck here in the small town of Hidden Falls forever. He'd wanted to see the world and football had given him the opportunity to do that while allowing him to help support his parents' cattle ranch. But when his brothers, Andrew and Benjamin, left the ranch to pursue careers as a police officer and fireman, then Linc left to pursue his music career, that had left only the twins, Jackson and Jefferson, to help their father run the place, including the fence he'd promised to help fix. Guilt ticked at the edges of his conscience, making him consider canceling his park date. Disappointment instantly filled his chest but he wasn't sure if it had more to do with the pretty woman who would be there or her son.

"You should ask Maddie. She works at the school a couple days a week. She probably knows at least a little about the kid."

Their sister, Madison, the only girl allowed into their boy's club, was a speech therapist. She would probably be able to fill him in on everything he needed to know about James, and his wary mother. But Grant wondered if he wasn't just asking for more trouble than he needed right now. He hoped to be leaving town come spring. He wasn't looking for another reason to tie himself down in a small town, and a romance, even a casual one, with a kid involved would do just that.

"Mom, I CANNOT believe James did this to me."

The next morning Bethany paced the small master bedroom of her tiny cottage home with the cell phone pressed to her ear. It wasn't fancy, but the house was hers and had a huge yard for James to play in. Plus, it was walking distance to Hidden Falls Elementary. She'd easily fallen in love with the two-bedroom house when she'd move to town over the summer.

"Honey, you don't really think he did it on purpose, do you?" Her mother's laughter rang through the phone. "He's six and he just met one of the Mustangs face-to-face. Your father would have done the same thing." Her mother paused for a moment. "You could have just said no," she pointed out.

"I did say no. But you didn't see James' face, Mom." Bethany began swiping hangers aside, trying to find something to wear to work. "And this wasn't just *one* of the Mustangs, this was Grant McQuaid, the *only* Mustangs player in James' eyes. Then they pinkie promised."

"They what?"

"You know, where you link pinkie fingers . . . it doesn't matter." She waved a hand in the air. "If you'd seen him, you'd know this was probably the greatest thing to ever happen to him. How am I supposed to keep telling him no after that?"

"So go to the park. Have a good time."

"I just don't want James to get hurt. If he gets too attached—"

"Honey, it's not like you're marrying this guy. You're going to the park, with your son. Relax."

She was right, Bethany was reading far too much into a simple afternoon at the park. Just because Grant McQuaid had asked her to dinner didn't mean he would again. And she could talk with James before they saw him, make it clear to him that this was just some time at the park and nothing else. She felt the muscles in her shoulders relax slightly. Her mother always had a way of calming her worries. Bethany only prayed she could be the same kind of mother for James.

"Besides," her mother began. "Maybe it's time to start dating again."

And there is was. The suggestion that there *might* be more to this.

"Mom," Bethany scolded. "This guy's a football star. He has his pick of a million women. I'm sure the last thing he's looking for is a single mom. Besides, you saw what happened with Matthew. He couldn't handle *things*."

Couldn't handle the pressure of his job, couldn't handle being a father, couldn't handle a son with a disability, couldn't handle saying goodbye in person.

"It's hard enough to explain to James why his father isn't around like his friends' dads and why he sounds different from everyone else when he talks. He doesn't need to get close to someone else only to have that person bail on him. I won't put him through that kind of emotional turmoil. The move and making friends has already been hard enough."

She heard her mother sigh into the phone. "James is a tough kid, Bethie. He can handle more than you give him credit for."

"But he shouldn't *have* to, Mom, and I'm going to make sure he doesn't have to as long as I can."

She pulled a white sundress from her closet. Paired with a jean jacket and her boots, it would be a casual look without looking like she was trying to impress anyone.

Are you?

Bethany didn't want to listen to the nagging voice in her head, let alone acknowledge the idea that she might want Grant McQuaid to think she was attractive. It had been a long time since she'd felt attracted to any man, and to think that a man who could have his choice of women would give her more than a passing glance was flattering. Okay, maybe exhilarating was a better description, she realized as her heart pounded against her ribs. Her body was just going to have to settle back down and control its hormonal outbursts because she was not about to risk falling for someone like Grant McQuaid when she had a responsibility to watch out for James. A guy like him would never want more than a quick hookup with a small-town girl like her and that was the last thing she would give in to, regardless of her excitable pulse. She was too responsible for that.

"I'd better go, Mom. I still need to take a shower and dry my hair."

"What," her mother teased, "no ponytail? I thought that's all you wore."

A shirtless James came and stood in the doorway of her walk-in closet, watching her, patiently waiting for her to get off the phone. "Not always, Mom," she said with a laugh. "We'll call you later. I love you."

"Give my boy hugs and tell him Grammie loves him."

"I will," she said as she disconnected the call. Bethany tipped her head to one side and smiled at her son. "What's up?"

"Do you know where my football jersey is? The one Grandpa got me?" He looked at her nervously and she wondered why.

"It should be in your dresser. Let's go look."

She took his little hand in hers, his blond hair still wet from his impromptu bath. She was amazed at times with how grown-up he acted for a six-year-old. He'd already surpassed her signing skills and could read lips like a pro, but it was his calm acceptance and beguiling charm that won over everyone who met him. It was a strange feeling to wish to be more like her son but Bethany did. If she could face adversity with even half of his upbeat attitude, she'd consider her life well-spent.

He paused at his doorway, his little bare feet planted firmly. "Are you mad?"

"Me? No, baby, why?" She squatted down so she was eye level with him.

"Because you looked mad on the phone." He brushed his little fingers over her forehead, smoothing out the wrinkles of her frown. "Did I make you mad?"

"Oh, James, no. It's just that Mommy doesn't usually meet with strangers at the park so I'm a little nervous about it."

"But Grant plays football and said I could play with him. That means we're friends."

She smiled at his simplistic views on the way life worked, wishing again that she could see the world through his eyes. "I guess you're right but, sometimes, grown-ups like to know each other a little better before they go places together. Even when they're friends."

He pursed his lips, thinking about what she was trying to explain to him, so she stood up and opened the drawer where he kept his shirts. She found a bunch of t-shirts already stuffed inside and knew he must have been trying on several, trying to decide on what to wear. *Like mother like son*, she thought. She moved the shirts aside, tugging the jersey from the bottom of the drawer.

"Here it is," she announced. James raised his arms and she slipped it over his head. "There, now you're all set."

"I need his football."

"What football?"

"Grant forgot to take his ball when he left yesterday. I need to bring it back to him at the park today."

She smiled. "Oh, honey, I think he was giving that to you."

James planted little fists on his hips and gave her a disapproving frown. "I can't take things that aren't mine,

Mom. He forgot it so I was taking care of it until I can give it back."

She pinched her lips together, trying to hide her smile as he repeated her own words back to her. She'd taught him from a very young age that he shouldn't take things that didn't belong to him. It was nice to see he listened and understood. "Okay, you're right. Let me finish getting dressed and we'll make sure the ball is still in the car."

"Hurry up, Mom," he scolded, tapping his finger where a watch would eventually sit on his wrist. *You'll make us late*, he signed.

Okay, she signed back. *Be patient.*

She was trying to share his excitement for their afternoon plans, and there was a part of her she didn't want to acknowledge that was excited. The last time she'd had a date was in high school, with Matthew. But the thought of her ex-husband was enough to squash any anticipation that might be building.

This is not a date, she reminded herself as she hurried into her bathroom, checking the time on her alarm clock as she passed. She was going to have to forgo the shower if she didn't want to be late for work. She fluffed up her dark hair with her fingers. Maybe she could manage to curl it. Bethany glanced back at the bedroom doorway and saw James waiting and smiled at her reflection. It looked like she was going to have to put it into a ponytail after all.

Chapter Three

BETHANY WAS EXHAUSTED. The last thing she wanted to do was to head to the park but James hadn't stopped talking about meeting Grant McQuaid there today. She'd tried to shush him, especially when several of the older kids had suggested he was lying, but he wasn't having any part of it. He was meeting with his hero today, at the park, and nothing was going to change that. Not even his mother's exhaustion.

"Wait, James," she warned as he unbuckled himself from his booster seat before she'd even put the car into Park. "You have to stay buckled until the car is stopped."

"Sorry." She glanced at him over her shoulder. He didn't look one bit apologetic as he bounced in his seat, trying to see if Grant was already there waiting. "There he is!"

James rose onto his knees and waved at Grant out the back window of her car. Reaching for the football on the seat, he held it up. Bethany quickly glanced into the rearview mirror, checking her makeup, even though she realized there was nothing she could do about it if she wanted to. She saw the reflection of Grant jogging toward them and quickly took a deep breath, trying to mentally prepare herself for the next hour or so. Surely he didn't expect them to stay longer than that.

She opened her door, surprised to see Grant had gone to James' door immediately. He lifted his brows in question and, when she nodded, he opened it for her son.

"Hey, little man, I've been waiting for you." *Ready for some fun?* he signed.

James scrambled from his booster seat in the back of the car. "Yeah!"

"Wait a minute. You can't just run through the parking lot." She walked around the back of the car and held out her hand. Instead of taking her hand the way he always did, James reached up and grasped Grant's index finger.

She felt a twinge of jealousy at her son's choosing someone else over her but she couldn't be too angry. At least her competition was his hero. She knew it meant James was growing up, even if it made her heart ache for it to happen. Grant looked over at her, as if recognizing the poignancy of James' actions, his eyes filled with apology.

"So, what do you want to do first?" Grant asked as James looked up at him with wide blue eyes.

"Football."

Bethany tried to bite back a grin. "Of course." She

shrugged a shoulder at Grant. "Would you expect anything else?"

"Probably not." He pointed to an open area along one side of a field and headed toward it. "Why don't we go over there?"

His gaze slid over her and she felt the blood move through her veins slowly, growing hot, warming her from the inside out. "Your mom looks too pretty in her dress to play football so I guess it's just the two of us boys."

She couldn't deny the pleasure that swirled through her at Grant's compliment. Even if she didn't plan on dating him, it felt nice to know Grant thought she was attractive. She'd seen him in plenty of magazine articles with beautiful women beside him and, while it might be nothing more than a charming line, she couldn't help the pleasure that swirled through her. Before she could thank him, Grant had turned his attention back to James.

"Go long."

James immediately knew what to do and began running, looking behind him so he could turn when Grant threw the ball. In spite of Grant's instructions, James turned toward him after only running about ten feet and Grant lobbed the ball into her son's arms. She clapped for James, even though it was an easy catch. James was beaming from ear to ear, even when Grant ran toward him and scooped him into the air.

"Blindside," he teased, setting James back onto his feet. "Gotta watch out."

She settled herself in the shade of several trees, tucking her feet beneath her, and watched the pair as they played. She'd never seen James so happy, not even with his Grandfather. Granted, it wasn't like her father had really been able to take James out and play with him this way. But it was almost like Grant had a connection to James, as if they could understand one another without words.

Her worries about James' safety faded as she watched Grant play ball with him, careful not to get rough but also discreet so that James didn't notice his diligence. She laughed when James tucked the football in the crook of his elbow and acted like he was going to tackle Grant, only to run through his legs and spike the ball on the other side. It was obvious to her that Grant had known exactly what her son was doing but had allowed him to do it anyway.

After almost an hour of watching the two play, Grant stumbled to where she sat and crumpled to the grass, flopping onto his back. James ran over and mimicked Grant, even folding his arms under the back of his head, just like the man lying beside her.

"Whew, kid, you wore me out."

"I did?" James frowned for a moment, his brow furrowing, his lips pursed in an adorable pucker. He looked across the grassy knoll at the jungle gym nearby. "Since Grant is too tired, can I go play on the slides?"

"It's Mr. McQuaid," she corrected. "And, yes. Just stay where I can see you, okay?"

"Okay!" James ran off, heading for his favorite slide that twisted like a corkscrew.

A nervous flutter began in her belly as soon as James

left. She adjusted the skirt of her dress, fidgeting, all the while wondering why she was so nervous. She was acting like a girl on a blind date and this, most certainly, was *not* a date.

"He's a great kid."

She barely glanced in his direction but had already seen him cross his ankles. "Thanks."

Silence fell between them as they both watched James. But it wasn't the awkward silence she expected, the ones where the longer it continued, the more uncomfortable it became. This was . . . nice. It was a companionable silence, like that of two people who'd known each other forever, who could just relax and be around one another without needing words. She wasn't sure she'd ever felt that way with anyone but her parents.

And it scared the hell out of her.

Whether she wanted to admit it or not, this was the closest she'd come to a date in over eight years, and sitting this close to *this* man was making her feel things she hadn't realized she missed.

Grant sat up quickly, turning toward her. "Hey, you okay? You look a little pale."

She fanned herself, feeling her cheeks heat even as she spoke. "I'm fine. It's just warm out."

"We can leave if you want." He started to rise.

"No, I'm fine, really," she insisted when he looked doubtful. Grant sat back down, even closer she realized.

"You're sure?" She nodded, trying to ignore the way her heart was beating at twice its usual pace. "You do look like you have a little color back."

His eyes twinkled with mischief and she realized he knew exactly why there was color in her cheeks. It was exactly the cocky arrogance she needed to see in order to get her hormones in check.

"So, are you in Hidden Falls to recuperate from your injury?"

She saw his jaw clench slightly before he answered. "Yep."

"You grew up here, right?"

He nodded. It was pretty obvious he didn't want to talk about why he'd returned to Hidden Falls. But thanks to his charming her son and practically conning her in to acquiescence, she was out here with him instead of grading papers, so he could make polite conversation.

"Then you'd know all the best places to take a six-year-old who likes to explore, wouldn't you?"

He turned to her with a slight grin, looking relieved at the change of subject. "I do. Have you taken him down to the river yet?" She shook her head. "Some great fishing." His gaze caressed her again. "But if that's not your thing—"

Bethany sat up straighter. "What makes you think fishing isn't my *thing*?"

"I don't know." He shrugged a shoulder nonchalantly. His gaze fell on the princess-cut neckline of her dress before he laughed. "You seem sort of . . . girly. In a good way, of course."

"Girly? I'll have you know, Mr. McQuaid, James didn't learn how to juke just from watching you do it on T.V."

"Oh, really?" She could tell he was humoring her.

"I was an All-State hurdler and Powder Puff quarterback, thank you very much."

"Well, well, I stand corrected." He acted impressed. "I think you might be able to show me a thing or two."

"I might be able to at that." She looked over at the jungle gym to see James standing on a bridge, waving at them. Grant waved back before she could.

"You're a lucky mom." His voice sounded wistful and she wondered for a moment at the regret she could easy read in his face.

"It's not like you're Rip van Winkle." She grabbed a handful of grass and threw it at him, watching the blades rain onto the t-shirt stretched over his flat abs. "You sound like you'll never have kids."

He plucked one of the blades from his shirt and twirled it between his fingers. "The life I've got doesn't exactly lend itself well to having a family. Maybe down the road a ways, but I'm not the kind of guy who'd want to leave my wife and kids behind six months out of the year. Serious relationships and football travel don't work for me."

Bethany saw a shadow of a frown cross his brow before it was gone just as quickly. "You want to be a hands-on dad."

"Exactly."

She felt her stomach do one of those gymnastic flips. What would it be like to love someone who loved you back enough to stick around? He rolled onto one arm and playfully tossed the grass in her direction.

"Although I'm sure there are days you'd like to run away, huh?"

"Not so many now, but when he was a baby . . ." She nodded. "Colic is the worst but it's almost intolerable when you can't console your child."

"Was he . . . nevermind."

"It's okay." She looked across the grass to where her son was climbing over monkey bars, hanging upside down. "He was born deaf and the doctors diagnosed it just before he was two months old. They never did figure out a reason why." She looked back at him, knowing that she should get James and head home but unable to keep from bragging about her son. "But he's smart. So smart. He was learning signs by the time he was six months old."

Suddenly a country song blared from his back pocket. Grant slid his phone out and looked at the picture on the screen. "I'll be right back, okay?"

Without waiting for a response from her, he got up and walked away to answer the call. But not before she saw a pretty woman on the screen. It was enough to kill any girlish crush she might have been feeling toward Grant McQuaid. She was not about to be "the other woman," not for any man, even if he was famous, good-looking and charming.

She brushed off her hands and stood up, slapping her skirt to knock off any grass and made her way to where James was swinging.

"We should get going. I have to fix dinner."

"Awwww!"

She'd expected his discontentment, even an argument, but she hadn't expected her own frustrated disappointment. Grant seemed like a nice guy, someone who would have made her think twice about her no-dating policy. But she had James to think about and, obviously from the picture on his phone, Grant already had someone else in his life, regardless of his comments about his job not being compatible with relationships. It was serious enough that he didn't want whoever she was to know he was with another woman.

It was better this way. The fact that she would even consider him dating material was reason enough to stay away from him.

SWIPING THE PICTURE of his mother on his cell phone, Grant answered. "Hey, Mom, what's up?"

"You brother tells me you're not coming to dinner tonight? Were you planning on letting me know?"

"I was going to call when I knew for sure." He turned back in time to see Bethany rise and head toward the playground where James was. He began walking back in their direction. "Don't hold dinner for me tonight but thanks for thinking of me, Mom." He hated feeling like a thirty-two-year-old child, living with his parents again, even if it was only temporarily.

"Jackson said something about a girl?"

He was going to kill his brother when he got home. "I'm actually just hanging out with her kid here at the park. He's a fan."

"Jackson said his mother was really pretty and . . ." She squealed in surprise, making him cringe and hold the phone away from his ear. "Hi, Maddie. I didn't know you were coming tonight."

"Mom, I'll let you go since Maddie's there." Grant disconnected the call before she remembered what they'd been discussing. He'd only managed to avoid the "when are you going to make me a grandmother" discussion because his sister had chosen that moment to arrive. He'd be sure to give her an extra tight hug of gratitude when he saw her next.

He hurried over to the jungle gym. He'd heard Bethany telling James they had to leave but he really wanted to talk to her again before she left. He liked her, more than he knew he should, and he liked her son. He knew he shouldn't get in any deeper, he'd even explained to her why, but it was the first time in a very long time Grant felt completely at ease with someone.

Even though Bethany knew who he was and what he did for a living, she didn't treat him any differently than she would anyone else. His missed that. He missed being nothing more than Grant McQuaid from Hidden Falls.

"I'm starving," he announced as he walked up to the pair. "What do you say we go grab a bite to eat, James?"

Bethany scowled at him. He wasn't sure what he'd said or done but she seemed suddenly aloof, the way she had yesterday when dinner was suggested. He knew she could see through his tactic and fought the urge to recant his invitation. But he also knew, like yesterday, she probably wouldn't agree unless James pressured her to accept.

James turned his face up toward his mother. "I'm hungry too, Mom."

Thanks, kid. I owe you one.

She ran a hand over his tousled, blond hair. "You can eat when we get home." Bethany turned her hazel eyes on Grant. "Thank you for joining James today. I'm sure it's one of those moments he'll never forget, playing football with his favorite Mustangs player."

"It doesn't have to end." He squatted down in front of James, praying this was one of those times he could ask for forgiveness after the fact since he doubted she'd give him permission to do what he was about to.

"It doesn't?" The little boy's eyes were wide with excited wonder and he brushed back several sweaty strands of hair that had fallen into his eyes.

"You promised to help me work on my sign language, remember?" Grant's eyes twinkled mischievously as he squatted down to James' level again. "We can do that while we eat. Where do you want to go, James? I'll take you wherever you want for dinner."

"I don't think—" Bethany began.

"Dino's."

"The pizza place?" he asked, impressed by James' selection.

Bethany sighed. "He likes the sports memorabilia," she explained, sounding defeated.

"Dino's it is, then." A half-smile curved the side of his mouth, and he deliberately avoided meeting Bethany's gaze, hoping any irritation she might feel for him would fade before they arrived at the pizza place. "We'll have a guy's night."

"Can Mom come? She's not a guy." James looked up at

Grant with every ounce of wide-eyed innocence he possessed and Bethany bit back her laugh. Grant wanted to hug the boy right then and there for helping break the tension he could feel mounting between him and Bethany.

"You're right, she's not." Grant frowned and pretended to be thinking about the dilemma before leaning closer to James and lowering his voice. "I think we can let her come this time. We'll just *pretend* she's a guy, okay?"

James' lips pursed as he thought about it. "But she's a mom," he insisted. "That means she's a girl so we can't have a guy's night."

Bethany crossed her arms and cocked her head at Grant as if to say *now what?*

Bethany wasn't kidding. James was smart but he was still a six-year-old. As an idea took hold, Grant smiled back at her.

"I guess I'm just going to have to take both of you out on a date then."

"What's a date?" James asked, curious about what must be a new concept.

"It's *not* a date." Bethany shot daggers his direction. "Mr. McQuaid, I'm afraid—"

James tugged at her skirt. His fingers moved quickly. *I'm hungry, Mom. Let's have pizza. Please.*

Grant knew the instant she decided to give in. Her face lost the frown as she looked into the angelic face of her son, her eyes tender and soft. Adoration was written there clearly. She would rather give in to her son, in spite of her trepidation, than disappoint him.

She sighed and signed back, *Fine.*

Grant couldn't help but feel a bit jealous of Bethany's relationship with her son. She loved him and he adored her. There was no mistaking it. They might not be the perfect family, but they were a family nonetheless.

Grant longed to have a family of his own. Instead, he had football. Until now, he'd never longed for anything else more. Until today, he'd never resented his career choice.

Chapter Four

GRANT PULLED INTO the half-full parking lot at Dino's, wondering again if he shouldn't just head home. Even he knew this went above and beyond the typical fan experience. But this was no longer about James' being a fan. He couldn't even convince himself this was just about James anymore. He liked the kid, had fun with him at the park today, and he liked Bethany. Somewhere between playing ball and his conversation with Bethany on the grass, he'd begun to wonder what it would be like to have more in his life.

As he climbed out of his car, he looked around for any sign that Bethany and James might already be here waiting for him. She'd insisted on taking her own car, making it painfully obvious that she didn't want to be here with him, even though he'd been nice, polite, even gentlemanly.

Maybe you're not her type, he thought. *Maybe she's already got a boyfriend.*

Grant felt a swirl of guilt center in his stomach. What if she did?

The more he thought about it, the more it seemed likely. Her discomfort, the way she tried to keep her distance, it would all make sense if she was already taken. A woman as pretty as she was wasn't likely to be single. But she'd repeatedly made it clear she didn't date.

Seeing Bethany's sedan, he slid his Camaro over the center line of two parking spots beside it. He wasn't taking any chances with his baby. The '69 candy-apple red Camaro had been his first big purchase after he'd been drafted and he still loved this car. It might be cliché but there was something about a man and his muscle car that just couldn't be denied—it felt great to have that kind of power in his hands and adrenaline rushing through his veins when he opened her up on a stretch of highway.

When he didn't immediately see Bethany or James waiting for him, he made his way to the front door, glancing at his watch. He'd been caught at the stoplight but they couldn't have arrived more than a few minutes ahead of him. The bells over the door jingled loudly but no one even looked up as he entered. Every eye was focused on one of the pool tables. A cheer went up in the room and he moved closer. The last thing he'd expected to see was James, standing on a bench, shooting pool.

The boy looked up as he came closer. "Hi, Mr. McQuaid!"

James' face beamed with pleasure as he hopped down from the stool, knocking one of his implant microphones off. He reached and slid it back into place.

"Come play pool with me." James slid his hand into Grant's and dragged him toward the table.

Grant didn't miss the way every eye turned his direction when James said his name, or the way people around the table moved to let him through. Or the frown that slid to Bethany's brow as soon as she saw her son holding Grant's hand. James reached for his small cue stick and chalked it like a pro.

"I'm winning."

"Who are you playing?"

"Me," Billy, the youngest son of Dino's longtime owner, complained. "I should really get back to work. Here." He shoved the cue stick into Grant's hands. "See if you can do better."

Grant looked at the crowd surrounding the table, unsure what to do. The easiest move would be to miss his shots, let James win and pretend it was a fair game, but one look at Bethany was enough to cast that idea aside. She stared at him with a slight smirk on her lips, as if she was daring him to beat her son. For a moment, he got the same feeling he did when a linebacker shot him a grin during the snap count. Bethany knew something he didn't and there was a good chance he was about to get destroyed. It also hadn't escaped his notice that James wasn't using a regular pool cue from the stock the pizza place kept. He had a custom-made cue stick, just the right size for him. It was unusual and kicked his curiosity into high gear.

Grant worked his way around the table toward Bethany, not missing the flicker of apprehension in her eyes as he got closer. "Okay, Mom, how good is he, really?"

She couldn't hide the pride that swelled and her smiled broadened. "I could probably survive off his winnings if he ever wanted to start hustling people."

"Great." Grant rolled his eyes. He wasn't a great player to begin with and now he was about to get schooled by a kid. He bumped her hip playfully with his own, moving her aside. "At least you can say you warned me." He pointed at the ball nestled in the corner pocket. "I'm solids, right?"

"Yep." James smiled at him and Grant noticed one of his bottom teeth was missing. Damn kid was adorable. "I only have one left," he said, pointing at the eight-ball.

Grant shook his head, mentally preparing himself to be spanked by this kid and humiliated in front of at least twenty people from town. *Please don't let any of them be reporters*, he prayed.

It took all of five minutes for James to win the game. As soon as he'd sunk the eight-ball, he climbed down from the bench and threw his arms around Grant's legs, giving him a warm hug. Without even thinking, Grant bent down and picked him up, lifting him so he was at eye level.

"Want to play again?" James asked, a bright gleam in his blue eyes.

"Maybe later. Let's order our pizza and we can visit for a little bit first."

James wiggled in his hands and Grant put him back onto the floor, following him to the front counter where Bethany joined them. Reaching his hands to the top of the counter, James hopped up, trying to see over the top even though he was far too short. Grant picked him up again and pointed at the menu.

"What kind do you want?"

"Pepperoni and cheese." The boy bounced up and down in Grant's arms excitedly, until his mother cleared her throat beside them. "Please," he corrected with a sheepish grin.

"You heard the man," Grant said, laughing at James' infectious excitement. "A large pepperoni and cheese. Make that light on the sauce and heavy on the cheese with as thick a crust as you can."

"Will that be all?" Billy gave James a mock glare, sending the boy into peals of laughter again as he shook his finger at James. "You just wait until next time," he warned.

"I *always* beat you, Billy."

"Not next time. You want the usual drinks, Bethany? I can bring them over in a couple minutes."

Grant looked at her, confused and shrugged. "Sure."

"You're awfully daring. How do you know it's not all the soda flavors mixed into one pitcher?" She turned and headed toward a nearby table and slid into the booth.

"Ah," Grant said on a long, nostalgic sigh. "Long live the suicide soda." He slid James into the booth beside his mother and took the seat across from them.

"It's nothing that bad, just cola and root beer mixed," she informed him.

James was like a human jumping bean on the seat, unable to still his little body. "Can I go play video games?"

"Puh—" Bethany began.

"Please," he added quickly.

"Yes, you can." Bethany reached into her purse and pulled out several dollars. "You remember how to get change?"

Grant had never seen a kid so young give a look of such teenage condescension but James pulled it off without a hitch. "I know, Mom."

"Okay, James." She mimicked his tone with a laugh and, shaking her head, turned back to Grant, rolling her eyes.

"He's got to be the coolest kid I've ever met."

"Yeah, he's pretty great," she agreed, her eyes filled with affection for her son as she watched him run to the change machine. "Mr. McQuaid, I just wanted to apologize again for yesterday. James doesn't usually take off that way but he loves football and when he saw you and your brother playing, coupled with the fact I wouldn't let him play at recess . . ." She shrugged. "I don't want to even think about what could have happened." He could see even the idea left her shaken. "And, while you probably don't understand what it means to him for you to have played at the park with him today, it means a lot to me."

Grant opened his mouth to tell her how he'd been happy to do it, how he'd like to do it again, but she didn't give him the opportunity to speak.

"But I hope you don't have the wrong idea."

"Wrong idea," he repeated. He had a sinking suspicion he knew where this conversation was leading.

"James is a great kid and he's easy to like. It's also not hard to see that he's my life and I'd do anything to make him happy, which you know because you used it to your advantage to get us here. But I'm not sure what you're hoping to gain from this . . ." She sighed as she searched for whatever word she might be looking for to describe the torture she looked like he was putting her through.

"Don't say *date*. It's not one—you said so yourself." He couldn't help himself, any more than he could help the grin that lifted one corner of his mouth. "Relax, okay? This is not a date. I get it. You aren't looking for a relationship and neither am I. Message received loud and clear. But I do like your kid and there's nothing wrong with the three of us being friends, is there?"

She narrowed her eyes skeptically, searching his expression. "I guess not," she finally agreed.

"Good because I had fun with him today." Grant looked at the boy intent on the video game and furiously pounding at the buttons on the ancient machine. "I was surprised he knew as much about football as he did. Does he play for a team here in town?"

"Football?" Bethany's brows shot up and her pretty brown eyes widened in surprise. "He has to be seven for the youth team here in town but he wants to. His doctor in Tennessee said he could, but I just don't know."

"You don't want him to play?"

Grant watched her as she played with the straw in her soda, swirling it nervously. Even though they'd come to an agreement to be friends, she still seemed on edge and he wondered how he could get her to relax and take him at his word. Usually women threw themselves at him, whether he wanted them to or, more often, not. But not this woman. She was strung tighter than his brother Linc's guitar.

It was contradictory to the put-together, in-control illusion she was trying so hard to convince him of. While she might look perfect, he knew she was hiding behind the fantasy. Her white sundress made her look fresh and innocent, showing off just enough leg to rev his imagination into gear but still be appropriate for a park outing. With her long hair pulled back into a ponytail, it made her look younger than she claimed to be—twenty-six if he'd done his math correctly—and sweet as a spring shower. Her purse matched the color of her boots and the entire look screamed flawless. But he wasn't buying it.

He could see the anxiety in her eyes. She was hiding something. Her eyes scanned the pizza place, moving quickly from watching James to watching the others in the room curiously. She was fidgety, skittish, but trying to conceal the fact.

Part of him felt the same way. As attracted as he was to her, those cowboy boots made him want to turn tail and run. She might not be a local but she was still a small-town girl through and through. He'd dated enough of them to know a real one from a fake and the real ones were full of far too much piss and vinegar for his liking. Between those boots and the curves she was sporting, he heard warning bells going off. But couple that with the fact that he found himself *wanting* to spend more time with her, in spite of the fact that he didn't want anything to interfere with his return to football, and those warning bells turned into full-fledged sirens.

Bethany's hand stilled the straw and she tipped her head to the side, giving him an identical look to the one James had just given her, like he'd just asked her the world's stupidest question. It took him a moment to even remember what he'd asked.

Football, about James playing, that was it.

"I'm his mother. I don't want him to get hurt." She went back to twirling the straw. "But I also want to see him happy, which is the only reason we're here now. Mr. McQuaid—"

"Grant," he corrected.

He hadn't missed the disapproving tone of her voice and could tell she was gearing up to tell him again why she shouldn't have come. He wasn't about to take the bait.

"What made you decide to move from Tennessee to California and leave your family?" he asked, changing the subject.

She looked up at him through her dark lashes suspiciously, as if she wasn't sure how much she wanted to reveal to him. She bit the edge of her lip with straight, white teeth and desire began a slow descent from his stomach to his groin before he could halt it.

"It wasn't exactly my idea. It was my Mom's. She thought it was time for us to have a fresh start. Then, when I landed the job at the school, it seemed almost like kismet. I miss them terribly, so does James, but I can also see she was right. The move has been good for us. Hard but good." She glanced at her son, now standing on a chair in front of an old Centipede arcade game. "Although he really misses his Grandparents."

"Grandpa?" Grant guessed, looking up as Billy delivered their pizza. "Thanks. James," he called. "Food's here, buddy."

"Okay, I'm almost done." Grant laughed to see the boy maneuvering the video game controls better than he ever could.

Bethany gave him an odd look, as if she was trying to figure out his motives and Grant wanted to ask her about it but held his tongue. He didn't want to give her the chance to clam up on him again when she was finally opening up a little. "Is that who taught James to play pool?"

"Pool, how to swim, baseball. My Dad's been the closest thing James has had to a father, so leaving . . ."

She let her words trail off, eyeing his reaction before sliding a slice onto a plate for her son and one for herself. She only picked at her food and Grant wondered how she'd been expecting him to respond, or what she hoped he'd say. From the way she was acting, he suspected the two were completely different things.

"And James' father?"

"Gone."

Simple, to the point and leaving no room for discussion. In other words, she didn't want to talk about it and the topic was off-limits for further discussion. Her standoffishness suddenly made sense. A prickly single mom, dad out of the picture for whatever reason, who'd just moved out of her parents' house? Definitely not the kind of situation he needed to stick his nose into. Grant wondered if he wasn't smarter to dodge that bullet.

Before he could say anything else, James came running over and climbed into the booth beside him, sliding his plate across the table from next to his mother.

"I almost got the high score."

At least someone was scoring tonight, Grant thought. It certainly wasn't going to be him. From Bethany's reserved reception, his brother had been right on the mark with his assessment—she'd rather scratch his eyes out than kiss him, and while she was tolerating him, she wasn't being overly friendly. He hadn't expected her to throw herself at him, but was an amiable dinner too much to ask for?

BETHANY WATCHED THE man across from her as he laughed with James. Her son was already enamored of him, but that was to be expected since he was James' favorite player on the Mustangs. She, however, was an adult. The same excuse didn't work for her but, somehow, in less than thirty minutes, Grant McQuaid had been able to weasel more information from her than anyone else in town had in six months. She wasn't sure what it was about him that made her want to spill her guts and she cursed herself for falling under his spell so easily.

She wanted to blame it on being slightly starstruck, which wasn't altogether untrue. She was trying to hide the fan in her but, since her father was a huge Mustangs fan, she'd grown up one as well. She'd watched with the rest of Tennessee when he'd taken his team to the playoffs and she'd been just as disappointed when his injury sidelined him. She'd heard the reports that his injuries might be career threatening but that no decisions had been made yet and, more recently, the rumors around town that Grant McQuaid, the star running back for the Memphis team, had returned to his hometown of Hidden Falls.

Watching him yesterday and today at the park, she wouldn't have guessed he was injured in the slightest. It had been amazing to watch him with his brother and she hadn't been the only one who thought so, if the groups watching from under the trees had been any indication. She pinched her lips together, trying not to think about the way the tanned muscles of his back and shoulders had rippled as he ran for a pass but the image was burned into her mind. It hadn't helped the rapid fluttering of her heart to see him playing with her son today either. He looked just as incredible now in nothing more than track pants and a t-shirt showing off every muscle in his arms. He'd shaved this morning but now she could see the dark shadow on his jaw, making him look slightly dangerous. However, his dark eyes were warm, like hot chocolate, as he listened to her son regale them with his video game conquests. Looking down at James, his smile welcoming and wide as James maneuvered Grant's long, tapered fingers into the correct sign, he looked more like a big teddy bear than a football player.

Yeah, a big teddy bear whose clothing you're mentally removing, she scolded herself.

Her heart thudded against her ribs, her stomach fluttering like a baby bird taking flight. She normally had no problems separating herself from any sexual attraction she had for a man. Usually dredging up some reminder of her ex-husband's abandonment did the trick, but even Matthew's betrayal wasn't working when it came to Grant. And she *never* let herself open up. Grant McQuaid was worming his way past every door she'd nailed shut years ago.

Maybe it's high time you open a few.

Bethany frowned at the sound of her mother's voice in her head. Fantasizing about the football player on television was one thing but having the living, breathing, very enticing man sitting across the table from her was completely disarming. It was that kind of thinking that was causing her to slip up and tell him too much, like her comment about her father. She needed to shut this dinner, and her girlish crush, down before Grant was able to cross any more lines she'd drawn in the sand for herself.

She watched as Grant pulled out his cell phone and looked at her expectantly. "Earth to Bethany," he called, wiggling the phone, eliciting a giggle from James.

"Call Grandpa, Mom. So he can talk to Grant."

"Oh, um . . ." She slid the phone from his hand and dialed her parents, dreading what either of them might say.

She didn't want anyone to realize how Grant was affecting her and she knew her mother was far too discerning. She chanced a quick peek at Grant through her lashes and saw his eyes twinkling mischievously just before he arched a brow.

Too late, he already knows.

Her mother picked up on the second ring. "Oh . . . hey, Mom, it's Bethany," she stammered, trying to regain her composure. "James and his friend would like to talk to Grandpa. Is he around?"

"Are you kidding? He's been waiting by the phone all day. Here." She heard the rustle from their end as the phone was passed to her Dad.

"Hey! Where's my boy?"

Bethany felt the familiar hero worship she had for her father well up in her at the sound of his voice. He'd been the best role model she could have wanted for her and her son. It broke her heart to move across the country, leaving him behind.

"Hang on, I'll put you on speaker but it might be a little loud. We're at the pizza place." She pressed the button.

"Hi, Grandpa!" James' face lit up with excitement. He had a story for his Grandfather, a gift to give him, and couldn't wait to bestow it with every ounce of six-year-old enthusiasm. "Guess who I'm eating pizza with."

"Who?" Beth knew her mother had already told her father they were with Grant McQuaid but James didn't. She adored her father even more for playing along with James' excitement. "Is it your Mom?"

"Yep, but guess who else." James didn't give him the opportunity to guess again. "Grant McQuaid. He's right here. Say hi, Grant."

Grant laughed. "Hello, sir."

Bethany realized he didn't know her father's name.

"Grant, this is my Dad, and your biggest fan next to James, Craig Jenner. Dad, this is Grant McQuaid."

"We played football today, Grandpa."

"You did? I have to admit that I'm a little jealous of you, James." Her father's tone was playful and she couldn't help but smile at his banter with his grandson. "But I hope Mr. McQuaid realizes he's only allowed to play with you and not your mother, though, or his neck injury will be the least of his worries."

"Why, Grandpa? Because she's a girl."

Her father laughed. "Yep. Because I don't want to see her get hurt."

Grant's eyes immediately jumped from the phone screen to meet Bethany's and she felt the color drain from her face at her father's threat. She scrambled for the phone but Grant beat her to it, smiling broadly as he lifted the cell phone from the table and pressed the button to take the conversation off the speaker. Bethany covered her eyes with her hand, wondering what her father might say next.

"Yes, sir." Grant didn't take his eyes from her but at least his lips spread into an even wider grin. "Yes, you're right, she is beautiful." She saw his eyes travel over her face, pausing at her mouth. "That's not my intention at all, sir. You have my word."

Bethany's eyes widened and she felt the heat creep over her face as his gaze met hers again, the corners of his eyes wrinkling with humor. "He's a pretty great kid. Bethany told me you were the one who taught him to play pool too." Grant's laughter rang out. It was a rich sound that warmed her all the way to her toes. "Yeah, he crushed me in about five minutes."

She couldn't listen to any more. Bethany reached for the pitcher and carried it to the counter, waiting as Billy refilled it for her and forced herself not to turn around and stare at the man seated at the table with her son. How could her father embarrass her that way? At least now she wouldn't have to worry about Grant McQuaid getting any more ideas about this being a date. Even if he hadn't gotten the point from her, her father had sufficiently taken care of that. She felt a trickle of disappointment slide through her, settling in her chest, and she cursed the feeling. She didn't want to date him.

Or do you?

She stuffed the confusing thoughts deep into her psyche. She didn't have the time or inclination to date anyone. Her first loyalty was to her son. It just wasn't the right time to bring a man into their lives, especially one in the public eye like Grant McQuaid. As Billy took the pitcher of soda to fill, she looked back to the table to see Grant, now off the phone, with his head bent close to James as he worked on his signs.

Bethany knew that James was a charming child, dazzling most people he met, but she'd never met someone quite so enamored of him. Nor had she ever seen her son quite this taken by another adult, although, in fairness, Grant was his favorite player. She smiled as she recalled how telling James they were moving to Grant McQuaid's home town was the only way she'd been able to convince him about the move. She'd never, in a million years, expected to run into the man with his schedule, let alone be on a date with him.

This isn't a date, she reminded herself again. Why was she having such a difficult time remembering the fact?

"Because you want it to be," she muttered to herself.

Billy slid the pitcher across the counter at her. "What was that, Bethany?"

She shook her head, embarrassed at being caught staring at Grant. "Nothing. Thank you." She carried the pitcher back to the table, steeling herself to apologize for her father's comments.

"Mom, can Grant come to our house and see my room? He said he'd buy us ice cream too."

Grant turned his dark eyes on her and gave her a disarming smile. "Sorry, I probably should have checked with you first."

He didn't look sorry at all. In fact, he looked certain she would give in.

Please, James signed.

Please, Grant copied, his lopsided smile deepening as his gaze locked on hers and she saw a dimple cut into his right cheek.

A sizzle of heat coiled in her, ready to break free as she tried to force herself to deny James. She hadn't had anyone over to their house since they'd moved here last summer. It was her sanctuary, the one place she could hide from the rest of the world, where she and James could just be themselves, instead of "the single mother and her deaf kid" she'd heard people whisper about when they thought she couldn't hear. Having him over wasn't something she was comfortable with. Not one bit.

Grant cocked his head to one side and narrowed his eyes, trying to read her reaction and, suddenly, reached into his pocket, pulling out two dollar bills. "Here, James, why don't you go play a few more video games and let me talk to your mom for a minute, okay?"

James knew a good deal when he heard it and plucked the bills from Grant's fingers. "Thank you," he said as he signed it too.

"You didn't have to do that," Bethany said, frowning as she watched James hurry off. "I'm sorry for my Dad. I can't believe he said that."

"Don't worry about it, Bethany. I've met plenty of protective fathers."

I'll bet you have.

Bethany tried to keep her lips from pinching to a thin line. His smile slipped and he grew serious.

"Have I done something? Or are you always like this?"

"Like what?" She bristled but she knew exactly what Grant meant. He wanted to know what made her act so cold, why she was keeping him at such a distance. But she didn't owe him any explanations. He didn't know her past and had no right to judge her, and she had no plans to explain herself. That would mean opening up and letting him in even more.

"Tense. You need to relax," he coaxed.

That wasn't what she'd expected him to say.

"At first I thought it was just your being upset at the

near miss with James yesterday at the park but even now you look like you're about to just . . . snap."

She looked down and caught herself wringing her hands. Bethany laid them flat on the table.

"Breathe," he instructed. "I'm not going to bite you."

Oh, if only she could be so lucky. The sizzle of heat that had been simmering in her belly sprang to life.

Stop it! she warned herself.

Grant was breaking through her walls faster than she could hide behind them and that scared her. She tamped down six years of pent-up sexual frustration as well as any thoughts of romance with every ounce of heartache she could dredge up from her failed marriage.

"I don't do this," she muttered. It wasn't a good explanation but it was all she could offer him right now.

"What? Eat pizza, have a conversation with someone? Make new friends?" She rolled her eyes and glared at him. Grant wagged a chiding finger at her but didn't bother to hide his grin. "Oh, no. You said this wasn't a date, remember?" His eyes practically danced with humor, daring her to challenge his observation.

She rose from the table and smoothed down the front of her dress. "You're right, I did. That means we don't need any sort of escort home, Mr. McQuaid, or your ice cream nightcap. Thank you for the pizza but James and I should be going. James," she called to her son. "Come tell Mr. McQuaid thank-you."

She didn't miss the disappointed frown on her son's face as he walked back to the table, his shoulders hunched over as if it might delay the inevitable departure. "But I thought—"

Grant eyed her questioningly. She knew she was over-reacting. It would have been far better if she'd just listened to her initial instinct yesterday not to come at all.

"Not this time, buddy." Grant looked almost as disappointed as James.

"I brought your football. It's still in the car. Mom made sure." Bethany saw James' lower lip quiver as he tried not to cry.

"I'll tell you what, let's go out to the car and I'll sign it for you to keep." He reached down and lifted James, swinging him up onto his shoulders as they headed for the door. "Duck your head."

Grant squatted low so that James wouldn't come close to the door frame but exaggerated the movement, making James bounce as he popped back up to his full height outside. Her son giggled, forgetting his disappointment, more carefree than she'd seen him since their move, and Bethany wondered why doing the right thing for them both suddenly felt so wrong.

Chapter Five

GRANT ARRIVED AT his parents' house, far earlier than he'd planned on returning, to find three extra vehicles parked in the driveway. That meant the entire family was still here for dinner. Well, everyone but Linc since he was on the road touring with his band now. He sighed and rolled his shoulders, trying to work out some of the tension.

It was loud and rambunctious when he entered the kitchen, sounding more like a circus than a family get-together. Knowing better than to try to sneak past the McQuaid clan, he walked directly into the kitchen and grabbed a beer from the refrigerator.

"Hey, you're home early," Jackson pointed out. "Thought you had a hot date."

Grant shot his brother a withering scowl. The last thing he wanted was to discuss the way he'd crashed and burned tonight, especially when his brother had predicted it. For the life of him, he couldn't see why Bethany had run out of the pizza place like her ass was on fire. And she hadn't just been tense, she'd been pissed, but he had no clue what he'd done to cause it.

"Oh, hot date? Anyone I know?" His sister, Maddie, wiggled her eyebrows at him as he popped the top off his beer, tossing the cap onto the counter.

"Garbage," his mother ordered without even looking up.

Grant picked up the cap and took it to the can in the pantry, hoping the brief pause would be enough for someone to change the subject, but Jackson didn't seem inclined to let that happen.

"Probably." Jackson grinned now that the entire family was listening. "Pretty brunette, rockin' curves."

Maddie rolled her eyes. "Yeah, that helps a lot. Thanks for narrowing it down to half the females in town."

Grant glared at his youngest brother. "Bethany. She has a little boy, James."

"Oh!" Maddie exclaimed. "Bethany Mills. I've been working with James since they moved to town last summer." She laughed. "That explains why you're home early."

"What does *that* mean?" Jefferson, Jackson's identical twin, had suddenly taken interest in the conversation now that it might involve their oldest brother's humiliation.

"It means she doesn't date. Trust me, Grant—give up on this one. I've tried," his brother Ben warned. Six pairs of eyes rounded on Ben. It was well-known that Ben hadn't dated since his last relationship had ended badly over a year ago. Really badly.

"What? The fire chief had three of us do a presentation

at the school, and after the kids headed out for recess, I asked her out for coffee. She shot me down so fast I barely got the words out." He turned toward his sister. "I thought women couldn't resist a guy in uniform."

"Most of us don't have any problems," Andrew laughed. "I don't get turned down nearly as often as you do."

It was a constant playful battleground between the two since one was a fireman and the other a police officer. It didn't help that the town held the annual Red versus Blue Football Game each year around Thanksgiving to raise funds for the local homeless shelter and the firemen had won three years straight.

"Only because you've usually got the woman in handcuffs and she'd agree to anything to be rid of you. Tell me again how that worked out for you?" Ben teased, knowing full well the last woman Andrew had asked out had been pulled over for going twenty miles over the speed limit at the time.

"Don't even remind me," he conceded.

Grant took the playful banter as his chance to sneak out before the interrogation continued and his family began to pry for answers he didn't have. He took his beer out to the back patio and slid into one of the chairs his Dad had circled around the fire pit. It had been the family gathering spot on evenings since he was a kid and, honestly, he missed it. Right now, he welcomed the quiet retreat from the chaos of the kitchen.

Sighing, Grant took a long draw from the bottle, unable to stop thinking about Bethany and the way she'd reacted. He certainly didn't consider himself a dream guy but she'd acted like he was some serial killer. He wasn't even sure why he was continuing to let this bother him. So this chick didn't want to have him over for ice cream, or call their night out a date. So what? It didn't make him a total loser. This was her loss. But Grant couldn't help feeling like it was his and that bothered him more than he wanted to admit.

"Hey." Maddie plopped into the chair beside him, passing him another open bottled of beer. He set it aside as she sipped hers. "You aren't going to let those guys bother you, right?"

"No. It wasn't them."

"Bethany?"

Grant shook his head. "I just don't get it. I'm not *that* bad, am I?"

Maddie laughed. "Don't kid yourself, Grant. Women are still lining up to try to get your attention." Grant shot her a dubious look. "Ask Mom how many messages she's taken in the past few weeks."

"What?"

"You didn't realize women find the number to the ranch and call?" She bumped her brother's leg with her toe. "Don't let Bethany's rejection bug you. She's a pretty tightly closed book. I know a little of her story from working with James so trust me when I say, it's not you. She just doesn't seem to want a man in her life, or in James'."

Grant grunted and finished off his bottle. "She made that clear tonight."

"He's a pretty special kid, though. Funny, adorable—"

"Smart as a whip," Grant filled in, rubbing his index finger and thumb against either side of his jaw.

Maddie arched a brow. "Are you interested in the kid or his Mom?"

Grant shrugged. "Maybe both. You didn't see how sad he looked when he talked about leaving his Grandfather. I get the feeling he misses that male attention."

"That's actually pretty likely. Are you offering?"

Grant shrugged again. He wanted to offer but it seemed pretty unlikely that Bethany would agree. He wasn't even sure why he wanted to make the offer. He had more than enough to worry about with his upcoming medical clearances but he couldn't seem to get James' melancholy expression out of his mind.

"You know," Maddie hinted, "I could probably set up some sort of assembly or something at Hidden Falls Elementary if I knew a big football celebrity willing to talk to the kids. Maybe about staying in school, following their dreams, all that jazz."

He rolled his eyes. "You know I'd do anything for you, Mads, but why?"

She shrugged and her lips curved up into a mischievous smile. "I know for a fact what a huge Mustangs fan James is. It's all he's talked about since he saw the picture of us at the playoffs in my office. I'm sure if he was able to show off his favorite player at school and elevate his playground status a bit, his mother might be willing to show a little appreciation. Maybe I could put in a good word for you." She tipped her beer bottle toward him clinking the top of his.

It would probably work, but Grant wasn't sure it was a good idea. Bethany had made it perfectly clear that she didn't want anyone using her son as a way to get close to her. Not that he'd need to *pretend* to like James. He couldn't help himself. Any more than he could help being attracted to Bethany.

He needed to stay away and not put himself into that sort of predicament. Grant needed to focus on getting back into spring training, not spend what little time he had left trying to convince some woman he was worth dating when he could offer her nothing but a short-term fling. But he'd be damned if he could think of anything else.

"WHY DIDN'T YOU tell me you were going out on a date with Grant McQuaid?" Her aide, Julie, dropped the morning paper on the table in the lounge before class started.

"What?" Bethany nearly spilled the coffee as she set it on the table and looked at the newspaper. The front page showed a picture of Grant holding James at the counter as they ordered pizza. Somehow, someone had caught the moment on film and now it was headline news for their small town.

Wonderful. "It wasn't a date."

"So, it *is* true?" Julie's voice pitched several octaves higher. "Do you know how many women are going to hate you now? How did you meet him? What happened?" She lowered her voice to a whisper. "Is what they say about him true?"

"It wasn't a date," Bethany repeated. "James almost tripped him in the park the other day. He was just being nice to take him out to pizza, that's all."

Julie's eyes twinkled wickedly. "Sure it is."

Bethany clenched her jaw before pinching her lips together firmly. "Julie," she warned. "Nothing happened. We had pizza and I took James home."

"Well, that's not how this article makes it sound."

Julie tapped the paper and Bethany cringed as she skimmed it. It repeatedly insinuated that there was far more to the picture than just a pizza and some pool. It didn't even mention the fact that Grant and James had been playing football at the park. Instead, it implied they'd shared intimate moments and stolen glances. It was Bethany's worst nightmare come true.

"How many times do I have to tell you—"

"You don't date. I know." Julie looked like she'd just lost her best friend. "Do you have any idea how much I was looking forward to the dirty details of your wild night with a football star? If I can't have Grant McQuaid myself, I wanted to live vicariously through you."

"Sorry. But I guess this means you can have him now. It's just one of my personal rules."

"Tell me again why you don't date?" She pulled the paper closer, looking at the picture wistfully. "I mean, if I had a guy like Grant McQuaid taking me out for pizza, I'd be showing him just how grateful I was, maybe even twice. I'd break every rule in the book. I might even make up a couple just so we could break them." Julie winked at Bethany.

Bethany shook her head and rolled her eyes. Julie was the first person Bethany had met after the real estate agent showed her the house, and they'd quickly become friends, but as much as Bethany adored the aide, it didn't stop her from keeping her private life exactly that—private. That meant not sharing the details about her afternoon with Julie, not that there was anything to share.

"It was nothing more than James meeting his hero and Grant McQuaid spending some time with a fan."

"Who's the bigger fan? James or you?" Julie winked.

"A guy like him is the last thing I need in my life, the last thing *James* needs. What I do need is to get these kids ready for our field trip next week."

"What you need is to get laid."

"Julie!" Bethany felt the blush burn her cheeks.

Her friend laughed. "It's true. I bet you haven't had a good man in your life in years. You're *not* in a convent," she scolded, waving her hand, indicating the teachers' lounge. "You need someone who'll come in and rock your world off its matronly axis, Bethany."

"No, I don't. What I need is to get into the classroom before I have twenty-five monkeys jumping on desks."

Bethany rose, trying not to glance down at the picture staring back at her. James looked happy. No, he looked over-the-moon ecstatic, but what really caught her attention was the look on Grant's handsome face. He was facing James but he was looking at her with more than a little interest. She felt the sizzle of desire curling in her belly again.

Would it have really been so bad to let him come to

the house for ice cream? She had no doubt she could have had a good time with him if she'd let herself. Instead, she'd pushed him away, upsetting her son and making sure that the one and only man she'd been attracted to in the last few years would want nothing more to do with her.

Chapter Six

GRANT GRUNTED AS he finished his bench press set and
his brother slid the barbell back onto the rack. "Not too
shabby," Ben commented, not bothering to hide his ad-
miration. "You've got me beat."

Grant sat up and reached for the towel to wipe the
sweat dripping into his eyes. "I've gotta do better than
this."

He eyed the barbell. He was going to need to push
more than the two-sixty he was using now if he wanted
back on the team. This wasn't going to be enough, not
with so many young guys gunning for his position in the
Combine right now. And with the draft coming up . . .

"What exactly are you trying to prove, Grant? That
you can kill yourself?" Ben shook his head at his brother
and leaned over the bar, crossing his arms. "Why is it that
you can't just accept that it might be time to retire? Do
you want to finish out the next sixty years of your life in

a wheelchair? Because that's what the doctor said could happen if you take a hit wrong. Or worse. You know that."

Grant stood up, throwing the towel into his gym bag, and tugged his t-shirt over his head, zipping up the bag without answering his brother. He knew the consequences and didn't need the reminders of how likely he was to fail. He'd read every prediction from various sports writers, heard the commentary from the correspondents and read enough doctor's reports that he knew the risks.

But he wasn't ready to give up. Not yet. Not while there was still a chance for him to get back into the game. He had to give this last shot his all. He had to make a comeback and prove everyone wrong. Not succeeding was not an option. He couldn't afford to not make a comeback.

Grant hurried for the door of the firehouse, trying to head off any arguments. "Thanks for letting me use your gym."

"Anytime, brother. You know you're always welcome here." He didn't miss the note of curiosity in Ben's voice.

This burning desire to push, to excel, wasn't something he could explain to his family. It was just a part of him, what drove him every day. He had to play football; it was the only way for Grant to help provide for them. His entire family kept that ranch running and, since he wasn't around, his contribution was purely monetary. In fact, he'd sunk a hefty chunk of his savings into several new wells and an irrigation system to combat the drought that had struck the entire state and also helped with the start-up funds for Jackson to start his own horse breeding facility on the ranch. If he couldn't continue to support his family, what kind of man was he? He had no right even thinking of starting a family of his own until he had more than just his name to offer them.

Hurrying from the station toward the parking lot, the school across the street caught his eye. At least sixty kids ran around the blacktop, playing on the swings and monkey bars or caught in a game of what looked like baseball on the grassy field. Except for one small boy who stood alone in the back corner of the field, tossing a football into the air and catching it.

Grant couldn't mistake that blond hair for anyone else and felt the breath catch in his lungs painfully. Poor James stood off from everyone else, ignored completely by the other kids.

Leave it alone.

Without permission from his brain, his feet carried him toward the front doors of Hidden Falls Elementary. He'd no more stepped inside when he heard a stern voice from his right.

"Excuse me, sir, you need to check in." The receptionist stopped him before he could get past the desk. "Oh, you're—"

"Grant McQuaid! Maddie told me you might be willing to come talk to the kids. You have no idea how excited they would be to meet you."

As Grant turned to face the secretary, he recognized Raif Hunt, one of his former high school teammates. In fact, they'd graduated together but Grant hadn't seen him in years and had no idea he'd become the elementary school administrator.

"It's been a while. Didn't Maddie tell you I'm the principal now?" Raif held out his hand and chuckled at Grant's obvious confusion.

"She might have mentioned it, but I don't remember. It's good to see you, bulldog." Raif cringed at the nickname his teammates had called the boy who growled at the opposing players on the line of scrimmage.

"Yeah, these days it's just Mr. Hunt," he chuckled.

Grant glanced toward the door as he shook Raif's hand, wondering how quickly he could get out to the playground to talk to James. The slouch of his shoulders seemed so forlorn and lonely as he stood in the field, even from a distance, that Grant didn't want to hang out in the office chatting, but he couldn't exactly walk onto the school playground without permission. There were rules these days. Procedures to follow, and he doubted those included letting some strange man just walk out to see kids.

What had he been thinking? This spontaneity wasn't like him. He usually thought everything through.

"What are *you* doing here?"

Grant heard Bethany's voice and spun to see her looking prim and proper, albeit slightly shocked, in her frilly peasant blouse and jeans. Grant couldn't stop himself from letting his eyes travel the length of those long legs, taking in every curve she didn't seem to realize she showed. Her hair was pulled back into a tightly restrained ponytail again and he wondered if it didn't speak to her personality.

"Oh, Ms. Mills, have you met Mr. McQuaid? He's one of our local celebrities." Raif rolled his eyes and shook his head. "Surely, you've already heard about him from Ms. McQuaid. She's pretty proud of him."

Bethany's eyes shifted from Grant to her boss. Confusion flickered over her face before fire sparked in her eyes, igniting her anger, and he could practically feel the tension emanating from her.

Great. What in the world did I do now?

"From Ms. McQuaid?" she repeated.

Heat flooded her face as Bethany nodded, trying to ignore the sharp slice of envy coupled with the shame at having had dinner with a married man. She didn't remember hearing in the news that he'd married, but that didn't mean it hadn't happened. She didn't pay much attention to gossip about the private lives of football stars, and there were always those guys who kept their family lives hidden. She recalled the phone call he'd received at the park and cursed her naiveté. Now with the article in the paper, everyone would think she'd been trying to steal her co-worker's husband. The nightmare just seemed to get worse.

Indignation rose up in her as she glared at Grant. *He* was the one who'd cheated on his wife. She was grateful now she'd insisted that their trip to the pizza place was not a "date." Although, terminology had little to do with the disappointment she wanted to deny right now. Mr. Hunt cleared his throat and she realized she was staring at Grant, silently.

"Huh, I probably should have made the connection but I don't usually spend much time in her office. As a matter of fact, I'm seeing your wife today with James."

Grant couldn't hide his shameless grin and Bethany thought about smacking him for a brief moment until Mr. Hunt choked as he laughed aloud.

"Oh, no. Ms. Mills, Maddie, is Grant's *sister.*"

Grant cocked his head at her, his dark eyes glinting with humor. Bethany had no idea it was even possible to blush more than she was. She couldn't remember ever feeling this embarrassed. Unless it was after her father's comment last night. It appeared she was bound to make a fool out of herself repeatedly in front of this man.

"Mr. Hunt," Mrs. Bale, the school secretary, interrupted. "I'm sorry, sir, but you have Mrs. Davis on line two. She says it's important."

He rolled his eyes. "I'm sure it is. With her and her son, everything is. Ms. Mills, would you mind taking Mr. McQuaid on a quick tour while the kids are at lunch? I'll meet up with you at the kindergarten classroom in a bit so we can figure out a good day and time for an assembly."

Bethany opened her mouth to protest but Mr. Hunt had already vanished into his office, shutting the door behind him. Mrs. Bale shot Bethany a look of pure jealousy, practically swooning as Grant opened the door for her.

"Ladies first, Ms. Mills."

Sighing in resignation, Bethany ducked through the

doorway, scooting past him. "You never answered my question," she muttered as the door closed behind him.

"And which question was that?" She cocked her head to one side, crossing her arms over her chest. Grant chuckled at her disapproval. She might be used to this tone working on kids but he was no child. "You mean, why I'm here? Maybe I came to see Raif."

She continued to glare at him silently, waiting for n better answer. "Okay, you want the truth?"

Bethany couldn't hide the irritation in her voice and arched a brow high on her forehead. "No, by all means, please lie to me, Mr. McQuaid. That's exactly why I asked, for you to lie."

Grant shook his head and tried to bite back his laughter. "Why, Ms. Mills, do I detect a note of sarcastic smart ass in you after all?"

"Watch your language," she chastised. "There are kids here and the last thing I need is a parent complaining because you want to mock me."

He frowned and she could see the remorse in his face. "Sorry, I didn't think."

"I'm sure you didn't. I thought after last night—" Bethany planted her fists on her hips, letting her words fall away. She hadn't done much thinking either, if this morning's front page was any indicator. Parents were likely to be far more upset about her *extracurricular* activities than his language.

He held his hands out in front of him. "Trust me, you made your position very clear. I'm not here to ask you out again."

She glanced at the long fingers extended out in front of her, noticing the callouses on his palms. Her father always told her you could tell a hard-working man worth keeping by the callouses on his hands. She wondered what he'd say about Grant.

He'd love him and you know it.

She felt disappointment course through her as she thought about how many women would have reacted differently to Grant's dinner invitation. Hell, Julie had practically throttled her this morning. But, as much as she might want to date this attractive, hard-working, kind man, she had to think of James first and what was best for her son.

Grant's words sank in slowly. He was making it clear he wouldn't make the same mistake again. She'd had her shot at this guy and had thrown it away with both hands.

"I was with my brother at the fire station and was actually heading to my car when I noticed James playing out in the field alone." He clenched his jaw and she wondered at his sudden obvious aggravation. "I don't know what I was thinking I could do, but it bothered me to see him off by himself. The next thing I knew, I was in the office with Raif and you walked in."

Bethany couldn't help but be touched by his heartfelt honesty, feeling the wall around her heart chip slightly. Regret assailed her as she realized how unfairly she'd judged him, without any indication he deserved it. She couldn't believe how arrogant she must sound, assuming he'd come here to see her.

"You really came over here just to see James?"

He ducked his head slightly. "Look, Bethany, I swear I'm not some creepy stalker, but that kid of yours has gotten under my skin. He just looked so sad out there by himself and—"

She could see from the look on his face that he really cared about James. Not just as a fan, but on a personal level. Bethany didn't need to hear any more. "Come on."

She hurried with him toward the open field. Scanning the area, Bethany saw her son near the fence on the right, tossing the ball high into the air and dancing beneath it. He missed more often than he caught it but she didn't doubt for a second that he was acting out some brilliant Super Bowl fantasy in his imagination.

"Here." She reached into a bin nearby and pulled out a worn youth-sized football with tattered laces barely hanging on. Her fingers brushed over his and she tried to ignore the sizzle of pleasure that skirted up her arm. The ball was tiny in Grant's hands but smaller than the one James was trying to catch now. It would be just the right size for him. "Go out there with him. When the other kids see you, they'll come over but don't tell them you know me. Let them see you as James' friend."

The corner of Grant's mouth turned up when he comprehended why she was sending him out to James without her. It would give James more credibility with the other kids to be seen with a football hero that was *his* friend rather than one that his mother knew.

"You're a good mom, Bethany." His gaze caressed her face, warming her cheeks.

He didn't touch her but the tenderness she could see

in his eyes shot straight to her heart, and she returned his smile. His gaze heated, smoldering slightly with what looked like longing, before it was gone and he spun on his heel, jogging out to the field where James played.

She felt the butterflies in her stomach bounce wildly against her ribs as she tried to catch her breath. *Goodness, what have I gotten myself into now?*

GRANT WAITED AT his car for Bethany and James to finish up inside the classroom. He'd spent the rest of lunch recess entertaining nearly forty kids who'd come running over when they realized James knew a professional football player. The smile that lit James' face when he introduced Grant had been well worth the discomfort he'd faced trying to explain why he was at the school to Bethany.

He couldn't blame her for being standoffish with him when she first saw him there. What kind of weirdo showed up at your job the day after you told him to take a hike? But something had shifted in her today. He'd seen it in her eyes when he tried to explain why he'd come. Enough that he was willing to push his luck and see if she wasn't up for having ice cream today.

Grant saw her heading toward her older model sedan in the school parking lot, juggling an armload of books, papers and teaching supplies. James wore a small back-pack with a cartoon character he didn't recognize on his little shoulders but Bethany carried an overfilled tote bag that had to weigh more than she did.

"Hey! Here, let me get that for you." He hurried to her side, sliding the bag from her shoulder. Apprehension colored her hazel eyes and, for a moment, he wondered if she wasn't going to tell him to leave again. Instead, she unlocked her car.

Grant wasn't sure if he should ask but knew it would look far more suspicious if he didn't now. "What are you guys up to? I thought maybe I could convince you to get that ice cream today."

James' face brightened and he looked up at his mother. "Can we?"

Bethany bit her lower lip. "We can't."

Grant tried not to take the second rejection to heart and nodded in understanding.

"Our downstairs toilet broke this morning and I had to turn it off. Now I've got to run to the store for the part and figure out how to fix it," she explained.

Relief he hadn't expected coursed through him. Maybe she wasn't shooting him down after all. He let the corner of his mouth tip up playfully. "Ms. Mills, that sort of sounds like a load of C-R-A-P," he spelled, laughing at his bad pun.

Her eyes widened but she smiled at his audacity. "Mr. McQuaid," she scolded.

James giggled beside her and Grant immediately realized his mistake. "Mom, he spelled a bad word."

"How did he . . . never mind. I should have known this genius could spell that," Grant said, trying not to laugh. "How about if I help you fix your toilet?"

She popped open the truck, indicating that he should

set her bag inside. "You want to fix my toilet?" Bethany crossed her arms and leaned a hip against the side of the car as she closed the trunk. "Really? That's the line you want to go with?"

Grant shrugged but the smile never left his lips. What was it about this woman and her kid that made him feel so comfortably at ease? He hadn't felt this relaxed in a long time. She made it easy for him to forget about his injury, the pressure of his upcoming training camp and his possible job loss.

"What do you say, little man? You think between the two of us men, we can fix the toilet for your mom?"

"Yes!" he yelled cheerfully. James climbed into the back seat of the car and buckled himself into his booster seat.

"I'll meet you at the hardware store." Grant turned to walk back to his car.

"I'm not going to get rid of you, am I?"

Grant paused and looked back over his shoulder at her. "Why would you want to?" he asked with a wink and jogged the rest of the way back to his car.

THE THREE OF them stood in front of the plumbing display in the hardware store as Bethany's gaze slid over the rows of pipes, valves and fittings that might as well be car parts as far as she could figure out what to do with them. She had no idea what part to get, what size or where any of it would go, let alone how to install any of it. She'd hoped it would be far less complicated than this and that she could fix it herself. Spending several hundred dollars on a plumber was the last thing she could afford when her car was already making some strange grinding noise that she needed to get checked out.

"So what do you need?"

Bethany bit the corner of her lip and turned embarrassed eyes toward Grant and shrugged. "I literally have no clue."

His laughter was the last reaction she expected. Irritation for wasting his time, maybe. Annoyance for being a helpless female, likely. Probably even some frustration for her lack of plumbing knowledge. But instead, his rich laughter carried across the nearly empty aisle, surround her in warmth and making parts of her body tingle in ways she'd forgotten they could.

"So what you're saying is you've got a broken toilet and no idea why it's broken?"

Bethany looked down at James as if he were going to offer her some assistance, but he only laughed along with Grant. She wouldn't have thought her boy would turn on her quite so easily. She smiled down at James. "Other than the fact that I managed to turn off the water, yes, I guess that about sums up the situation."

"Why don't we start with how you know it's broken," Grant suggested.

"There was water everywhere, spraying from the back," James said, his little hands moving quickly as he signed while he spoke. "My shoes got all wet and I had to find my other ones. And Mom got sprayed in the face."

He tried unsuccessfully to hide his giggle as he looked up at her. "Mom said there wasn't pee in it but—"

"Okay, that's enough James." She arched a brow at him but Grant didn't even bother to control his laughter and she found herself giggling with them at the recollection. "It was just water coming from the wall."

Grant nodded, trying to hide his grin and appear solemn, before grabbing a couple of items from the brackets on the wall. "Was it leaking *in* the wall or outside of it?"

"Outside, where it goes into the back of the toilet," she clarified.

Grant nodded. "That's a pretty simple fix. And, for the record, there's no pee in the water that got on your mom, buddy."

James frowned and Bethany shook her head, poking her fingers into his ribs, making him squeal. "Don't look so disappointed that your mom just had regular water spray her, you stinker."

James laughed, wiggling and squirming until he hid behind Grant, peeking at her from behind his legs. Bethany tried not to notice how muscular Grant's thighs were when James arms wrapped around them or the jealousy that crept in when James reached his hand up and tucked it into Grant's much larger one as the pair headed for the cash register at the front of the store. As she reached the clerk, she saw Grant already paying for her purchases.

She tugged her wallet from her purse. "I've got it."

"It's fine," he said, barely looking up at her.

"No," she argued. "You're already fixing it for me. You have to let me pay."

"Too late." He accepted the receipt from the clerk and glanced back at her. The glare she shot him didn't seem to faze him in the slightest as his lips curled up in that charming boyish grin that deepened the dimple in his cheek. His gaze swept over her. "You'll learn pretty quickly that I tend to get my way most of the time."

"I've noticed," she muttered, following him and James as they led the way out to the parking lot, wondering why his comment didn't have her running for the hills the way it would have with anyone else.

Chapter Seven

BETHANY WATCHED FROM the doorway as Grant Mc-
Quaid, star running back, lay on her bathroom floor
repairing the seal on her toilet. Thank goodness she'd
cleaned the tile after the water had soaked it.

"That should do it," he announced, standing up and
handing James the wrench he'd purchased. "Go put that
in a safe place so your mom has it when she needs it next
time."

His shirt had several wet spots on it from his less-
than-stellar handyman skills, plastering it to him in several places and making it difficult for Bethany to keep
from staring at the way the muscles of his upper body
shifted, flexing with his every movement. Her fingers
itched to run down the lines of his rib cage where the
shirt clung to him like a second skin.

"Ice cream time," James announced, running past her
into the hallway.

"Put it into the drawer by the phone, baby," she called after him.

Grant washed his hands at the sink and wiped them on the towel sitting on the counter before he turned toward her. "Ice cream time," he repeated, his voice low and husky.

It didn't sound like a fun outing when he said it. It sounded like a dark promise of sweet, sinfully dangerous things to come. He took a step toward her, eliminating any distance between them and looked down at her, his dampened chest only inches from her face. Her fingers twitched, desperate to reach out and touch his skin, to see if it was indeed as hot and hard as it looked.

"Are you ready?"

Bethany glanced up at him, the heat from his skin warming her without a touch, setting every nerve ending in her body on high alert. She felt his breath wash over the top of her head. "Are you sure you want to do this? You don't have to."

The smile that spread over his lips was warm. And slightly wicked. "Bethany, there is nothing I'd rather do right now."

His eyes met hers and he lifted a finger under her chin. His hand was cool and still slightly damp from washing up but his gaze was hot. Bethany felt the sizzle of electricity from his touch as it stole her breath. She licked her lips, wondering what she could say, if she could even form words to speak.

His gaze fell to her lips and she felt her knees weaken,

her breaths coming in shallow pants. "I take that back. I *can* think of a few other things I'd rather do with you."

Grant took another step toward the doorway and she moved backward, molding her back into the door frame even as his chest pressed against her. She inhaled the scent of him, earthy and all male. Not cologne but simply soap and the heady, heavenly scent of his skin. Every part of her tingled, a raging inferno sparked in the long-dry tinder she'd forced her body to become. She felt the coarse hair of his forearms under her fingertips as she clung to him for balance. Grant's head tipped to one side and he leaned closer.

He was going to kiss her and, heaven help her, she'd never wanted anything as desperately as she did his kiss at this moment.

"Grant." She had no idea what she wanted to say, whether it was to ask him to stop, or beg him not to. Her voice was barely a whisper of sound but she saw his eyes darken as her fingers dug into the muscle of his arm.

"Come on," James appeared at her side in the hall. *We are going to be late*, he signed.

Grant laughed quietly before signing *okay*. He plucked his t-shirt from his skin. "I'd ask to borrow your dryer but I think it'd be better if we don't keep James waiting."

Bethany glanced down and saw several damp spots on her own shirt where their bodies had been pressed together. Goodness, if he took off his t-shirt, she'd faint on the spot.

THE EXTRA ATTENTION they received while waiting in line at the small ice cream parlor didn't pass Grant's notice. There had been several people slowing as they walked past the front window, a few daring to point at them. Luckily, Bethany seemed oblivious but it wouldn't take long before she caught on to what was happening. After their failed dinner last night, he didn't want anything to add any more pressure to today.

"What do you say to taking these cones back to the house so I can throw the ball around with James for a bit?" he suggested.

It wasn't a complete lie. He'd much rather play football with James than sit in a booth with people staring at them, speculating about who she was and why he was with her and her son. Bethany hesitated and he could almost see the excuses running through her mind.

"What if I promise you that this is not me making a play for you? I'm just really enjoying the time I've been able to spend with you guys and being treated like a normal person. Plus, I get the feeling you could use a friend around here."

"Friend, huh?" She arched a slim brow dubiously.

He gave her a lopsided grin and raised two fingers into the air. "Scout's honor."

She laughed and shook her head, lifting his ring finger and pressing them all together. "It's obvious you've never been a Scout or you'd know how to do it right." She shook her head and looked up at him through her lashes. "How am I supposed to trust someone who impersonates a Boy Scout? And poorly?"

"You're right, I was never a Scout." Grant tucked his hand into his pocket as they headed toward the door, shaking his head. "I was too busy playing ball. But my Dad did raise me to always keep my promises."

She paused with the spoon lifted partway to her mouth and tried to read him with those beautifully expressive hazel eyes. He could see the questions swirling in the depths of them, curiosity waging a war with her vulnerability.

After what seemed like hours, she agreed. Grant held open the door as Bethany and James went through, escorting them back to his car. He'd wondered at the frivolity of taking it for such a short distance when they'd left her house, but now he was grateful for the tinted windows that would hide her and James from prying eyes. Unfortunately, he wasn't sure if he was protecting her privacy for her sake or his own.

"MOM, WATCH!"

James turned his back on Grant and ran across the backyard. Just when he stopped and turned to face Grant again, the man she'd already seen easily pass a football forty yards to his brother, acted as if his ten foot pass to James was a tremendous effort. She clapped as the ball landed squarely in James' hands and he spiked it with zeal, performing his version of a wobbly-kneed touchdown dance. Grant danced around as well, copying James with every step, before falling onto his back on the grass as Bethany cheered for them.

"That was amazing." She directed the words at her son but her eyes were taking in the man lying supine on her back lawn. James ran up to him and threw one leg over Grant's stomach, plopping down and making Grant grunt loudly. "Be careful, James," she scolded.

She watched him sign an apology to Grant before being scooped up and swung over Grant's shoulder as he stood up. "What do you say, Mom? Didn't you tell me you were going to buy a sack of potatoes?" He tickled James, laughing along with the boy's squeals of delight.

"Okay, you two." She slid James from Grant's arms and put him back onto his feet. "You need to go get cleaned up for dinner."

"We had dinner," James argued. *Ice cream*, he signed.

She tipped her head disapprovingly. "That wasn't dinner and you know it. Go wash up." She swatted his bottom lightly as he hurried into the house and up the stairs. Grant chuckled as he held open the back door for her.

"I'll say it again, Bethany. You're a great mom."

She looked back at him as she moved past, trying not to notice the way he was watching her, like he wanted to finish what had almost happened in the bathroom. She cleared her throat. "He's a pretty great kid. I wish I could take all the credit."

He gave her an odd look.

"What?"

"Well, you said that his father was gone. You've been the only one raising him. So who else would you give credit to? Learn to take a well-deserved compliment, woman." He followed her into the kitchen, leaning a hip against the island as he watched her move to the refrigerator.

Bethany hadn't meant to open this can of worms. She pulled a head of lettuce and two tomatoes from inside the crisper, trying to figure out what she could say without revealing too much.

"Well, my parents for one. My Mom watched James during the day so I could finish school and, when I started working, she took care of him and made sure he got to the therapy appointments I couldn't get to."

"Need help?" he offered as he moved closer.

She pointed at the drawer beside his hip. "Knives are inside but it has a child lock." She showed him how to open it. "And then there was always my Dad. He's been the only father figure James has ever known, but I couldn't have asked for a better one."

Bethany pulled several chicken breasts from the freezer to thaw. She should ask him to stay for dinner, especially when he was helping her fix it, but she was worried he might get the wrong idea. She'd made it clear that she wasn't interested in dating but if that were true, why was her body humming from his nearness, every nerve ending on edge? Asking him to stay would be like lighting the fuse on a stick of dynamite, but she could already hear her mother's voice scolding her about how rude it would be not to ask. Not to mention that she couldn't deny that it felt good to have him look at her the way he had all day, like she was more than just a mom, more than someone to pity. He treated her like a woman he respected, and made her feel desirable. Paired with the raw sex appeal this man had, it was a dangerous combination. She spit out the words before she could second-guess herself.

"Did you want to stay for dinner?" Her breath caught in her throat as she waited for his answer.

Grant turned back toward her, his eyes dark with a yearning her body instantly recognized. Her heart slammed in her chest, pounding furiously. "I do."

Her stomach did a backflip.

"But I can't."

"Oh." She hoped she didn't actually sound as disappointed as she felt. She shouldn't be feeling this way. She needed to rein in her fantasies and regain control of her wayward libido. "Maybe another time."

She set the chicken onto a plate and washed her hands, avoiding looking at him. She reached for the towel on the counter before grabbing a bowl for the salad from the cupboard beside him. "Here," she said, passing it his way.

Grant's hands covered hers on the side of the bowl and she could feel the jolt of electricity shoot up her arm, striking her square in the chest and coiling into a molten desire low in her belly. She caught her breath in a quick gasp and her gaze lifted to meet his.

Bethany could read the heated, primal desire in his eyes, was sure he could see it in hers as well, and wondered why she didn't just lean forward a couple of inches and make the first move. Her gaze fell to his mouth, his lips so full, perfect for kissing. With her lower back against the edge of the counter, she should have felt trapped, pinned between the granite countertop and wall of muscle that would likely burn her if she touched it. His fingers moved over the back of her hand, sending shivers of anticipation through her.

"Grant, I—" Her voice was barely a whisper of sound. She rocked forward on her toes, leaning into him, giving in to the need she'd forgotten existed between a man and woman. And, goodness, was he all man.

His head tilted, dipping toward hers, but his gaze never left hers. She could stop his kiss at any moment but there wasn't one part of her that wanted to.

Footsteps pounded on the staircase, breaking the spell he'd woven over her, making her jump backward against the counter.

What was she thinking? She couldn't have James see her with him, not like this. Bethany quickly slid away from the counter, setting the bowl aside and hurrying to the sink. Bracing her hands on the counter, she tried to regain her bearings and her self-control. She bit her lower lip, wondering where she'd lost her sense of self-preservation.

"Are you staying for dinner?" James asked as he trotted into the kitchen and pulled one of the chairs toward the sink to watch his mother ready the chicken.

Bethany felt her stomach clench and cursed her reaction. How could she feel this strongly attracted to a man she barely knew? "Mr. McQuaid can't stay tonight, baby."

Grant moved to the other side of James and she was grateful for her son between them. It was a great reminder of her priorities and who she needed to put first.

"I don't know. I guess maybe I can stay."

Her eyes lifted to his, questioning, but he wasn't looking at her. His gaze was focused on James and she could see the worship reflected in her son's blue eyes as he stared up at his hero. James wasn't looking at him like a sports star now—he was looking at Grant the way he looked at his Grandfather. Bethany couldn't help but wonder how that had happened so quickly.

How had Grant scaled the skyscraper of a wall she'd kept around her and James for the last six years in only a few days? And why couldn't she seem to convince herself to do more to stop it?

She took another chicken breast from the freezer, running it under hot water to defrost it before placing it with the others.

"Mom, can me and Mr. McQuaid watch T.V.?"

"Mr. McQuaid and I," she corrected as she signed *yes* to him.

"Come on," he said, jumping down from the chair and reaching for Grant's hand.

"Well, now, buddy, I think we should probably help your mother in here. Why don't you show me where to find the plates and silverware and we'll set the table for her." He leaned down to James' level. "And, you can call me Grant."

James looked to his mother for permission and she couldn't help but smile at his glee. She didn't usually let James call adults by their first names but, she also didn't usually have strange men setting her dinner table. Grant was proving to be an exception to many of her rules. She nodded slightly and turned back to ready the chicken while the pair set the table, signing in between their chatter about football.

It was hard to keep herself from slipping into the fantasy—the one where this was just another ordinary day in her life—when a husband and children were all she'd ever wanted. She'd always pictured herself a mother with several children, the white picket fence and, maybe, a dog. She'd imagined dinners and birthday parties and vacations as a family. Never, before or after she and Matthew married, had she dreamed she'd be barely scraping by as a single mother, worrying about things like toilets and car repairs . . . or dating.

She looked at her son, basking in the attention from Grant. It could be far worse.

James was well adjusted and bright. They had a home in a beautiful town. And even though she rarely let people get close, they had a few friends. Melissa and . . .

Bethany paused, realizing there was no one else. She had never let anyone else close enough for more than a casual greeting. She didn't let anyone see inside her world because then no one could make judgments, about James or about her.

Suddenly, her life felt lonely and pitiable. And that was something Bethany refused to be—pitied. She turned around and slid the chicken into the oven.

"Are you okay?"

Bethany stood and saw Grant watching her, his brow furrowed as if he was trying to figure her out, while James climbed into one of the chairs and waited for them to finish in the kitchen.

"Yeah, why?"

She wasn't okay, but she wasn't about to admit it. These little white lies were just another part of keeping walls up and pretenses in place. Of not letting anyone see her need for protection from others.

Grant shrugged. "I don't know, the way you sighed." He took a step closer, making her want to retreat but she had nowhere to go. "The way your shoulders are all bunched around your ears." He moved even closer, lowering his voice so that James couldn't hear. "The way your eyes looked all sad again."

He reached up a finger and brushed a strand of hair from where it caught in her eyelashes. Her heart immediately began pounding against the inside of her chest, heat flooding her body. He didn't touch her, didn't have to, but she felt the warmth emanate from his body to hers. She licked her lips, unable to speak, and saw his eyes darken even more.

"You can talk to me, Bethany." The corner of his mouth curved up in a beguiling half-smile. "My sister says I'm a great listener and I'm a great guy to have as a friend."

Friend? It was what she had told him she wanted, more than once.

Longing and disappointment crashed through her simultaneously, like two conflicting waves of the emotional spectrum and threatened to drag her into the undertow. She reached her hands behind her, gripping the rolled edge of the counter top to regain her balance and returned his smile, glancing over his shoulder at James, watching them intently.

"I guess we could probably use another friend. Right, James?"

"Yes," he agreed, jumping down and hurrying to where they stood, wiggling his way into the small space between them. Bethany breathed a little easier and ran her hand over James' head, feeling the strength of her willpower return. "Mom says it's good to have lots of friends."

Grant's gaze flicked from James' back to hers. "Your mother is a very smart woman, buddy." He took a step backward, leaning his hip against the island but not breaking eye contact with her. "She knows that friends are important. They are the people you can count on to help you."

"Like you, fixing our toilet."

Grant laughed, looking back down at James. "Exactly like that."

Chapter Eight

GRANT LEANED AGAINST the back of the couch and looked down at the little blond head curled against his stomach as the end credits played on the Disney movie. They weren't even twenty minutes into it when he'd crawled over his mother and planted himself firmly between them on the couch, leaning against Grant's side. He'd never seen a movie about talking cars before but James had loved every minute. Bethany leaned forward and reached for the remote on the table before turning off the television and rising from the couch. She looked down at James, curled against Grant.

"I should probably get him to bed." She bent down, her dark ponytail swinging toward his face as she tried several times to scoop James from his lap without touching him. Grant could smell vanilla and sunshine with just a hint of wildflowers. It was just too damn tempting for him not to inhale deeply.

"I'll do it." Grant stood, effortlessly lifting the boy to his shoulder.

"Wait, I need to take these off." She leaned against his arm and unplugged the microphones over each ear from the battery pack, slipping the packs from where they were held with Velcro strips around his upper arms. With her body pressed against him, Grant felt every muscle in his body clench with need. He willed parts of his body straining against his jeans to settle down before he embarrassed them both.

"There," she said, stepping back. "Just follow me upstairs and I'll turn down his bed."

Grant felt his chest constrict as he watched her lead the way to the stairs, her hips swaying gently as she walked. "Pajamas?"

"He can just sleep in his clothes tonight." She plugged his batteries into the charger and tucked the microphones into their case before tugging down the blankets on his twin bed. Grant felt her eyes on him as he settled James on the mattress and pulled the covers over him. "Thank you for bringing him up."

"My pleasure," he murmured, his voice husky even to his own ears.

His words held far more impact than they should have and he wondered if she would read too much into them. They'd come to a sort of truce today—friendship and nothing more—and he didn't want to destroy the headway he was making at getting to know her, to know them both.

She smiled slightly. "You do realize you don't have to whisper now, right? He can't hear you."

Grant dropped his head sheepishly. "I didn't even think about it. Sorry."

She laid her hand on his arm and he felt the skin ignite under her fingers, heat sizzling up to his chest. "Don't apologize for being considerate, Grant. Come on."

She stopped to turn on a night light in the bathroom across from James' room before heading back down, pausing at the foot of the stairs. "Did you want something to drink? I don't really keep anything stronger than coffee in the house with James but I'm sure I could find something if I look hard enough."

His gaze skimmed over her. He wanted to kiss her, wanted to pull her into his arms, drag her up against his body and give in to the temptation to taste those perfect, plump lips. Instead, Grant shook his head.

"I should really get going." He glanced at the door to his left but didn't make a move toward it. "Thanks for dinner, Bethany."

"It was my pleasure."

His own words repeated back to him made the yearning ricochet through him and he felt his body clench again with longing. How in the world could she affect him this way when he'd only known her a few days? Bethany cleared her throat and he wondered if she could see the hunger in his eyes, if he was making her uncomfortable.

"I mean . . . after how nice you've been to James and helping me with the toilet, it was the least I could do."

Grant sighed and stuffed his hands into the pockets of his jeans. It was a good reminder for himself. *Hands off.*

"That's what friends are for."

As attracted as he was to Bethany, they were two different people wanting completely different things from life. She was stubborn and slightly skittish when it came to men, but he suspected it had more to do with her past than anything he'd done. She'd been on her own with James for some time and that had made her autonomous and almost too self-reliant. But he'd seen the loneliness and sorrow reflected in her face, especially when she watched him with James. She deserved a man in her life to treat her—to treat them both—with the devotion they deserved.

Unfortunately, he couldn't be that man.

He was leaving, heading out of town and back to Memphis as soon as the doctors gave him his medical clearance to go. He had a job to get back to, a team waiting for him to help them get to the playoffs again next year. He'd already seen the toll that football wrought on relationships, tearing them to pieces and leaving broken hearts and shattered marriages. He'd made a vow early on that he would never do that. Not until he'd finished his career. But, staring into Bethany's eyes, he felt the ache of loneliness.

Would it be so bad if the doctors didn't clear him and he could stay here, with someone like her? Someday be a father to a kid like James?

Grant clenched his jaw, squeezing his hands into fists in his pockets. Yes, it would.

Bethany needed a man who would stick around this town, and love every moment. Not a guy who had no interest in being tied down in the sticks when he really wanted to hear the rest of the world chanting his name while he strode onto the field. They were heading in two different directions in life. He could be her friend, but that was all. And that meant keeping his hands off her, regardless of how drawn he was to her.

"So, I guess we'll see you around." Her voice trembled slightly, hesitantly, reminding him again of that vulnerability she tried so hard to disguise.

He nodded and glanced at his watch. "Tomorrow. Remember, I promised James I'd take him for a ride at my parents' ranch."

Her brows dipped in a frown. "Wait, you did? When?"

"When we were setting the table. You don't remember us talking about it?" He moved toward the front door. "We have a picnic planned, football with my brothers, swimming in the pond, the works."

She narrowed her eyes. "You didn't ask me about this. I would have remembered." Bethany shook her finger at him, looking every inch the scolding mother. "You and James cooked this whole plan up and you were going to spring it on me, but he fell asleep first."

Grant could barely hide the smirk tugging at his lips. "Okay, guilty as charged." He opened the door, prepared to escape. "But, Bethany, he really wants to come and I told him I'd ask you. I don't know how you didn't hear him jabbering about it."

Grant wasn't sure how to broach the importance of James coming over without making her feel inadequate. But he had to try. He'd seen the longing in James' eyes.

"You're an amazing mother and you're doing so many

things perfectly, but James needs guys in his life, even if it's just a male friend, especially when your father is so far away. He needs someone who can show him how to do 'guy' things."

He saw the light in her eyes doused by his comment, but he didn't see anger there and thanked his lucky stars. He'd been worried she'd take it as criticism. What he saw instead was disenchantment, concern, perhaps even a little regret. Her shoulders slumped slightly in defeat as she chewed at the corner of her lip. She might be a skittish spitfire when it came to men, but she was also a realist who loved her son.

"You mean like fixing a toilet."

Grant chuckled. "Yeah, or a car or spitting or peeing standing up."

She arched a playful brow at him but wouldn't meet his gaze. "I'd better not catch my son spitting." He dipped his head toward her, forcing her to look up at him. "Okay, I get what you're saying. James needs some male bonding time."

"So you'll bring him?" Bethany held the door frame, looking thoughtful as she pursed her lips, twisting them to the side as he stood on the front porch, waiting for her answer. "We'll have a good time."

"Fine, but I don't want him on a horse." She smiled up at him as if she knew that would be a deal breaker.

Tricky woman. He wasn't about to play into her hand that easily. He made an X over his heart with a finger. "I won't put him on a horse."

He might not do it, but he knew Jackson would, not

that he'd tell her that. Not when the opportunity to see her in a bathing suit hung in the forefront of his mind, tempting as all hell. She squinted her eyes at him in distrust and he wasn't about to wait around for her to read his intention.

"I'll pick you guys up in the morning at eight." He turned and jogged down the driveway to his car. He opened the driver's side door and turned back to her, folding his arms over the top. "And, Bethany, be prepared. The whole family will be there."

Before she could change her mind, he climbed into the car and sped away. He was probably making a mistake, but thinking about the smile James would have on his face when he got to sit on a horse was enough to curb any second thoughts.

GRANT JAMMED HIS cell phone back into his pocket. "Son of a bitch!" he muttered, looking at the morning paper his father had left on the kitchen table.

"Language," his mother warned as she flipped a pancake on her griddle. "You might be grown, but this is still my house."

"Sorry, Mom." He pressed a kiss to her cheek and gave her shoulders a quick squeeze. She might be small but his mother had run their home with the discipline of an army general and they all knew to obey immediately, even if it was just to humor her into thinking she was still in charge.

"You were home late last night," Andrew pointed out.

"Did it have something to do with this?" His brother spun the paper on the table so that Grant could clearly see the picture of his car parked outside Bethany's house last night.

Didn't reporters have anything better to do than to keep following him around? What kind of news was a parked car? But he knew it was more than that. He was a local celebrity, a *single* local celebrity. For some reason, reporters took great pleasure and went to incredible lengths to report on his love life. All of the starters on the team complained of the same thing. Most of the time, it wasn't an issue because Grant made sure to steer clear of romantic entanglements and there had always been other players who fed the media fodder mill. Grant didn't have room in his life for relationships when he spent most of his time playing or training. But now, here in his hometown, there were no other players to draw the media's attention. His injury left him with too much time on his hands, and a certain teacher wouldn't stay out of his mind—he'd slipped up.

He prayed Bethany didn't read the paper.

"Nothing happened. We watched a cartoon with her kid on the couch, I carried him to bed for her and then I left."

Andrew laughed. "Sure it wasn't her that you carried to bed?"

"Andrew," his mother scolded. "Leave your brother alone. I certainly don't want to hear about him carrying *anyone* to bed over the breakfast table."

Grant ignored his brother's taunting as he grabbed

a plate and piled pancakes high, smothering them with butter and maple syrup. He reached for several slices of bacon as his mother set the plate on the table.

"You'd better start watching what you eat unless you want to get that middle-age spread," Andrew warned. "You *are* getting up there now, old man."

Grant didn't want to think about his age, or what he hadn't accomplished yet in his thirty-two years. "Mom, come sit and eat."

She slid a mug of steaming coffee in front of him. "I will when your father and Jackson come in." She glanced his way. "They were up helping pull a calf early this morning while you two were sleeping."

Grant and his brother recognized a guilt trip when they heard one. Before either of them could say anything, Andrew pushed back his chair. "Okay, I get it, I'm heading out to help."

His mother pressed a hand on his shoulder, stilling him. "They are heading in right now." She jerked her chin toward the back door where they could hear his father banging the dirt from his boots. "But next time, it would be nice if either of you at least offered to take a shift."

His father came through the doorway with Jackson on his heels. "Oh, look, the girls are up," he teased. "Did you two get enough beauty sleep?"

Andrew rolled his eyes and Grant shook his head. Their father had always been an early riser and expected all of his sons to follow suit. It was part of the reason each and every one of the boys had decided to move into the bunkhouse on their eighteenth birthday. Even now, they stayed there together, dorm-style, in order to maintain some sense of independence.

It didn't stop their father though. He had no problem popping his head in at the crack of dawn, claiming to be looking for the twins, Jackson and Jefferson, and waking everyone else in the process.

"Dad, I have to get down to the station, but I'd be happy to feed tonight when I get home." Andrew shoved another piece of bacon into his mouth before heading for the door.

"Hey," their mother called, holding her cheek toward him. "Don't forget."

He pressed a kiss to her cheek and grabbed the lunch she'd packed him from the counter. "Maybe by the time your birthday rolls around next month, you'll learn to fix your own lunches, huh?" Grant teased.

"Says the guy whose laundry Mom just put into the dryer." Grant rolled his eyes as his brother scooted out the door.

"Mom, I told you I'd switch it."

His father gave him the evil eye. "Sarah, this boy is plenty old enough—"

"I know and it's fine. I was doing our sheets anyway, Travis." She ruffled Grant's hair the way she used to when he was growing up and pressed a kiss to the top of his head. "You might be a grown man, but you'll always be my boy."

It didn't matter how many years he'd been at college or how long he'd lived in Memphis, to his mother, all of her kids would always remain children and she adored them. It was only slightly aggravating.

"Sit, Mom, and have some breakfast." Grant pulled her hand so she slid into the chair beside him as his father moved to the other side and set his plate on the table.

"Isn't that your car?" Travis McQuaid didn't miss much. He slid the newspaper closer, inspecting the caption. "Grant?"

"Yes, Dad, it is, but nothing happened."

His father's brow tilted upward in disbelief before giving Grant a stern look. "Is she nice?"

Grant inhaled slowly. Nice didn't begin to encompass all that Bethany was. Incredible, extraordinary, stunning. Those were good places to start.

But he knew what his father meant. He wanted to know if Bethany was like the usual team groupies, like the "cleat chasers" his father had seen hanging around the locker room in Memphis or stalking him like she-wolves here at home.

"Yeah, she's nice."

His mother looked more interested and he could see the visions of grandchildren already floating through her mind. "Is this the woman you were talking about before?"

"There is nothing going on. I fixed a broken toilet and then we watched a movie with her kid."

His mother grinned but his father simply tipped his chin down and looked at him somberly. "Then don't let this happen, son." He tapped his finger against the paper. "You plan on leaving before next month but she's got to live in this small town with whatever reputation she gets. Don't be the cause of something she can't live down."

Grant stared at the picture on the front page that

clearly showed his car parked in front of Bethany's home. It was blurry but there was no mistaking the house, not with the bird bath she'd placed in the middle of her front yard. This was the fourth time since arriving that he'd been photographed and, even after his irate call to the paper this morning, it didn't seem likely it would be the last.

As far as he knew, Bethany hadn't seen yesterday's article, practically calling her out as a gold digger and now this one, letting anyone in Hidden Falls find her and James. It was irresponsible sensationalism at its finest and he had to figure out a way to squash it. As long as he was around Bethany and James, people were going to talk and that *talk* would lead to plenty of speculation and rumors, if it hadn't already. He couldn't do that to her.

Grant rubbed his hand over the stubble on his jaw. The problem was, he also wasn't sure he could stay away.

Chapter Nine

BETHANY RUBBED HER eyes as she made her way past James' room. His bed was already made and she could just barely hear the sound of his cartoons coming from the living room. She backed up a step and went into his room to see his implant batteries and microphones still on the charger. Shaking her head, she slipped the equipment into her hand and carried it all downstairs. James always preferred to return to hearing slowly in the mornings, easing himself into waking before putting on the implant microphones that would bombard his world of silence with noise. She had just reached the foot of the stairs, deliberately trying to avoid the memories of last night with Grant that left her weak-kneed and her insides quivering with hungry anticipation, when there was a knock on her door.

She sighed, letting James enjoy watching his show for a few more moments as she headed for the door, running her fingers through her loose hair. It was barely seven, too early for Grant's arrival, but she'd have to get James to hurry up or they were going to be running behind when he arrived. She pulled open the door to see Grant holding two cups of what she could only assume was coffee, giving her a sheepish grin.

"Grant, you're early." The last thing she wanted was for James to come tearing around the corner and see him there. She'd never get him to settle down long enough for her to put his earpieces on.

"I come bearing gifts," he said, holding the coffee aloft.

"Yes, but why?" She glanced back over her shoulder and moved between the door and the frame, so James wouldn't notice if he did come running past.

Grant quirked a questioning brow at her. "I brought breakfast." She glanced down and saw the bag in his other hand. Was that her paper tucked under his arms? He must have seen her looking. "We need to talk. Can I come in?"

"Grant, if this is about last night—"

His face fell. "Sort of." He looked back over his shoulder. "Would it be alright if I moved my car into the garage?"

Bethany's brow furrowed. "What? Why?"

Grant sighed. "Trust me, it's for your own good."

"I guess." She shrugged and held the door open for him. "Let me just put these on James."

"Where are your keys and I'll switch the cars while you do that?"

She arched a brow and looked over her shoulder at

him while he followed her. "You can't wait five minutes?" The worry she could read in his eyes was enough of an answer for her. "They are by my purse on the counter, by the refrigerator."

She tapped James' shoulder, grateful when he didn't spot Grant before he walked back outside to move the cars. Her son's joyful smile was enough to brighten her morning immediately as he took the equipment from her hand and connected it himself. Bethany reached for the remote and turned the television sound lower so that it wouldn't be too much at once for him.

"Morning, Mom."

She smiled and ruffled his blond hair, feeling her heart swell with love for her son yet again. "Morning, James. I have a surprise for you." His eyes widened, his show forgotten as he shifted himself away from the television. "Why don't you go into the kitchen and see what's in the bag on the island?" He jumped up and started to run ahead of her. "Hey, no kiss?" He spun on his heels as she squatted down and held her arms out, barreling into her embrace.

She heard the rumble of Grant's car engine and saw James' eyes widen. "Is Grant here?"

It hadn't taken him long to recognize the sound.

She frowned at him. "Yes, and I hear the two of you made plans without asking me yesterday." He looked down, guiltily staring at his bare feet but not before she saw his grin.

How in the world was she ever going to protect James from being disappointed when Grant left town?

You sure this is about James and not you?

Bethany didn't want to listen to the logical voice of her mother in her mind. She was attempting to protect *both* of them. She heard the garage door closing as she followed James into the kitchen.

Looking into the bag Grant had left on the counter, James' blue eyes widened like saucers and a smile spread across his entire face, making them light up. "Donuts? Can I have two?"

She reached into the cupboard and pulled down a plate, slipping the donuts from the bag and arranging them. "We'll see. Why don't you just start with one and see how many are left?"

"But there are . . ." He paused as he pointed a chubby finger at each one, counting them. "Twelve."

"Those two are Danish and those two are bagels, honey, but yes, there are twelve. But you aren't the only person who needs to eat, you know." She glanced up as Grant opened the door into her utility room and saw them. James had his back to him but he spun as soon as he heard the door shut.

"Grant!" Bethany didn't think it was possible for his eyes to get any bigger or his smile to get wider, but somehow he managed it as he threw himself at Grant with even more enthusiasm than he'd shown her. "Are you here for breakfast?"

"I am," Grant replied, the frown he'd been wearing we he first arrived disappeared as he squatted down and accepted a hug from James.

Bethany had to turn away. This was exactly what she

was trying to avoid. After only a few days, James had become attached to Grant. She didn't even want to think about how she was going to break the news to him that Grant would be leaving soon for training camp and not returning. She felt her own heart lurch at the thought and had to admit James wasn't the only one getting attached too quickly.

She reached for the coffee, passing one to Grant when her eyes fell on the paper he'd brought inside. She instantly recognized the front of her house, and unfolded it, quickly scanning the headline.

Most Eligible Bachelor off the Market?

It wouldn't take much for anyone to recognize Grant's car. There weren't many people driving classic Camaros around the small town, and showing it parked in front of her house late at night gave the impression he'd stayed for more than just a movie. As much as she dreaded it, Bethany couldn't help but read the article insinuating a local woman had removed Grant McQuaid from the dating pool. It didn't mention her by name, but it wouldn't take much deduction for people to realize the house was hers. Between this article and the picture of them at the pizza place the day before, it would be an easy assumption that she was the unnamed woman.

"Crap," she muttered under her breath.

"Mom, you said a bad word," James pointed out.

Grant came up behind her and reached for the coffee, one hand on her shoulder. She felt heat spread across her shoulders and down her arm from that one simple touch.

"Now you see why I wanted to put the car into the garage. I'm sorry for this, Bethany."

He tapped the paper and she dropped it onto the counter, moving away from his hand. She reached for a paper towel and grabbed one of the donuts for James, setting it on the table. "Sit and eat, baby." She reached for a cup from the cupboard, avoiding Grant, and pulled the milk from the refrigerator. "Here you go."

"Bethany." His voice was quietly cajoling and she dropped her hands at her sides. "Look at me, please." She turned to meet his dark gaze, resigned to the fact that she couldn't seem to deny him anything. "I should have realized this would happen. There have been a couple stories about me ever since I got home a few weeks ago. I just thought they would figure out I wasn't doing anything headline-worthy and disappear. I didn't know they followed me here yesterday."

"Or the pizza place, apparently."

"So you saw that one too?"

She sighed and ran a hand through her hair. "Look, Grant, I don't blame you. I should have known something like this would happen. You're a professional football-player in a small town. Of course, it will set the gossip mill on high alert, but this is exactly why I said no to pizza." She lowered her voice. "I don't even want to think about what people are saying. Anyone can tell that's my house."

Grant let out a long sigh. "I've been thinking about that. There is one sure way to keep this from blowing up into a local tabloid story." She looked up at him and his dark eyes begged her to hear him out. "You need to start dating."

GRANT HAD TRIED to convince himself during the entire drive to Bethany's house that there was another way, but the fact was that she was a kindergarten teacher, a single mother of a hearing-impaired child and new to town. People were probably already talking about her but if his name were to suddenly become connected with hers, if they were to become a couple, this small-town newspaper would be the least of Bethany's worries. It was the broader news outlets he worried about—networks, tabloids and social media. Once the smoke cleared and he went back to the team, she'd be the one left trying to live down a reputation that was undeserved, trying to pick up the pieces of what had once been a normal life. He couldn't do that to her. She was already struggling; he didn't want to make her life more difficult. He liked her and James too much, even after the short amount of time he'd known them.

In truth, the best option for her would be if he turned around and walked away completely, putting as much distance between them as he could. If he didn't show any interest in her, neither would the reporters. But he couldn't do that. He'd offered her his friendship, offered it to James and, like he'd told her yesterday, he was a man of his word. He wouldn't just turn his back on either of them. So the next best thing would be for them both to be seen with someone else. If her name was linked with another man, he could convince reporters they were nothing more than friends. She and James would be off their radar once they saw her with someone else.

"Date?"

"Look, I like you and I like James. I don't want to cause you any trouble. To make this go away, this reporter, whoever it is, needs to see you involved with someone else."

"Wouldn't it be more important to see *you* with someone else?" she pointed out. "I'm a nobody and it isn't me they want to follow."

"They do now, because they think we are together." Grant ran a hand through his hair. "Look, Bethany, I messed up. I wasn't even thinking about this the other day when I invited you two to the park or last night. I'm so used to it that I don't even notice it most of the time anymore, but you're not."

She studied the paper again. "No, this is not the kind of attention I really want James dealing with." Her gaze sought his. "But what makes you think my dating is going to change anything? It would be far easier for you to go out with someone else."

Grant didn't miss the flicker in her eyes as she said it but he didn't dare hope it was because she might not want him to date someone. He had no right, not unless he was willing to give her what she deserved.

"And I will. But we need to create the right image here, to tell a story that shines a good light on you. If I date someone else, you're the poor, single mom screwed over by the football star. That's going to create attention you don't want too. If *you* date, then they'll second-guess the validity of us as an item altogether. Rather than admit they were wrong, the story will drop with the attention disappearing altogether."

Grant didn't even want to think about the way his stomach was churning at the words coming from his mouth. He was honest enough to admit he wanted her for himself, but he was realistic enough to know that wasn't possible, not while he was still playing ball. Not while he couldn't offer her any sort of security or a future. Shit, if he didn't get back on the team, he'd be forced to live in the bunkhouse for the next two years until he started seeing a return on the money he'd invested into Jackson's venture.

"Bethany, you agreed that James needs a man in his life."

Bethany crossed her arms over her chest. "I thought that was why we were going to meet up with you today," she pointed out. "For him to learn 'guy' stuff."

"It is, but we both know I won't always be around." He saw the flicker of regret in her eyes but he had to press on. "I'm heading back for training soon. He's going to need someone besides just me."

Jealousy ate at him. The thought of another man playing ball with James, teaching him how to fish, or how to throw a baseball, grated on his nerves. He'd grown far more attached to this pair in the past few days than he'd ever thought was possible. He relished the sight of them, longed to be with them when he wasn't. It was as if there was a common thread that had drawn them to one another. The thought of someone else making either of them smile or laugh made him feel hollow inside.

But he couldn't offer them what they deserved and it wasn't fair to pretend he could. He'd meant what he said about being her friend so he needed to get her out of this mess he'd gotten her into, which meant forgoing what he wanted *someday* for what she deserved today.

James slid from the kitchen table and came running toward them. "I'm finished. Can I have another one?"

"You can have one more, but after you go put your clothes on." She looked at Grant. "We *are* still on for today. Right?"

Grant could see the hesitation in her hazel eyes again, the anxiety creeping back. He felt like every bit of the headway he'd made at gaining her trust had been destroyed.

"Make sure you wear long pants and bring your bathing suit with you. Go, hurry." Grant gave James the sign for *hurry*. The little boy scooted past him and ran up the stairs. He could hear drawers opening and slamming shut. "Bethany."

She met his gaze but he wasn't sure what he wanted to say. He wanted to go back to the easy friendship they'd had last night. Hell, he wanted to go back to that moment in the doorway of the bathroom when it had taken every ounce of self-control to keep from kissing her. She moved past him toward the kitchen and grabbed the coffee cups, passing one to him.

"It's okay, Grant. I appreciate your honesty. I'll have to think about it though. I told you I don't date, and I have reasons. That's not going to change just because of a newspaper article."

"Or two," he reminded her.

She nodded in agreement. "Or two. But I'm not sure dating someone else is the right answer either."

Grant needed her to agree to this plan. He hadn't realized how much until he'd come this morning. Seeing her looking pretty and sweet, her eyes half-closed with sleep, her hair mussed and she still in her pajamas, he'd been able to convince himself that he wasn't ready for the permanence that she and James made him long for. But it was a lie.

And this plan of his wasn't only for her benefit. Until there was another man in her life, he was going to continue to want things he couldn't have. However, if she was happy in a relationship, he would gladly step back for her and James' sakes.

"I know what you said, but—"

She waved him off. "I'm not saying I won't date, just that I haven't, not in a long time, and I need to take some time to consider it. I'm out of practice and I don't really know anyone here." She took a sip of the coffee and looked over the rim at him. "Any recommendations?"

Grant felt his gut tighten in knots. Wasn't it bad enough to have to see her with someone else? How could he pick a guy out for her when he wanted her for himself? Crap, who did he know that deserved a woman like Bethany but whom he wouldn't see often enough for it to rip his heart out and make him want to beat the man senseless?

BETHANY TRIED NOT to stare across the car at Grant as he drove them out of town toward his parents' ranch. The man was a complete enigma.

Last night, she'd thought several times that he was going to kiss her. She'd even lain awake most of the night reconsidering her no-dating policy again, knowing it would be a huge mistake to go out with Grant but wanting it nonetheless. That rule had kept her and James away from heartache for the past six years. However, after seeing James with Grant last night, she realized it might not have protected James the way she'd thought it would. It might have sheltered him from heartache, but she'd also confined him to living in an overprotective fantasy that kept him from developing into the man she hoped he would someday become. Grant was right—James needed some male influences in his life, especially now that the only one he'd known was thousands of miles away, across the country from him. She'd spent most of the night contemplating her options, which really only came down to two courses of action: continue the way they had been and risk stunting James' development or take a chance and risk heartache both for her son and herself.

After making a decision in the early morning hours, she'd actually been excited to see Grant this morning, ready to spend the day getting to know him without the walls she usually erected. After all the flirting he'd done the evening before, she was looking forward to the warm thrill she felt when his eyes swept over her, the way his touch sent goose bumps over her flesh and a tremor through her. She'd been looking forward to the moments, like this one, when she could steal a glance at his profile, see his ruggedly handsome features and relish the heat seeping through her veins at the anticipation of their first kiss.

And then he'd made the suggestion she date someone else.

Finding out that people had seen her picture in the paper with him at the pizza place had been disconcerting enough, but to see the picture of his car parked outside her home, to read details of their imaginary love affair as if it were reality, had rattled her. She understood the small-town dynamic, how everyone involved themselves in everyone else's business, but she hadn't expected a complete fabrication to circulate so quickly. It had definitely made her think twice about her decision the night before. However, Grant's suggestion had crushed it under the heel of his very expensive-looking cowboy boot.

Regardless of how much he'd flirted, he obviously wasn't interested in anything more than friendship, exactly what she'd been insisting on from him since from beginning.

She'd brought this upon herself with her stupid rules and the way she'd pushed him away. She couldn't blame the man for taking her not-so-subtle hints. Unfortunately, she'd changed her mind and made her decision too late. Now she'd have to live with the consequences, which meant she could have nothing more than friendship with the first man she'd found herself attracted to in years. It was all he offered and, while embarrassment would have her turn tail and run, she owed it to James to at least accept that from him. It wasn't James' fault she'd been foolish.

Grant turned toward her, catching her admiring him. "Whatcha thinking about? You've been pretty quiet during our ride."

She shrugged. "The article, what I should do about it." It wasn't a complete fabrication. She glanced over her shoulder into the back seat where James was playing with two of his superhero figures and lowered her voice. "I'm hoping there's no real backlash from some of my more judgmental parents at school."

"And that is part of the reason I suggested you . . ." Grant looked back at James who smiled his way, obviously catching at least part of their conversation. "I suggested what I did," he amended.

"You don't think that will make things look even worse?"

"If I get asked, I'll mention that James and I were paired by my sister because I know sign language. If you've been seen with someone else, it will just give it credence that there is nothing more going on and the story will drop."

"I'm not going to use someone just so—"

"I'm not telling you to *use* someone. I'm suggesting you find a nice—" She cleared her throat in warning. "Friend to spend time with," he clarified, turning his chocolate eyes on her again, melting her refusal. "Go see a movie, have a cup of coffee, take a walk in the park."

"I like the park," James chimed in from the back seat. "Can we go to the park too?"

"My house is sort of like a park, James. You'll like it." Grant looked out the windshield again. "Bethany, you've been letting life pass you by. I have no idea what happened in your past, but you need to find your future. Find someone, be happy again."

Grant's voice held a note of regret and she wondered if he wasn't wishing he'd done things differently as well. He wasn't wrong. Everything he mentioned was what she wanted for herself again, someday. But until now, there hadn't been anyone who made her want to take the risk. Unfortunately, the one man who had made her want to reconsider was telling her to find someone else.

GRANT SLOWED AS he made his way up the driveway and
stopped the Camaro in front of his parents' home. He
knew his father and the twins would be coming in soon
from feeding cattle, which was exactly the reason he'd
arrived when he did. He didn't want Bethany to feel like
he was throwing her to the wolves nor did he want James
to feel overwhelmed by too many people at once. Only
his mother and sister were at the house right now, since
Andrew and Benjamin would still be in town until their
shifts were over.

Maddie came out to the front porch to greet them.
"Well, hello there, James! I think you're the first of the
kids at school to see where I grew up."

"Hi, Ms. McQuaid. Do I get to see your room?"

"Sure, why don't you come with me so your mom and
Grant can grab a cup of coffee." Maddie winked as she
turned and he prayed Bethany didn't see it.

The last thing he needed right now was any match-making from his mother or sister. As much as he might want more with Bethany, his father was right. He couldn't leave her with a "baller" reputation as a noose around her neck in this small town. It was bad enough in a big city, but at least there she could disappear if things didn't work out. In Hidden Falls, she'd become a spectacle for the rumor mill.

"I'm betting Mom has a fresh pot in the kitchen and breakfast ready if you want something more substantial than donuts." Grant held open the front door for her. They might only be friends but his mother had raised him to be a gentleman. Of course, that didn't explain the way his fingers itched to lie at her lower back as she entered.

"I had one of the bagels, remember? That was plenty." She smiled at him as she walked through the door. "But I'd love another cup of coffee."

"Then come right in," his mother said, appearing in the hallway like a magician's assistant, wearing a smile just as cheesy. "I have a pot that's just about finished brewing. I'm Sarah McQuaid."

Bethany held out her hand. "I'm Bethany M—" Her voice was cut off when his mother pulled her into a warm embrace. He could easily read the surprise on Bethany's face and laughed.

"Sorry, forgot to warn you about how Mom gets a bit overfriendly with company."

His sister came back down the stairs, leading James with his little hand in hers. "Oh, I see Mom got a hold of you. Watch out, James, she loves little boys. So much that she had six of her own," Maddie teased. "You're so sweet, she might want to keep you here forever and send Grant home with your mom instead."

Grant felt the yearning bubble up in his chest. He'd love to go home with Bethany. Hell, he'd settle for just spending an hour alone with her.

Stop right there, his brain warned. *Wrong timing, wrong woman. You are the wrong guy, remember?*

If only his life wasn't in limbo right now, if there was some sort of concrete foundation for his future, if only he wasn't nearly broke. Until he had an answer from his doctors, until he knew where he'd be spending the rest of the spring or the year—hell, until he knew whether his football career would continue or be finished—he couldn't be anything more than a friend to anyone.

But it didn't stop the wanting.

Releasing poor Bethany, his mother looked up at a giggling James. "Well, hello. And just who might you be?"

"Mom, this is James, Bethany's son and my favorite fan."

"I thought I was your favorite fan," she teased.

"I don't know," he teased with a wink at James. "You might have some competition now."

James took a step forward holding out his hand the way Grant was sure Bethany must have taught him to do but he too was enveloped in a big hug. His laughter rang through the hallway and another kick of longing hit Grant square in the chest.

This is what I want.

He shoved the thought away, but he couldn't completely eradicate the vision of children running down the halls of his parents' house, his children . . . his and Bethany's children. His eyes fell onto the woman who haunted his thoughts and he saw her smile tenderly as James hugged Sarah back. He didn't know her well enough to have these sorts of thoughts but, in that moment, he realized what his mother was asking for when she begged him for grandchildren. She wanted a family, for him. She wanted this sense of undying legacy, of loving someone unconditionally and being loved the same way in return. Something that would last longer than football and be stronger than his desire to succeed. For the first time, he realized his career wasn't enough to satisfy him.

"Oh! I'm so sorry."

Grant was jerked back into the moment and glanced up at his mother to see James adjusting one of the microphones over his ear.

"I didn't mean to—"

"It's okay, they come off, see?" James pulled the magnetic piece from the side of his head to show her. "It doesn't hurt. They help me hear," he explained.

His mother's eyes flicked to Grant and caught his gaze. He could see the emotion in them, a sheen that hadn't been there before, and he wondered what she was thinking. He felt tenderness well up in him as he watched James easily explain how his implants worked in a way that no six-year-old should understand. When he looked at Bethany, he could see the fierce devotion in her face. She had every right to adore this child; he was strong and brave. He was amazing.

Grant took a step closer to her, his hand slipping to her lower back as he leaned to her ear. "It takes a pretty awesome mother to have a kid that great."

She jumped, turning toward him, her forehead brushing his cheek, bringing his lips just inches from her skin. He inhaled the sweet vanilla scent of her hair, pulled back in a ponytail again, and felt her tense just a moment before she relaxed into his touch. His hand burned where it rested against her and his fingers itched to travel the curve of her spine, to trace the indentation of her waist and pull her closer.

He moved away quickly, only able to put a few feet between them before his mutinous body reached out for her hand. "Let's get that coffee."

BETHANY SAT ON the back patio watching the four men playing football with her son while Madison and Sarah chatted beside her. They cheered loudly as Grant picked up James and ran him to the end of the yard for another touchdown. Travis, Grant's father, ran over and gave James a high five as they walked back toward the women watching from the patio.

"And *that* is how you show two young pups how it's done."

Jackson and Jefferson jogged over to the deck and reached for the bottles of water their mother held out to them. "We let you win, old man," Jackson teased. "We didn't want to hear you crying when we beat you at football and fishing today."

He flipped the cold perspiration from the bottle of water at his sister.

"Hey! Unless you want to ice down your pants, you'd best keep that cold water over there," Madison threatened.

Sarah stepped between the pair, diffusing their playful bickering and Bethany couldn't help but smile at how quickly they both fell into line. "I've got lunch packed already for you guys whenever you're ready to head out. I think you father put all the poles into the trailer."

"The horses are in the corral just waiting to be saddled," Jefferson added.

"Horses?" Bethany's smile fell as she looked toward Grant, a tremor of fear creeping into her chest. He'd promised that he wouldn't put James on a horse. Neither of them had ever been around the animals and she certainly wasn't about to put her son onto a beast that could tumble him six plus feet to the ground. Not that she was too keen about sitting astride one either.

Grant's eyes twinkled with merriment. "It's how we're getting out to the pond, unless you want him to ride the quad with Dad?"

Bethany glared at Grant. "You said you wouldn't put him on a horse."

"And I won't. You will."

She shook her head slowly. "No, I won't."

What in the world was he thinking? There was no way she was going to let him manipulate her into allowing this.

"Mom, I want to ride a horse too."

"Before you say no, just come out and see the horses, okay?"

She shot Grant scowl and noticed that the rest of his family had already headed back toward the house, leaving them to argue about this privately.

Grant held his hands up in front of him. "Bethany, have I done anything that would indicate you can't trust James with me?"

"No," she admitted, look at his throat instead of those eyes that begged for her give in to him.

So far, he'd been more than careful with her son. He seemed to inherently understand James' need for adventure, but somehow he managed to balance that with her need to protect him. He pretended to play rough with him, all the while, wrestling so carefully he hadn't even knocked off one of James implant microphones. He'd been just as vigilant of James as she was, but without smothering him the way she tended to do. In spite of her desire to disagree, Grant was right. He hadn't given her any reason to distrust him. In fact, she found herself wanting to let him lead the way, to teach both of them how to trust again.

Whoa, Bethany, her mind warned. *Just friends, remember?*

She remembered. But watching him play with her son, watching Grant interact with his family and the warm, loving dynamic they shared, was making it difficult to confine him in the friend zone when she longed for more.

Maybe he was right, maybe she did just need to get back on the horse, so to speak, and go out on a date with another man. Maybe these feelings she had for him were simply because he was the first man in years to pick the lock of the vault she'd kept bolted around her and James for so long. The same way being around his family made her long for close friendships again. Maybe she just needed to take that first step with someone.

"Bethany, look at me." Grant's voice was soft as his fingers twined with hers, the rough callouses on his palms sending a shiver of heat up her arm and straight to her heart. "I won't do anything to hurt either of you."

That's where you're wrong. I think you're going to break both of our hearts.

"MOM, LOOK!" JAMES was bouncing in place, delighted as he pointed toward the miniature black and white horse Jackson led from the corral. "He's little, like me."

Bethany stopped short and Grant laughed, dragging her closer to the corral where Jefferson and his father were quickly saddling the other mounts for the adults. "Come on, slow poke. Let's go introduce James to Shorty."

She followed his lead, but he could tell she was still hesitant, dragging her boots through the dirt and kicking up puffs of dust behind her. Grant let go of her hand and picked up James, taking him to Shorty's head. "James, meet Shorty. He's a quarter pony. That means he's exactly the same as the quarter horses there—" he pointed at the other mounts "—just smaller. Just like you're a smaller version of us grown men."

James reached out a hand to pet the horse as Shorty dropped his head. "See, he likes you already."

"Mom, look!"

"I see." Bethany's voice held a note of doubt, but Grant could see it was less than it had originally been.

"Okay, cowboy, here are the rules. You have to stay quiet and calm around horses and never, ever, walk farther than their front shoulders without an adult with you. That's a sure way to get kicked and, trust me, horse kicks hurt."

James looked into his eyes somberly, absorbing everything he said with a focus far beyond his years. "I don't want to get kicked. Julie kicked me once at school and it hurt."

Grant glanced back at Bethany and could see that this bit of information was news to her. She frowned, but refrained from saying anything.

"The second rule is that you have to wait for one of us guys or your mom to help you on and off. I want you to stay right here with your Mom while I saddle him for you, okay?"

James nodded and, when Grant put him back onto the ground, he held his mother's hand in a firm grip. "Mom, I get to ride him?"

"Grant, are you sure?"

He could see the fear in her eyes and knew this wasn't just a question of her allowing James to ride a horse. This was about her relinquishing control of her son's welfare to someone else. This was about whether she could trust someone to protect James in a situation she couldn't control. It went far deeper than apprehension and misgivings. She was asking if she could place her faith in him. He wouldn't let her down.

"Shorty is a great boy to learn on. In fact, Maddie learned to ride on him too."

James' eyes grew wide. "She did? He's very old then."

"James!" Bethany corrected.

He turned and signed something to her that Grant couldn't make out but couldn't hide his grin as Bethany signed back that calling someone old was rude. He looked crestfallen that he'd disappointed her.

"He's old but horses can live a long time and he was really young when she learned. He just moves a lot slower now. See that big horse over there?" Grant said as he pointed to his bay gelding. "I'm going to ride him but I'll be holding this rope and I'll lead Shorty the whole way. But you get to steer him with these reins."

"You about ready?" Grant pulled the pony's cinch tight as Jackson brought his bay to the hitching post. Jefferson followed behind with the sorrel mare he'd chosen for Bethany. Ginger was as sweet as any they had on the ranch and would plod along beside his horse, babysitting her while he kept an eye on James.

"Yes!" James clapped his hands and jumped into the air.

"Remember what I said about staying calm and quiet." James immediately stilled. "Bethany, bring him over here and lift him into the saddle."

Her gaze met his again and he could read the hesitation in her stance. To her credit, she walked forward, albeit slowly, and ran a hand over the pony's neck. The old gelding turned his head to look at her and dropped his neck, waiting for her to rub his forehead. It was enough to win her over. She ran a hand over his face.

"Okay, little man, you do whatever Grant says, okay?" James nodded, excitement gleaming bright in his blue eyes as she settled him into the saddle. Grant moved to her side and slid James' feet into the stirrups of the child-sized saddle and put the reins into the boy's hands.

"Hold the reins right here, just like this, and keep your feet right here."

Grant instructed him on how to steer the pony although he wouldn't really be directing him with Grant holding the lead rope. He knew how important it was to let James think he was doing it himself. When he felt like James was comfortable and settled in the saddle, Jackson came and held Shorty's rope. Grant's hand slid to Bethany's back and he felt the tension in her ramrod-straight spine.

"Come here, Bethany, so you can meet Ginger."

He guided her around the hitching post to where his brother had tied her mount. He slid the bridle over the mare's head and moved the reins over her neck before taking a step closer to the woman fairly trembling with worry. He slid his hand to Bethany's upper arm, trying to allay her fears. Electricity shot through him but he ignored it as he moved his hand to her waist.

"You ready to mount up?"

She put one foot into the stirrup. "Hold on here, right?" Her voice was shaky as she reached for the saddle horn. He could see she was trying to cast her fears aside and trust him.

"Yep. Now push off and swing your leg over carefully." With his hands around her waist, he helped her into the saddle, the way she had James. As she settled herself into the seat and slid her other foot into the stirrup, his hand ran down her thigh. "There you go."

Bethany glanced down at him from atop her mount and he saw the look in her eyes. It was a mixture of trepidation and excitement, fear and yearning. His fingers burned where they connected with her denim-encased leg, and desire coiled in his gut, making his jeans suddenly uncomfortable. This wasn't like him, to feel this pull, the yearning for more that he felt with her and James.

He was the guy who hyperfocused on the task at hand and refused to even look away from his goals. And right now, his goal was still returning to his career, of proving himself and rebuilding the fortune he'd been forced to part with this past year. But Bethany had him rethinking his purpose completely. Grant had to get at least a modicum of control over his lust for this woman or he needed to leave her alone altogether.

He pulled his hand away from her leg and made his way to his gelding. "We'll head out first and meet you at the pond in a little while, Jackson."

His brother handed him Shorty's lead rope and gave him a thumbs-up, indicating his agreement. With their horses walking slower, there was no reason to wait for the rest of the family. They'd catch up and, most likely, pass them on the way to the pond. But he didn't want Bethany or James to feel pressured to keep up the faster pace his family would set. He preferred they feel comfortable and enjoy their first time in the saddle.

Grant looked down at James on the pony, his eyes sparkling with excitement and adventure, a broad smile covering his face. The kid actually had a relaxed seat, something that couldn't really be taught, and Grant felt his respect for the boy rise in him as James lightly held the reins in his hands. He was a natural. He looked over at Bethany.

He couldn't help the grin that spread over his face. She was having a bit more trouble. She had a death-grip on the reins like she was holding a baseball bat and was pulling back on them in order to keep both hands wrapped around the saddle horn. The movement made the mare back up, even while Bethany pressed her heels against the poor animal's side, indicating she wanted her to move forward. Confused, the mare tossed her head several times.

"Bethany, loosen your reins."

"What?" Where James' eyes were wide with excitement, Bethany's were fearful. "I can't."

"Honey, you need to relax. Pry your hands off that saddle horn. It's not going to help at all. You're not going to fall off. Just move your hands onto her neck."

She did as he said and the mare quit tugging against the reins.

"Now, press your heels down like you're trying to touch the ground with them." Her legs immediately dropped forward, away from the mare's sides and she began walking forward. "There you go, see?"

"I think I hate you a little for this, Grant," she muttered.

If she hated him for the ride, he was going to be in real trouble when the soreness set into her backside and inner thighs tomorrow, but he kept his mouth shut, not wanting to give her any more ammunition.

"You should bring Ginger to the other side and see James' face. That will be enough to make you fall in love with me."

Her gaze met his and he realized what he'd just said. *Crap.*

It wasn't what he'd meant. Well, it was, but not that way and now there was nothing he could say that would make it sound better so he chose to gloss over the comment.

"If he's this good at riding, I can't wait to see him cast a fishing pole."

With only a little trouble, she managed to move the mare to the other side of James and, seeing his smile, she began to relax in the saddle. "See, what did I tell you?"

Her gaze met his across the horses, the green flecks in her hazel eyes dancing with joy. He could see the relief that filled her. "I hate to admit it but you were right."

"Get used to it, Bethany." He shot her a wink as his lips curved into a lopsided smile. "I usually am."

Chapter Eleven

BETHANY WATCHED AS Madison, Jefferson and Jackson made s'mores around the fire pit. Madison waited for one to cool off before passing it to James, who was tucked snugly in between Grant's brothers, his new cowboy heroes. Andrew and Benjamin had arrived just in time for dinner and now leaned back in their chairs on the other side of the fire, finishing off two bottles of their favorite beer, something Andrew claimed to have brewed in the barn. Bethany glanced at Grant before she took a tentative sip, her eyes rounding in surprise at the sweet peach flavor.

"Your brother made this?"

Grant chuckled. "Yeah, it's a hobby. He's got this whole setup in one of Dad's stalls. Dad was so mad when he saw one of his foaling stalls turned into a brewery, but when he realized how much it helped Andrew blow off steam after a rough shift, he let him keep it."

"It's really good." She took a long swallow, savoring the sweet, yeasty flavor.

"So, you have Andrew, Madison, Jefferson, Jackson, Grant and Benjamin. Do I detect a theme?"

Grant chuckled and rolled his eyes. "Dad was a huge history buff and thought it would be a good idea to name all his kids after significant historical figures."

"At least he picked names that weren't too off the wall. You could have been Woodrow." She tried to bite back the smile tugging at the corners of her mouth when he glared at her.

"Thank goodness for Mom. He'd actually chosen Roosevelt and she put her foot down."

"You mean you could have been Rosie?" She couldn't help the laughter that bubbled forth and when he glared at her, she laughed even harder.

It felt good, she realized. For the first time since arriving in Hidden Falls she didn't feel like an outsider. She felt welcome and like she was part of a unit instead of someone trying to fit in. Grant had no idea how grateful she was for all he'd done for them in just a few days.

"Thank you for today. James has had a great time."

Grant leaned his head against the back of the chair and peered up in the sky filled with winking stars. "Just James?"

His head turned slowly to face her. She couldn't make out most of his features, especially with the way they were shadowed from the firelight several feet away, but his eyes practically glowed.

She looked away, straight ahead, where James sat with the twins. "I had a good time too."

Grant chuckled quietly. "We should do it again. I think Mom and Dad liked having you guys here. Mom's been on our cases for years to have grandkids so I think she's getting ideas. Maybe if James was around, she'd lay off."

"You think it'd be that simple?" Bethany watched as Sarah kissed each of the twins on their cheeks before hugging James from behind. She reminded Bethany of her own mother and a pang of homesickness washed over her.

"Nope," Grant said with a chuckle. "Mom wants to see us kids settle down, have families of our own. Until that happens, we're going to have to listen to the nagging."

Bethany frowned. "Guess she's not much different than the rest of the town, wanting to see their hometown hero settle down."

He shrugged and crossed his arms over his chest with a sigh. "I usually just ignore it, but then again, I don't live here all of the time. It'll happen when the time is right, but that won't be until after I retire and I hope that's not anytime soon."

She caught an edge to his voice and the way his answer almost seemed rehearsed and wondered at it.

"Have you thought about who you might want to ask out?" Grant's question caught her off guard.

"*I* can't ask anyone out." Her voice pitched higher, squeaking out the last word.

"Why not? It's not like you'd actually have to ask anyway. All you'd have to do is turn those doe eyes of yours at a guy and he'd be on his knees begging you for a date."

"Hardly." She took another swallow of the beer, wishing it would give her the bravado to tell him that he was the only guy she had any interest in.

"Any guy would be lucky to go out with you, Bethany." She could almost feel his glowing eyes caress her in the moonlight. "I know for a fact there are a couple of guys who'd give their right arm to go out with you sitting over there." He waved a hand at Andrew and Benjamin. "Didn't Ben already ask?"

"Are you seriously suggesting I ask your brother out?" *Because that might take the definition of* awkward *to a whole new level.*

She bit the corner of her lower lip and a frown furrowed his brow as Grant studied her. "What about someone from work?"

He looked back at the sky, but she could see the side of his playboy grin. He wasn't even bothering to hide it. "There has to be some guy who has made your insides all tingly and fluttery."

Yeah, you.

She shrugged. "Steven asked me out for coffee the other day."

"Who's this Steven guy? And what are you waiting for?"

"He's the other kindergarten teacher, and I already told him no." She finished off the beer, running her thumb over the dried glue where the label had once been, trying to avoid looking in his direction.

"Why?" Grant turned to face her again, but instead of his usual boyish humor, he looked entirely too serious. "Bethany, how long were you with James' father?"

"We were married for two years, but we dated for three before that."

She waited for him to ask what happened, to pry into the life that was her past, the one that barely seemed real anymore. She looked back at her son laughing with Jefferson, leaning close as they shared a joke. He'd blossomed today, been adventurous, living out boyish fantasies that she could have never given him without the help of Grant and his family. Today her son had been able to fully live, something she now realized she'd been keeping him from doing for too long.

Maybe he hadn't been the only one not living.

"And how long have you been without him?"

Grant's question caught her by surprise. She'd been preparing to give him her usual vague answer about the demise of her marriage, but he didn't seem to want to know *what* happened, he was asking about her and James. He didn't know any details other than the fact that Matthew wasn't in James' life. For all Grant knew, her husband had died.

In a way, he had. So had she. Their fantasy life, the tie that had once bound them, the ideal of family life they'd had when they married right out of high school had come crashing down around them with James' diagnosis. Matthew hadn't been able to cope.

"Almost six years," she whispered.

She heard Grant's slow exhale, saw his head drop back on his chair as he closed his eyes. "Six years is a long time to be alone, Bethany." She could hear the empathy in his voice. Grant turned toward her and a slow, sweet smile spread over his lips. "Don't you think it's time you shared James a little?"

This wasn't the direction she expected this conversation to take. "Shared . . . James?"

"I told you before—he's a great kid and you've been keeping him all to yourself." He sat up and braced his elbows on his knees, folding his hands and letting them drop between his thighs. "I think it's time you let someone else hang out with James for a while. Go out to the movies or something. Tomorrow, I'm going to be the friend you need. I'll come over to babysit James while you go out with Mr. Sexy Kindergarten Teacher."

"I never said—"

Grant held up a hand, cutting off her argument. "No need to thank me. Just call this man in the morning and ask him out to lunch and a movie. If it turns into dinner, even better."

"Grant, I don't—"

He stood and reached for her hand, pulling her to her feet. She tried to ignore the slow spiral of heat that curled through her limbs at his touch. Maybe he was right. Maybe her mother was right. Maybe it was time for her to date someone again.

She looked over at her son, leaning sleepily against Madison's side, enjoying the attention of so many adults. She'd spent so long being independent, allowing no one but her family close enough to either of them, and here was a group of people she barely knew, opening their home to her and her son, filling the void she hadn't realized had been growing larger every year of their solitude.

"I would," she agreed, "but I don't have his number."

"This is a small town, Bethany. It can't be that hard to track it down."

GRANT KNOCKED ON Bethany's door and wondered for the umpteenth time if he wasn't making a huge mistake by convincing Bethany to go out with someone else. It was like finding a million dollars and just handing it to a stranger. But the fact was, she wasn't *his* million dollars. As much as he might want her to be, he wasn't at a point in his career, or his life, where he could stop to focus on having a family. The painful realization had dogged him during his morning workout, helping propel him to his fastest sprint times since he'd arrived back home.

Just the thought of her sitting in a darkened movie theater with another man, his arm draped around her, on a date Grant wanted to be on infuriated him enough for him to increase his bench press max to what it had been a few years ago. Before the injuries. Before the commentators started talking about how he was getting too old. Before there was talk of retiring from the only thing that made his life worth living.

As much as he might want to pursue a relationship with Bethany, and suspected she would be the woman he'd been holding out for, he knew he couldn't give her what she needed, what she deserved. At least, not right now.

You still didn't have to encourage her to find someone else.

No, he didn't and, if he'd listened to his instincts, he'd have kept his mouth shut. But he cared about Bethany and James. Too much to see either miss out on an opportunity at happiness. His desire to see her move beyond the hurt that shadowed her eyes when she talked about her past was too strong. He wanted her to learn to trust again, which meant doing what was best for her and being a real friend, even if it meant losing his chance.

Bethany answered the door, flustered, with her cheeks flushed. She looked young and pretty with her dark hair flowing softly around her face, draping over her shoulders. It was the first time he'd seen it down and he could barely help the urge to run his fingers through it. He clenched his hands at his sides.

"Come on in," she said on an exasperated sigh. "James, I'm not going to argue about this," she called over her shoulder.

"Uh-oh." Grant handed her the tall to-go cup of coffee he'd picked up on the way.

He'd had no idea if it was something she'd like but figured most women wouldn't turn down a white chocolate mocha. And from the sound of the fit being thrown in the next room, she needed a sweet start to her morning.

"Sounds like someone got up on the wrong side of the bed."

"He's mad that I won't take him to the park this morning." She rolled her eyes and shrugged. "Maybe we should just call this off. I really don't know Steven's number—he could say no or have other plans . . ."

Grant tipped his chin down, pinning her with a dubious look. "This sound like a job I can handle. First, here." He reached into his pocket and pulled out a scrap of paper, holding it out to her.

"What's this?"

"The phone number for one Steven Carter, kindergarten teacher and lover of action flicks, Italian food and strong cappuccinos."

"What?"

Grant didn't even want to venture a guess at why her full lips slid into a broad grin or entertain the idea that she might be excited for this possible lunch date. He was too busy inwardly cringing, like he'd just taken a helmet to the groin.

"Madison?" she asked.

Grant shrugged. "I guess they went out a couple of times but there weren't any sparks." He made air quotes over the last two words. "She said he is a nice guy though."

Bethany closed her eyes and covered her face with a hand. "You told Madison." She shook her head and he saw the blush creep over her cheeks. "Grant, you're a terrible wingman."

"I told her I needed to coordinate an assembly with both of you for next week."

"And you found out what sort of movies and food he likes from that?"

Grant laughed out loud. "Have you met my sister? It wasn't hard. She will tell you her life story if you ask how old she is. That girl loves to talk." He slid the door shut and headed for the screeching child he could hear in the next room. "And this will be a piece of cake."

Bethany stopped at the doorway and crossed her arms over her chest. "Have at it."

"James, I can't take you out to play football if you're making so much noise."

The temper tantrum instantly stopped and James spun toward the sound of Grant's voice, jumping to his feet. "Grant!"

He squatted down as James ran into his arms and he swung him into the air. "Yep, we get to have another guys' day, this time without your mom."

James little blond brows instantly pinched together in a frown. "Why?"

"Well, because your mom is going to meet a friend for lunch today, so we get to hang out together and do guy stuff."

James looked from Grant to his mother and back. "But why can't she do guy stuff with us?"

Grant leaned close, as if he was about to tell James a secret. "Because sometimes moms need time to do things that make them feel special. It's been a long time since your mom got to feel special and spend time with a friend. When you don't get to be with your friends, doesn't it make you feel lonely and a little sad?"

"Grant, don't guilt-trip him."

James pursed his lips and looked toward the ceiling. *Damn, this kid is adorable.*

"Like when I have play alone at recess?"

Grant's gaze met Bethany's before focusing on the boy again. "Exactly like that. This way, your mom will get to spend some time with her friend and you can spend time with me."

"Because you're *my* friend," James finished.

"Right." Grant leaned his forehead against James'. "I think you're a lot smarter than people give you credit for, little man."

James nodded vigorously. "I am," he agreed.

Grant laughed before meeting Bethany's gaze. She was biting the corner of her lip again, which meant this conversation hadn't turned out the way she'd expected and he began to wonder if she wasn't using James as an excuse to remain reclusive and protect herself as well.

"Go make your phone call and get ready, Bethany. We're going to go play ball and then have a snack."

Grant didn't miss the hesitation in her eyes, the apprehension that slumped her shoulders before she lifted her chin and stood straighter, taking a deep breath. "Okay, you two have fun."

She pointed at James, giving him a stern look and trying not to smile when James grinned back at her. "No conning Grant into cookies for you until after lunch."

BETHANY TOOK ONE final look in the mirror that ran down the back of her bedroom door. Smoothing her long hair back over her shoulder, she considered pulling it into her usual ponytail.

"No, you're making a few changes, starting today," she scolded her reflection as she adjusted the elastic waistband of her favorite peasant shirt. It showed just a sliver of skin between the hem and her jeans and she wondered again if she could be courageous enough to wear a mini-skirt.

Better just wear the jeans. Small changes were one thing, but she wasn't feeling confident enough to completely cast all caution to the wind on her first foray into dating in almost eleven years. Steven had been more than a little surprised when she'd called.

He probably thought you were some sort of stalker since he never gave you his number.

She brushed the thought aside. He'd sounded thrilled once she told him Madison had passed along his number. And, sure enough, he'd suggested they have lunch at Rosetti's before going to see some action movie he said he'd been waiting for months to come out. She couldn't even remember the name of the film but it didn't really matter. She was taking the first step. She was actually taking two: going on a date *and* trusting someone other than her parents with her son.

She glanced at the clock on her nightstand and realized Steven would arrive in ten minutes. Hurrying down the stairs as quickly as her wedge sandals would allow, Bethany headed into the kitchen in search of Grant and James, wanting to make sure Grant knew how to buckle the car seat and how James liked his sandwich cut.

A low whistle stopped her in her tracks. "Wow, you look incredible."

She turned and saw the pair coming in from the backyard. James' hair was damp on his forehead from the exertion of playing ball with Grant. She tugged at the bottom of her shirt, self-consciously.

"We're supposed to go to Rosetti's. It looks . . . okay?"

Grant moved toward her and she felt her stomach begin the delicious flips it seemed to do whenever he was near. Pausing, he opened the cupboard and retrieved a plastic cup, filling it with water for James before handing it to him. "You look better than okay."

"You look pretty, Mommy."

Grant cocked his head to one side and smiled. "He's right, you look beautiful. I like your hair down. It suits you."

The compliment shouldn't have sent her stomach tumbling to her toes, nor should she have felt the sizzle of heat zing through her, especially when she was about to go on a date with another man. She *shouldn't* have, but she did, and there was nothing she could do to stop it.

"Thank you," she murmured as she moved toward James to kiss the top of his head.

"Poor Steven isn't going to be able to keep his hands to himself." Grant chuckled as his gaze swept over her, warming her insides. The chime from the doorbell interrupted anything else Grant might have said and he arched a brow, giving her a cocky grin. "I'll get it."

"No, you can stay with James. I'll get it." She moved toward the front door, aware of James and Grant edging into the entry hall so they could spy on her as she opened the door. "Steven, you're right on time." She opened the door wider so he could enter.

"I was so surprised by your invitation after you said

no to coffee, I wasn't about to have a strike against me for being late." He looked up and saw the pair in the doorway. "Oh! I didn't realize you had company." He looked back at her, confusion written on his brow.

"Grant has offered to stay with James today."

"Hi, Mr. Carter." James waved, smiling brightly, and Bethany felt her heart swell. Maybe this wasn't such a bad idea after all. "Sorry you have to make Mom feel special today instead of doing guy stuff with us."

Bethany felt the blush rise up from her toes, heating her face, and she wanted to crawl under a rock and die of embarrassment. Grant tried unsuccessfully to hide his amusement as James reached up and took his hand, but Steven laughed out loud.

"As much fun as it might be to do stuff with you guys today, James, I'm actually looking forward to spending some time with your mom. I get to see you at school for several hours a day. I hardly ever get to talk to her."

Steven turned his gaze toward her, his eyes skimming over her and coming back to rest on her face. It might have been a while since she last dated, but she still knew how to read attraction in a man's eyes when she saw it and begged her body for some sort of tingly response. Sadly, it didn't seem inclined to cooperate.

James nodded seriously. "Except for recess."

Both men laughed this time. "Yep, except for recess," Steven agreed, turning back to her. "Are you ready? I have them holding a table for us."

She nodded. "Let me just grab my purse." She hurried

into the kitchen as Grant followed her. "You remember how to buckle in the car seat, right?"

"Yes, and I know your rules: no soda, two cookies— but only *after* lunch—and no naked women." Bethany glared at him but Grant laughed. "Just wanted to see if you were really listening."

"Thank you, Grant. My cell number is by the phone and I'll call the house when the movie is over, okay?"

"Go, have a good time and don't worry about us. We'll be too busy having fun to miss you."

Oddly enough, that was exactly what she was afraid of.

Chapter Twelve

GRANT STARED AT the kid bouncing energetically beside him and wondered what he was supposed to do now. It was one thing to play ball and take him riding while Bethany was there to let him know if he was straying from James' interests. Thanks to his own not-so-bright idea, he was completely on his own for the next several hours. At the very least.

Grant looked at his watch. It was almost eleven. "Are you hungry? I'm thinking we should eat something." James nodded and Grant made his way to the refrigerator, peering inside and finding sliced turkey and ham as well as a few hot dogs. "Well, which do you feel like, little man?"

"Mom makes me peanut butter and jelly." James looked up at Grant expectantly.

"Is that what you want? I think I can manage to make a PB&J sandwich." James shook his head and signed *no*. "Then what would you like?"

A broad smile split the boy's face as he peered through his lashes at Grant and he knew this kid was going to hustle him. *Hamburger and fries*, he signed.

Grant arched a brow at James before grinning. "I like the way you think, kid. Burgers and fries it is."

It only took a minute to buckle James into his car seat before the engine of Grant's Camaro rumbled and they were on their way to an old-time drive-in. It had always been one of Grant's favorite burger places in town. At least, that's what he'd tell anyone who asked. The real reason he'd gone out of his way for it today was because it was directly across from Rosetti's and he had a clear view into the front of the restaurant.

He wasn't spying. At least, not exactly. He was just making sure things went well for Bethany.

Who are you kidding?

A big part of him had wanted to punch Mr. Kindergarten Teacher in the face for not telling Bethany how beautiful she'd looked the minute he got through the door. Because she had.

He'd never seen her look more gorgeous. Her eyes sparkled with renewed vigor and, with just a little eye makeup to accent the various colors reflecting within them, she'd fairly glowed with radiance. He'd loved seeing her let her hair down, both literally and figuratively. Speaking of figures, he wished he could fathom how any woman could look that damn sexy in a pair of jeans and a flouncy top but seeing that small strip of her stomach bared just before she pulled down the bottom of her shirt had sent his blood pounding hotly through his veins, pooling in areas well below his waistband.

Grant ordered the burgers and fries, paired with milkshakes he was pretty sure Bethany wouldn't have approved of, and carried the food to his car. He must have it bad if he was willing to take a chance with a six-year-old kid eating in his baby just so he could keep an eye on the restaurant across the street, praying for a glimpse of a woman on a date with someone else. He might try to tell himself it was to make sure this guy treated her right, or that he was hoping to catch a glimpse of the photographer who'd been stalking him in order to point him in a different direction, but the truth was, he wanted to see if she was enjoying herself.

Did she give him the same smile she'd given Grant before she left for her date? Did her eyes glimmer with the same look of yearning that he saw when she looked at him?

He watched the front window of the restaurant as James dug into the bag of fries. "Thank you for lunch, Grant."

A half-smile slipped to his lips. *Damn he liked this kid. You're welcome*, he signed back.

His cell phone rang just as Bethany came into view, a waiter seating them near the front window. He glanced at the number on his phone screen and saw it was the owner of the Memphis Mustangs, Randall Wolf. He had to take the call—there was no other option, so he looked at James with a finger to his lips, indicating he stay quiet.

"Mr. Wolf, it's good to hear from you, sir."

Grant felt his heart stop as he waited to see why the owner of his team, the man who had the final say on the direction of his career with the Mustangs, would be calling instead of the team's general manager. It didn't bode well.

"I should have called you sooner, Grant, but I wanted to give you some time to . . . get your priorities in order. Have you spoken with your doctors?"

"I have and I have another appointment scheduled for next week. I should be able to let you know their final recommendation then. But I feel great and my workouts are better than ever," he added quickly.

Grant heard the owner's sigh through the receiver. "Let's cut the B.S., Grant. You know I like you, I always have, but do you really think you're going to be able to come back this season at a hundred percent?"

"Sir—"

"You have two more years left on your contract with a buyout option. I was there when the doctor warned you about your neck and the dangers if you come back to play." The man sighed into the phone again. "I think it's time to accept that your playing days are over."

"With all due respect, Mr. Wolf, I disagree."

Even as he spoke to his employer, Grant stared at the woman across from him, admiring the tilt of her chin as she listened to her date, the way the sunlight played over her hair, the way her smile seemed to make even this conversation bearable.

The man on the other end of the line chuckled softly. "Damn if you aren't the most stubborn player I've ever had on my team. That's one of the things that's made you so good." There was a long pause as Grant waited for his boss to say more. "Grant, I'm trying to tell you that we're going to offer to buy out your contract. I understand that you're willing to take the risk for the team, but you're too much of a liability now. We have to focus at what's going to help the team this year and I just don't think it's you. I'm sorry."

It was obvious that Wolf wasn't just calling to offer a contract buyout or he would have gone directly to Grant's agent. Grant was impatient for the owner to get to the point of the call.

"I want to offer you a position on the Mustangs staff. You'd work closely with the offensive coordinator and move into a coaching position the following season." Grant opened his mouth to protest but the man caught him before he could utter more than a grunt of protest. "I know, you don't think it's time to retire, but you've been mentoring the rookies for years now and I think this is a place on the team where you could continue indefinitely and be a huge asset."

Grant took a deep breath, trying to control the rage threatening to erupt from within. With James in the car and no outlet for his fury, he clenched his jaw, hard enough that he heard it pop.

"We'll buy out the remainder of your contract and you'll be offered a generous salary. Think about it before you turn me down, Grant. This is a onetime offer. I just wanted to talk to you about it before I sent the details over to your agent. We'll give you a few days to think about your answer."

Taking another deep breath, Grant closed his eyes, pinching the space at the bridge of his nose. "Thank you, sir. We'll be in touch."

With his head pounding, Grant wanted to throw something and when he looked across the street, seeing Bethany smiling brightly at the man across from her, laughing at some brilliant comment, no doubt, it only made the fury roil in his gut. He tossed the bag with the uneaten burger into the front seat, losing any appetite he might have had.

Why couldn't he have gotten this phone call yesterday, before he convinced her to go out with this guy? How had his future managed to go from favorable to fucked up over burgers and fries?

GRANT LEANED AGAINST the back of the couch, his eyes closing as he tried to relax in the semi-darkened room. It was only early evening, but he was beat emotionally. He'd turned on some movie for James about a boy and his pet dragon, but the kid had been so exhausted from playing ball again after they'd returned from lunch, he'd fallen asleep only a few minutes after the opening song and Grant hadn't even bothered to wake him for dinner. He'd simply carried James up to his bed and, unsure how to remove the implant microphones, left them on for Bethany to remove when she arrived home in a few minutes. She'd already called and told him she was on her way back from the movies.

As if the thought conjured her from thin air, Grant

heard the front door close and the soft *clomp* of her shoes on the tile floor as she made her way into the living room. He cracked one eye open just enough to see her bend over and take off her shoes, kicking them to the side, before padding over the carpet to the couch to peer down at him. She bent over, not realizing the view she gave him as her blouse fell forward. His mouth dried up and he tried to force himself to look away from the delicate curve of the top of her breast and the barely-there decorative trim at the edge of her bra.

"Grant," she whispered as she reached for his arm, shaking him slightly.

He opened one eye and smiled, tugging her down onto the couch cushions beside him. "I'm awake, but that boy tired me out. I don't know how you do it every single day."

"He can be a handful sometimes." She laughed softly.

Grant slid his arm around the back of the couch and fought back a groan when she dropped her head against his shoulder. There was nothing inherently intimate about the gesture but the fact that it seemed so natural made him want to pull her closer against his chest and he forced himself to stifle the urge.

"So, how was the date?" He tipped his face toward her but it only resulted in the sweet scent of her perfume filling his lungs. It was like sunshine and honey, warm and sweet. Without realizing it, his fingers slid over her shoulder, caressing the curve of her neck.

"It was . . . nice."

"Honey, guys don't want to hear a woman say a date

was nice." He gave a quiet chuckle. "That's a sure sign you're being friend-zoned if there ever was one."

He could feel her smile against his shoulder, even through his cotton shirt, but she didn't look up at him. "I'll have to keep that in mind for the next time. It *has* been a while since I did this. I think I've almost forgotten how."

"It's like riding a bike. As soon as you start, it will all come back to you. The coy glances, the flirty smiles. I've seen them from you so I know you know how." Heat pooled in his groin and he fought the urge to lay his cheek against the top of her head. It was too comfortable with Bethany; it felt too right.

She pulled away and looked up at him. "I have not."

"The hell you haven't." Grant laughed deep in his chest. "But I'll just chalk it up to you being out of practice and its being an accident." He pulled her close again, hating the emptiness he felt when she'd sat up and cursing the circumstances that kept him from pursuing what he knew they'd both regret later. "So, are you guys going out again?"

She tipped her face toward him, her hand resting against his chest, and batted her lashes sweetly. "That depends on if I can get a sitter again."

"See, there you go." He shook his head, berating her gently with a laugh. "Don't tell me you don't know how to flirt," he teased.

Longing kicked him in the groin. It took every ounce of self-control he had to keep from kissing her. Even if she was joking, the pout on her lips and the tenderness he saw in her eyes was enough to make him forget. Forget football, forget leaving, forget what he needed. He wanted to cup her face, to run his thumb over that lower lip she bit so often and taste the sweetness he knew he would find in her mouth. If he waited even a moment longer, his willpower would cave and they wouldn't be able to find their way back to this place. He needed to leave before he made a mistake he couldn't undo.

He rose from the couch, causing her to flop back against the cushions. "I wasn't sure how to take James' implants off so you should probably do that. He's already in bed asleep."

She frowned, looking hurt and confused. "Um, okay."

Rising from the couch, she ran her hands over her thighs and trotted up the stairs. He could hear her footsteps, lightly padding overhead, before moving back down the hall. Grant knew he was a fool, knew he wanted this woman like he'd never wanted another. He'd known from the first night at the pizza place she was trouble, but he'd thought then that it was because she was a pretty, smart-mouthed, feisty small-town girl. Now that he'd gotten to know her, he realized it was because she'd given him a glimpse of what he wanted his future to hold, not just the idea of a family, but the very woman and child he wanted to call his own.

With one phone call from the owner of the Mustangs, his plans to return to football had been derailed. He wasn't sure it even mattered any longer what the doctor might tell him next week because it sounded like Mr.

Wolf had already made up his mind, which meant trying to negotiate a new contract with a new team, leaving his future even more up in the air. Frustration welled up in him. He'd risked everything to return to football, been willing to sacrifice everything. All of the time he'd spent training was wasted unless he was playing. There were so many things he'd given up over the years that he could never get back.

The realization made him think about the woman upstairs and wonder if this wasn't a second chance with her. He'd been a fool to tell her to date someone else when every part of his body was begging him to reach out to her, to touch her, to let her know exactly what he was feeling. He'd offered her friendship from the beginning, but deep down he'd known from the first that friendship would never be enough with Bethany. Even now, in his frustration about his future, he felt a small measure of relief. If he didn't go back, he would be free to stay and offer her more. He might be nothing more than a washed-up player, but he'd give her whatever she might want from him.

He heard her feet tapping against the hard wood flooring through the ceiling and it sounded like she was in James' room. For the first time, he was able to see a future without football. He'd wasted so much time on a game, gambled his future on a crumbling foundation and, from the sound of Mr. Wolf's call, he'd just lost. He wasn't about to risk the only other thing he wanted.

BETHANY TURNED ON the bathroom light in case James woke up then snuck into his room and slipped the microphones from behind his ears. She removed the battery packs from his arms and put them on the base to charge, taking a moment to watch her son sleep. It felt odd not being the one to tuck him in or read him a story at night. Her date had been exactly the way she described it to Grant—nice. Not overly exciting, but not horrible either.

Steven had spent most of the evening sharing stories about several of their co-workers and some of the kids they taught but their conversation never strayed far from work. While she loved her job, she'd hoped to get to know him better outside of their roles as teachers. What she'd really been hoping for was to feel the same shiver of heat that raced through her veins when Grant touched her hand, or to feel her stomach flutter nervously the way it did when Grant looked her way. But with Steven, as nice and attractive as he was, there were no fireworks. Not even a little flare. She assumed he'd realized it as well because he didn't even bother to try to kiss her at the door. Just a quick hug and a thank-you before he hurried off.

There was a distinct possibility that this was her worst-case scenario.

She was falling for Grant McQuaid, hard and fast, and that was something she simply couldn't do. He was leaving town in a week for his medical appointments and training camp. Starting a relationship that was bound to end in heartache, and hurt James, was the stupidest thing she could do. Logically, she knew it yet it didn't stop her from wanting him.

That moment on the couch, she'd almost given in to the feelings that welled in her chest. When he'd pulled her down beside him, it had taken every ounce of her control not to sigh and curl into his embrace, practically purring like a kitten. She hadn't been strong enough to keep from leaning against him, inhaling the musky scent of his soap or feeling his heart beating rapidly beneath her hand on his chest, its pulse matching the way her own heart raced.

She'd been sure he was going to turn his head and kiss her, welcomed it even, until he jumped up and made her head practically bounce off the cushions along the back of the couch.

She sighed. At least one of them had been thinking clearly.

She made her way back to the stairs and, from the top, could see him standing below. "Are you leaving?"

"I should get going."

"Oh."

Disappointment rang in her voice and she hoped he didn't hear it. Grant hadn't said anything about when, or if, they might see him again, even when she hinted at needing a sitter again. It was probably best to reconcile herself to the fact that this was as good a time as any to put this crush of hers to rest.

She made her way down the stairs. "I really appreciate what you've done for James."

"Just James?" Grant was looking up at her with those dark eyes of his. She might get lost if she continued to stare into them. There was emotion there but she wasn't sure she wanted to name it. Desire? Maybe. Apprehension? Definitely. She just wasn't sure why.

She gave him a slight smile. "No, not just James. You've helped me too."

Bethany gasped as she stepped down from the last stair and Grant's arm slid around her waist, pulling her close. Her heart pounded against her ribs and it stole her ability to speak. She sucked in a quick breath just before he dipped his head. The touch of his lips was gentle, warm and seductive. Her hands were caught between them, against the hard washboard of his stomach, and clenched instinctively. She needed to feel the rest of him under her fingers, to feel his skin, his heat. He brushed his mouth over hers, toying with her, teasing her, and she realized he was testing her to see what she would allow.

The problem was that she didn't know what she really wanted anymore. Her body craved being closer to Grant but fear warned her to move away, to hide from the storm of emotions he was creating inside her.

She hadn't even been kissed by a man since the morning her ex-husband kissed her cheek before turning his back on her and James without warning. She hadn't been this close to a man, or let one this close to her and James, since Matthew's abandonment. She'd forgotten how a look could send the butterflies in her stomach flitting, how a glance could make her tingle with anticipation and how a touch could make her limbs go liquid with desire. Grant was forcing her to come alive, making her feel things she hadn't felt in the last six years like she was awaking from hibernation.

Who was she kidding? She'd never felt this heady desire, not even with Matthew. They'd been friends and lovers, but there had never been this overwhelming hunger that made her feel simultaneously hot and cold, weak and powerful.

Grant curled his fingers into her hair, drawing her closer, and her hands found their way over his chest, climbing the granite wall of muscle to his shoulders. His tongue swept over hers and he tasted of sweet mint. She sighed, leaning into him for balance, for something solid to help her regain her equilibrium. She was about to wind her arms around his neck and give herself over completely to the reckless abandon her body craved, when he withdrew, brushing his thumb over her cheek.

She knew she should be trying to maintain a safe distance, for her heart and her body, but it was the last thing on her mind as the muscles of his shoulders twitched, tensing under her fingers. He didn't release her and she didn't try to move out of his arms.

Grant didn't even bother to hide the cocky tilt of his grin. "You're a pretty damn good kisser, Ms. Mills."

She could hear the soft drawl in his voice from his time spent in Memphis with the team and it made her want to melt against him. It reminded her of riverboat cruises up the Mississippi, afternoon barbecues and home. She felt connected to Grant in a way that went beyond football and she felt a few more of her reservations fade into the distance.

What if . . . her heart whispered.

She wanted to cling to the possibility for a moment

longer, before she allowed reality to crash in, spoiling her fantasy. Bethany arched a saucy brow at him and leaned backward, her hips pressing into his. "You're not so bad yourself, Mr. McQuaid."

Grant groaned deep in his throat, growing suddenly serious. His eyes became dark pools of desire as his hand slid to her hip, his fingers slightly curling into the flesh as he pulled her firmly against him. She could feel the evidence of his arousal against the front of her.

"Bethany, unless you want me to forget being the gentleman my Mom raised, don't do that again."

She felt the blush rise over her cheeks and took a step backward, bumping into the railing of the staircase. "I didn't . . . I mean . . ."

His smile was gentle again but the hunger didn't leave his eyes. "You really have no idea what you do to a man, do you?" he asked, leaning close to her ear. "You look at me with those big, innocent eyes and I forget."

She felt the shiver of yearning travel down her spine making her want to press against him again. His hand ran down her arm and back up her side, his lips brushing over the edge of her ear sending shivers of delight spiraling through her limbs.

"Forget what?"

Her voice was barely a whisper of sound. She couldn't chance speaking louder. Doing that might break the spell he'd woven over her and make her come to her senses. It might make her remember that these feelings weren't made to last.

He brushed his lips against hers, barely a featherlight

touch. His hand found the curve of her jaw and he cupped her face with both of his hands reverently.

"I have to go," he murmured, his lips moving over hers. "I don't want to, but I have to."

Without looking back, he hurried out the front door, leaving her standing at the foot of the stairs with the fingers of one hand over her lips. She heard the roar of his car engine only seconds before it faded down the street. Bethany refused to acknowledge the regret trying to creep up on her or give in to the angry tears welling at the back of her eyes. She'd known better and this was all a result of her not listening to the warnings she'd given herself, for plunging headlong into the vulnerable state she now found herself in.

I don't want to leave you, but I can't stay any longer.

How ironic that Grant had used such similar words to those in the note Matthew had left on the kitchen table the morning he'd left them behind.

Chapter Fourteen

"I THOUGHT YOU were putting an end to this?" Grant's father tossed the paper beside him as Grant sat down with a cup of coffee, rubbing the sleep out of his eyes. "I like her, Grant. Don't do this to her."

Travis McQuaid had never been one to mince words and, since he'd already been up for at least a few hours, he had little sympathy for any of his sons who slept in past six in the morning.

"Think you could give me five minutes to wake up first, Dad?" Grant slid the paper closer.

While the headline was about the upheaval in town over a new box store that had proposed coming in, the story just below it was yet another picture of him. This time, it showed Grant and the back of James head, having burgers, detailing how he was spending time with the unnamed child. He noticed they were careful enough not to show James' face, since they didn't have his parent's permission but, since there weren't any other hearing-impaired kids in this town, it would be hard for anyone to mistake the implants on James' head or who it was a picture of.

"Son of a bitch," Grant muttered. "At least this makes my story that I'm spending time with him as part of an outreach more believable. I told them we weren't an item and tipped them off so they would see Bethany on her date . That should have been enough to satisfy most people."

"Yeah, well, it's not that woman or her kid they're really interested in, son. It's you. You should have stayed out of sight." He sipped his coffee.

"I thought I did."

"They're going to keep following you around until you leave. Just like they always do."

"*If* I leave." Grant stared down into the mug, letting the steam from the coffee invade his senses, hoping the caffeine might give him some clarity on what to do next.

He hadn't told Bethany about the phone call from the team owner. Maybe he should have. Because what he really needed to do was find out how she would feel about his staying and if she felt the same connection sizzling between them. In truth, he wanted to know if she believed there was any possibility of a relationship between them that went beyond friendship. If that kiss was any indication, they didn't just sizzle, they could burn the town to the ground.

But there was a part of him that wanted nothing more than to hop on a plane today and fly out to Memphis to prove to Wolf that he still had it, that he could still keep up with the rookies coming in, that he wasn't a liability regardless of what the doctors might be telling him.

"What do you mean 'if'?"

Grant shook his head. "I got a call yesterday. They're ready to put me out to pasture, even if the doctors clear me. They want to buy out the rest of my contract and have me work with the offensive coordinator."

His father ran his finger and thumb over his jaw, the same way Grant did when he was thinking. He and his father were so much alike, enough to drive each other crazy, but in times like these, it came in handy to have someone who understood him so well.

"Hmm, are you considering it?"

Grant shrugged half-heartedly. In truth, it wasn't a bad offer for someone in his position. He'd risked everything he'd saved over the years on the ranch, knowing it would pay off in the end. He just hadn't realized the end of his career would come before the return came in. Still, being around the team but unable to continue playing would prove to be torture.

"Doesn't sound like something you'd want to do if there were other options," he pointed out.

"I'm not sure there are."

"What about going to another team?"

Grant sighed and sipped the coffee, willing the caffeine to give his brain a much needed jolt. "I'd need an offer from one and I'm not sure I could get one before spring training starts, which means I'd be fighting for a starting position. At my age, with my record . . ." Grant shook his head. He couldn't even deny the humiliation he felt.

"Aren't you doing that anyway?"

Grant knew it was a valid point. "I mean, I always knew a time would come when I'd retire, eventually. I just didn't expect it to come so soon."

"Could you? I mean, you've invested a lot into this place and with Jackson. Not to mention your little venture."

His father was talking about the business he'd started just before his family had needed his backing, a high-end camping facility that he had yet to put time into marketing.

"With the buyout they're offering, I could manage until things pick up around here. But if I take this position they're offering, I'd have to relocate to Memphis permanently. I mean, you need help here, the family is *here*."

"Would you really be happy in Hidden Falls forever, without all the attention and glory you get from football?"

The image of Bethany and Grant settled in his mind, warming him. "In the right circumstances, I think I could be."

His father arched a graying brow at him. "Son, I love you and ranching might be in your genes, but it's not in your blood like it is with the twins or the way it is with me. I'd hate to see you give up something you love for something you're just settling for."

Grant couldn't tell his father how much his words might apply to a completely different subject. He looked down at the picture of him with James again. Was he willing to give up his last chance at football, the only chance he'd have to prove himself again, for the chance at a future with Bethany?

"Thanks, Dad."

"For what?"

"Putting things back into perspective for me." He finished off the mug of coffee and rose to refill it, holding the pot out toward his father who nodded. Grant topped off his father's cup. "And for letting me off the hook as far as the ranch goes."

Travis McQuaid scrunched up his face in doubt. "I didn't let you off the hook. I just know where your strengths lie. Now go help your brother saddle up those horses. We have calves to band today."

Grant shook head. He should have known his father would make the most of the one day this week he had all his kids, minus the one on his national country music tour, at the house together. "Okay, let me change into old clothes. I know how messy this gets."

His father chuckled. "That's one way to put it. Be sure to wake up Andrew and Ben too. I just don't understand how the three of you can sleep the day away," he grumbled into his mug.

"Because we don't go to bed with the chickens like you, old man," Grant yelled back as he headed out the door for the bunkhouse.

If nothing else, the talk with his father had made him realize he didn't need to accept this new position with the Mustangs yet, unless he wanted to. His buyout wouldn't be enough to retire on long-term, but it was enough to get him by until next year when Jackson's first foals sold. In the meantime, he would just talk to his agent about setting up some endorsement deals or something, unless there was a chance he could get on another team, maybe one of the West Coast teams. Then he could turn his focus to the only thing other than football he was most interested in—the very woman who was probably pouring herself a cup of coffee with a little blond boy chattering away at her kitchen table. If last night had proven anything to him, it was that Bethany Mills had a way of making him forget his worries about the future to focus on the here and now.

I DON'T WANT to go . . . I have to.

Grant's words kept replaying through her mind, like a nonstop, degrading loop that made her feel like she'd slipped backward in time. Bethany rubbed her eyes and poured herself a cup of strong, black coffee, adding in far too much of her flavored creamer in hopes that it might sweeten her mood. She paused and poured in more, knowing that she was going to need all the help she could get this morning. She was surprised James was still sound asleep since he was usually an early riser but attributed it to the busy day he'd had with Grant yesterday.

She sighed, wishing she could go back and relive the last few days. If she had a do-over, she'd stick to her original plan and turned him down for pizza both times he asked and send him off the same way she had every other man who'd invited her to dinner over the past six years.

But Grant isn't like other men.

"You can say that again," she muttered into her coffee before taking a sip.

She might not be able to pinpoint what it was about him that drew her like filings to a high-powered magnet, but that didn't stop the force from working overtime. He seemed to draw everyone to him, the same way James did, but being with him in person was different than watching the man in interviews teasing the media and charming people from the field. It was like he had his own gravitational pull, and the more time she spent with him, the stronger it felt.

When he'd kissed her last night, every inch of her body had ignited in a fire she'd thought would burn her alive. Her fingers moved to her lips, as if trying to relive the memory of his kiss.

"But it didn't stop him from leaving either." Her words trailed off with a sigh. Matthew was the last person she wanted to think about.

Rising from her chair, she reached for the carton of milk in the refrigerator. She needed to do something, anything, to keep her mind off Grant, and maybe making pancakes for James would help. She gathered the ingredients and began mixing the batter. She had just lifted the container of blueberries to fold them into the mixture when her phone rang and she heard the soft pad of James' feet on the staircase.

She reached for her phone. "Hello?"

"Well? How was your date the other night with Grant

McQuaid?" Her mother's voice held far too much enthusiasm for this early in the morning.

"Mom, it was only pizza," she corrected as she gently stirred the mixture, turning on the griddle to preheat.

James made his way to the table and took a seat, resting his chin in his hands, his eyes still only at half-mast. *Good morning,* she signed to him. He smiled at her and climbed down from his chair, wandering closer to wrap his arms around her waist. Bethany kissed the top of his head and signed for him to set the table.

Is Grant coming for breakfast? he asked.

She shook her head at him, trying not to acknowledge the way her heart clenched at the disappointment she could see in his big blue eyes.

"So, when are you seeing him again?" Her mother's voice broke her focus on her son.

"Mom, weren't you the one who kept telling me to relax because it *wasn't* really a date? That I shouldn't think of it that way?"

Bethany heard her mother's sigh through the receiver. "I know but, honey, I just want to see you happy again. I hate seeing you lonely."

"I'm not lonely," she lied.

"You might be able to fool some people, Bethie, but you will never be able to fool your mother. I hear it in your voice every time I talk to you." She laughed sadly. "That would be like you not knowing James' moods the way you do. We mothers know."

Bethany took a deep breath. "James and I went to his

family's ranch last weekend," she confessed, wondering if her mother could hear how torn she felt from her tone. "He taught James how to ride a pony and they went swimming. They played football," she added.

"He's a good man," her mother said matter-of-factly.

She laughed at her mother's quiet confidence. "There is no way you could possibly know that."

"Bethany Marie Mills," her mother scolded. "Would I say something like that if I didn't know it? First of all, your father knows everything that has ever been reported about any of the Mustangs in the past twenty-five years since we moved here. I'm so tired of his sports shows," she complained before catching herself. "And, besides, I know *you*. You would never let someone close to James if he wasn't a good person."

Guilt swept over Bethany. As much as she wanted to agree with her mother's assessment of her, she wasn't nearly as confident in her own judgment, as a mother or a woman. Maybe a week ago, but now? She could barely meet her son's gaze, knowing that her decision to let Grant into their lives would hurt him, far more than if she'd just said no to dinner with him in the first place.

"So . . ." Her mother drew out the word.

"So?" Bethany poured the pancake batter onto the griddle and leaned back against the island, grateful that James hadn't put on his microphone receivers yet. "There's really nothing to tell. Even if there were, he's heading back to spring training soon. I'm not about to get involved with someone who is about to leave."

"And if he wasn't?"

"Of course he will." She heard the thud of the morning paper against her front door and headed to retrieve it, cradling the phone with her shoulder. She slipped the rubber band from around it and unfolded the newspaper. "There's no way he wouldn't at least go back and—"

Bethany couldn't believe the picture gracing the lower half of her paper. It showed the back of her son's head, while he ate a burger and fries in Grant's car. That would have been bad enough since Grant hadn't told her he'd taken him out, but the snapshot showed a profile of Grant with his cell phone to his ear, watching something directly in front of him. The restaurant where she'd had lunch with Steven was directly across from the parking lot he was in. There was only one reason she could think of for him to be there. But why would Grant spy on her?

"What's wrong?"

"Nothing, Mom. Let me finish getting James his breakfast and I'll call you back, okay?"

"Sure. Bethie, are you sure you're doing okay? I mean, I know it was my suggestion you move but—"

"I'm fine, Mom. We both are. I'll talk to you in a bit, okay?"

Bethany disconnected the call and studied the picture. She wished she knew for sure what Grant had been looking at. Obviously the photographer had been along one side of the street to catch this vantage point. However difficult it might be to figure out what attracted his attention, the look on his face was easily deciphered. He was angry. The question was what had made him that way— his call or the subject of his intense focus?

GRANT CLIMBED OUT of the shower and wound a thick terrycloth towel around his slim hips. He was in great shape, better than when they'd carried him off the field last season, but even the hot water couldn't ease the soreness already setting in from a long day in the saddle. He'd left the actual banding of the cattle to his father and the twins who were faster at it than he and Andrew were, but it didn't lessen the physical exertion he, Ben and Andrew expended herding and moving the cattle to and from the chutes. He'd forgotten how much work was involved on the ranch, and how it never seemed to end.

Or how much you actually enjoy working with your family.

It was true. It had been a long time since the seven of them had put in a full day's work together but he found it as exhilarating as it was exhausting. While there had been plenty of name calling and ribbing, there was also an unspoken rhythm to the work. Each person knew their part, like a well-oiled machine, and they worked together flawlessly. Now that the hard part was done, they were going to grill some burgers and have a couple cold beers apiece while they relaxed at the fire pit. They'd probably end up giving each other crap about stupid things they'd done as kids, reminiscing and reliving memories, the way they always did when they got together, but he couldn't think of anything else he'd rather be doing.

Nothing else?

Okay, there was one thing that he'd rather be doing, something he hadn't quite managed to get out of his mind all day. He couldn't help but think about the way Bethany's soft curves had felt in his hands last night. Ever since the conversation with his father this morning, Grant had been dying to call her, but he didn't want to push her. He wasn't exactly sure where he stood with her after that kiss. He couldn't expect to just go from being a friend— offering her advice and suggestions on dating—to *the* guy she was dating without letting her catch her breath.

However, he wasn't willingly walking away from the easy friendship they'd developed. That was as much a part of his attraction to her as her as her tender vulnerability and her quiet strength. In truth, it was the biggest part of his attraction to her. Of course, it wasn't that he didn't appreciate her beauty, but there was so much more to her. She was as sweet and innocent as she was feisty and flirty. She didn't mind standing up for what she believed courageously but she was also willing to keep an open mind. She was as honest as anyone he'd ever met and wasn't impressed by his celebrity. In fact, she'd been put off by it, and therein lay part of the problem.

Even when he walked away from the team and left that chapter of his life behind, the reporters wouldn't just go away. At least, not at first. Once your name was up in lights, that fame was a difficult thing to shed. For most players, it took at least five years of ducking the press and disappearing off the media's radar. She was far too private a person to ignore it. He'd seen the anxiety she'd tried to hide when she read the last article about his car at her house. He couldn't ask Bethany and James to live under that kind of scrutiny and media attention.

"Oh, hey!" He heard Jefferson's voice from downstairs

as he greeted someone in the bunkhouse living room. "I'll get him for you."

His brother's feet pounded on the stairs and Grant jerked a t-shirt over his still-damp head just as Jefferson banged on his door. "Grant, Bethany's here."

He opened the door, looking over the banister to see her looking up at him, her hair loose around her shoulders, looking gorgeous and agitated. He hadn't expected her to come by and, from the look on her face, this wasn't a friendly visit. James, on the other hand, looked ecstatic and Grant chose to focus on the boy's excitement first.

"Hey, little man. Are you here to whip Jefferson at Xbox? I have to warn you, he's pretty good at car racing."

James eyes widened with delight as Jefferson jogged back downstairs. "You have an Xbox?" He spun on his mother. *Can I play?* he signed.

Jefferson wisely looked to Bethany for confirmation before he agreed. Bethany pinched her lips together tightly. He could tell she was upset and wondered what had happened.

"Fine, for a couple of minutes while I talk to Grant." Her gaze slid past James and his brother, who were already heading for the couch, and lit on him again. The yellow flecks in her eyes glowed brightly.

"Why don't we go outside?" he suggested, opening the back door for her. She glanced back at James. "He'll be fine with Jefferson for a few minutes. You look like you need to get something off your chest and I'm thinking you might prefer to do it privately."

She pinched her lips together again and he knew he'd

hit the bull's-eye. He held open the back door for her, ignoring the surprised looks from Andrew and Ben as she headed toward the barn. This wasn't looking promising for him.

"Okay, what's on your mind?" he asked as he led her into the aisle of the barn. The horses greeted them with quiet nickers and the sweet musty scent of straw surrounded them.

"This." She pulled a folded newspaper from her purse and slapped it against his chest. "I thought you were watching James."

Grant scanned the headline of the paper, his gaze falling on the picture his father had pointed out earlier. "I was. He was hungry, so we went for burgers and fries."

"Looks like James wasn't what you were watching here. This burger place is across the street from Rosetti's." She tapped the picture. "Were you spying on me?"

Grant clenched his jaw. It was on the tip of his tongue to tell her the truth. He could easily confess that he'd been jealous of her date, but seeing the picture of him on the phone with Wolf reminded him of just how insecure his future really was. For all he knew, he could be out of a job by the end of a week and, as of right now, he had no real prospects. Regardless of the conversation with his Dad this morning, even though he knew he *wanted* her, he had nothing solid to offer her. He had no idea where his career was headed, or where he would end up. And there were plenty of guys in Hidden Falls who could offer her the privacy and security Bethany craved in her life, something he wouldn't be able to give her for some time. It wasn't fair for him to ask her to wait, or make her a promise he might not have the power to keep.

Chapter Fourteen

BETHANY WASN'T SURE what had possessed her to show up unannounced at his home like she really had any reason to be angry at Grant. But seeing the look on his face staring back at her from the front page, knowing he'd been across the street while she'd been on her date, realizing that James could have seen her and misconstrued even a handhold, had infuriated her. Almost as much as the damn guilty grin he had plastered across his face right now. She wasn't about to let him charm his way out of this.

"Okay, let me explain," he began, reaching for her hand.

She jerked it away. His touch had a tendency to scatter her thoughts and turn her into a puddle of Jell-O. She needed every ounce of her focus to confront him.

"Explain what? *You* were the one who convinced me to go out with Steven in the first place. What could you possibly say to make this okay?"

Grant took a deep breath, patiently waiting while she lashed out at him. When she paused, he answered. "Bethany, I called the paper and told them where to find you on your date. I was there, trying to make sure that reporter, whoever it is, showed up to get a picture of you with someone that wasn't me. That was the original idea, remember? To prove that *we* aren't a couple."

She'd forgotten. The revelation took the steam out of her tirade. After arriving home after her date and trying to recover from Grant's kiss, which had left her hungry for more, the reporter following him had been the last thing she'd worried about. After his sudden rejection, little else had commanded her thoughts. Assuming that he'd followed her because of jealousy gave her a reason to confront him and had taken some of the sting out of the way he'd walked out last night. Now, she wasn't sure whether to be grateful that he'd been trying to help her reputation or confused by his mixed signals.

"Then why do you look so mad in the picture?"

"I got a phone call I wasn't exactly expecting." Grant clenched his jaw, his tone suddenly clipped and almost angry, but he didn't seem inclined to share more information than that with her.

"I see."

"No, Bethany, you don't." Exasperation and sheer frustration colored his voice and he shoved his hands into the pockets of his jeans. "You think you understand, but you can't. Because I had a life all planned out, in every detail. I was coming back here to recuperate and returning to Memphis, back to my job but now, who knows?"

He ran a furious hand through his hair, making it stand up. Her fingers itched to brush through it and lay the strands back into place. She had no clue what he was talking about but she could see the aggravation in his face, the anger building in the way his muscles tensed. She'd never seen him lose his temper, not even during press conferences, and she wasn't sure what she'd said to cause it. Grant threw his hands into the air and spun in a circle, looking at the barn around him.

"I could stay here, but that isn't exactly a long-term option. I'm not a rancher and I'd go crazy." He beat a hand against his chest and it hurt her to see him feeling lost. "I'm a football player—it's what I do, who I am. *That* is the only thing I know how to be successfully. But I may not even be that anymore. I'm not a coach or a mentor. Those guys don't want to listen to me."

Bethany was confused and wasn't sure what she could say to help him so she simply remained silent, letting him vent his anger until it was spent. Grant slammed his palms against the wall of the barn, turning his back to her.

"Damn it," he muttered, closing his eyes. "I didn't mean to lay that on you."

"It's okay." Bethany stepped closer, suddenly understanding that his anger stemmed from fear—fear of what his injury might have caused, fear of whether he'd have a future with the team, fear of the unknown. She could understand that kind of fear.

Laying one hand over his against the wall and the other over his heart, she looked up at him, wanting him

to see her empathy. Regardless of what had happened between them on the stairs, he'd been a good friend to her
and James in the past week. He deserved for her to be a
friend in return.

"What do you want to do, Grant? What would make
you happy?"

He looked at her hand, splayed over his chest then
back to her face. As much as she might try to deny it, she
didn't miss the desire that flashed in his eyes before they
shadowed with regret. Grant closed them and shook his
head. "Don't ask me that, Bethany. Please."

"Grant, you've made me face some hard truths in my
life this past week. Maybe it's time for you to face a few
as well."

"Bethany," he warned, looking away from her. "This is
a Pandora's box you don't want to open, trust me."

"I do trust you." She reached her fingers to his jaw,
turning his face back toward her. "What about you? What
would make you happy, Grant? What do *you* want to do?"

His eyes were sorrowful and it hurt her to see him
agonizing over this decision she couldn't help him with.
Their meeting might have been unorthodox, but in the
past six days he'd made more of an impact on her life, on
James' life, than anyone other than her parents. He was
teaching her to trust again and it pained her to know he
didn't feel he could lean on her as well.

He looked into her eyes and she could see the inner
war he was fighting. He wanted to open up to her, even
opened his mouth to speak, but his eyes clouded and he
closed it again.

"Damn it," he muttered.

She took a deep breath, trying to ignore the agonizing rejection that wanted to steal her breath from her lungs. She couldn't force him to open up, to tell her what he was holding inside. Searching his eyes, Bethany questioned whether she was sure she wanted him to. It would change things, even more than their kiss had. She wasn't sure how she knew it, but Bethany was certain that Grant telling her whatever he was holding inside would alter their friendship.

"Okay." She nodded, unsure where they could go from here.

There was an unspoken wall between them now that hadn't been there before, not even when she'd been trying to keep barriers between him and James. He had secrets he couldn't share, or wouldn't. They were no longer on a level playing field and she couldn't allow herself to be open with someone who was closed off with her. She had to walk away, regardless of how much it hurt, if she wanted to save face at all. Otherwise, she'd look just like all of the rest of the football groupies throwing herself at *the* Grant McQuaid. She closed her eyes and fortified her resolve as she turned her back on him.

Grant's fingers brushed her waist as he reached for her. She paused midstep but didn't turn around. Bethany felt him move toward her, his chest pressing against her back, the heat of him scorching her through her clothing. She stood still, waiting for him to do something, to *say* something, to explain himself and reach out to her emotionally. His arms moved around her waist, enveloping her, and she felt the tornado of need spiral through her. He pressed a kiss to the top of her head.

"You make me happy," he whispered.

He didn't sound happy. He sounded tormented, like the admission was being ripped from him.

GRANT TRIED TO stop himself, tried not to confess the truth but the anguish he saw in her eyes was his undoing. When she'd turned away from him, he'd known he was losing her for good. She'd had enough hurt in her life. He refused to be the reason she had more.

His hands cupped her shoulders as he turned her slowly to face him. His fingers ached to touch her face, to slip into her hair and tip her head back. He wanted to kiss her—was dying to kiss her—but he knew that if he gave in, he would only hurt her more if he left. However, his mouth didn't seem compelled to listen to his brain's logic.

"I want you, Bethany, and I can't seem to stop it."

She smiled up at him, sweetly, her eyes lighting up with a pleasure he couldn't understand. As her hands cupped his face, her thumb traced the line of his jaw. "Then don't."

Bethany stood on her toes, pressing her mouth to his, surprising him with her sweet kiss. Wrapping her hands around the nape of his neck, she pulled him down toward her, insistent, stronger than he'd imagined someone so petite could be, and his arms circled around her back, lifting her higher. She opened to him, letting him explore and taste. Grant caught her quiet whimper on his breath as he turned, pressing her against the wall, hungry for more. She clung to him, arching into his body, as needy as he was. His hands skimmed the hem of her shirt, his fingers touching the bare skin beneath and she sighed, letting her head fall back against the wall.

As his lips found her jaw, pressing hot kisses over the delicate curve of her neck, his hand felt the slight indentations of her ribs. Moving higher, his hand cupped the soft mound of her breast and Bethany whimpered, her back arching, pressing it fully into his palm. His entire body seemed to tense as he fought to maintain some small semblance of control, but he knew he was losing the battle. He slid one hand over her rear and her entire body seemed to answer his, molding against him, as if they were made to fit together seamlessly.

"Grant," she whispered on a sigh.

"Hey, bro, are you out here? You've got a call. It's your agent," Jackson yelled from the back of the bunkhouse.

Grant froze, his palm filled with the flesh of her breast, as they both gasped for air, trying to catch their breath. Grant looked down into her face and could see the redness along her jaw from where his stubble had scraped her sensitive skin. Her lips were swollen and pink from his kisses. He could still taste her and, like a drug, it wasn't enough. He needed more.

"Grant?" Jackson called again, this time closer.

He knew they would be caught in a moment and moved his hand from under her shirt, but was unable to move away from her without pressing one last quick kiss to her lips. "You make me forget. That's dangerous."

"Grant?" Jackson's footsteps were just outside the barn and Grant stepped in front of Bethany, shielding her from his brother's view. One look at her would be enough for any of his too observant brothers to know what they'd been doing. The thought of doing it again was enough to force him to adjust his jeans.

"I'll be right there, Jackson." The footsteps stopped. "Tell him that I'll call him right back."

"You got it." Grant was grateful for the unspoken communication he had with his brothers.

Bethany's hand slid along one side of his spine, tracing the curve of the muscles in his back. He felt his body respond to her touch with a shiver of hungry desire and nearly groaned aloud at the pure, enticing pleasure of her touch. Her hands circled his waist from behind and he covered them with his own, looking back at her over his shoulder. "I'm beginning to wonder if you don't like living dangerously."

"You're a terrible influence on me, Mr. McQuaid. First horseback riding and now making out in a barn. What would my father say?" she teased, her eyes shimmering with humor.

He'd remind me that I gave my word not to hurt you.

If there was one thing he was, it was a man of his word. Right now, his word was the only certain thing Grant had left.

GRANT WALKED BACK to the bunkhouse with her hand in his. As much as she didn't want to let go of him or stop the way his thumb brushed over the pulse racing at her wrist, she couldn't risk James seeing them this way. She already knew she was risking her own heart, she couldn't take a chance with James'. Grant wasn't wrong; they were dangerous for one another.

"Grant?" She turned toward him before he reached the door and opened her mouth to explain to him why they needed to keep their relationship a secret from James when he put a finger to her lips.

"I know." His eyes were dark and shadowed with regret again. "I completely agree that it's best to keep what happened in the barn between the two of us. It'll confuse James."

Bethany frowned. James wouldn't be the only one baffled by their relationship. She was present, a willing participant, and still thoroughly confused as to where she stood, or what either of them really wanted from one another.

"Why don't the two of you stay for dinner? We were just about to throw burgers on the grill."

She looked at the door, picturing her son playing video games inside. "It's a school night and you have a phone call to make to your agent," she reminded him.

His eyes clouded even more and she wondered what she'd said to upset him. He looked like he was lost in his thoughts for a moment. Suddenly his expression cleared and he gave her a lopsided grin, that dimple cutting into his cheek and making her heart beat heavily and the lower regions of her body throb.

"What about dinner tomorrow? I'll meet you at your house and we can have a movie night."

"I'll have some work to take home."

He arched a brow. "Ms. Mills, are you trying to let me down easy?"

"No!" She cleared her throat and lowered her voice. "I just ..." She took a step toward him and let her fingers fall against his t-shirt, feeling the washboard abs tense underneath. Her eyes lifted to his, searching for the answer to the question she so desperately needed to ask. "What are we doing?"

Grant slid his arms around her waist and smiled down at her. The tenderness in his eyes made her want to settle into his embrace and remain there forever. "I know you're out of practice but this, Ms. Mills, is me asking you and James out on a date." He dropped a kiss to her nose. "A real date this time."

"What about the reporter following you?"

"He's going to have to find something better to write about for Wednesday's paper because I'm going under-cover. Nothing is going to mar our date. There won't be any evidence, I promise."

GRANT WATCHED AS Bethany and James made their way down the driveway in her sedan, which kicked up dust behind it. As much as he understood her need to get James home, he missed the two of them already, and that feeling worried him as he walked back into the bunkhouse. He'd spent so many years fixated only on his career that the thought of straying from that single-minded focus was overwhelming. Grant shook his head, trying to rid himself of the sappy soundtrack that seemed to be on a constant loop in his brain, but he couldn't keep himself from smiling.

"Shit." Andrew laughed as he reached into the refrigerator and grabbed him a bottle of his latest brew, a bitter IPA Grant hadn't tried yet. "If that goofy grin on your face is any indication, you've got it *bad*."

Grant popped off the cap and took a long swallow. "Shut up."

Ben looked over his shoulder at the pair, his hands wrist-deep in the hamburger mixture he was getting ready to form into patties. "You're just jealous, Andrew." His gaze met Grant's and Ben gave him an impish smile. "I think it's great, and maybe now Mom will just nag you to get married and leave the rest of us alone."

Andrew rolled his eyes as he set a beer on the counter for Ben. "Fat chance. Mom wants grandkids and she's going to keep at it until she has some. It's not going to matter which of us it is."

Ben shrugged and slapped a ball of meat onto the wax paper lining the cutting board. "Which is another reason Bethany's good for Grant. She comes with a ready-made family. It's a win-win for all of us."

"What the hell, Ben? You've already got us walking down the aisle? We haven't even gone on a date."

Ben and Andrew looked at one another before bursting out in raucous laughter. "You're kidding, right?" Ben asked. Grant frowned at the pair as the twins came in from outside.

"Fire's ready. What's so funny?" They looked from Ben and Andrew to Grant and back.

"Grant is trying to convince us he's not *dating* Bethany." Andrew made air quotes with his fingers. "Dude, you got a yes from her. That's more than any other man in this town has come close to."

The twins joined in, laughing with the other two, deepening Grant's scowl.

"Screw all four of you."

He stormed toward the stairs, ready to head up to his room and forget the evening altogether. He already had enough to worry about. He didn't need their crap.

"Whoa, big brother." Andrew clapped him on the back of the shoulder. "Take it easy. It's just that you've never brought a girl home to meet Mom. Ever."

"And I've never seen you act this way about a woman before, or look at one the way you do with her. Not even when we were younger." Ben shrugged. "I mean, it's not a bad thing. Like I said, she's great, but we all know you and your one-track mind. I've never seen you take your eyes off the ball, so to speak."

"Stop turning this into more than it is. We barely know each other," Grant pointed out.

As much as he might be trying to convince his brothers, he couldn't help but feel like they'd known each other far longer than a week. He and Bethany had connected from the first moment, like something far bigger than coincidence had brought them together.

Jefferson chuckled. "Like that matters? When it's right, it's right."

Grant rolled his eyes. "Don't try to convince me that you four believe in love at first sight? Andrew will date anyone who says yes."

Andrew perked up. "I'm not an idiot and who said anything about love?"

Grant knew he'd just slipped up and given his brothers far too much ammunition to use against him. Thank God his sister and mother hadn't been here to hear it. They'd have them walking down the aisle next week.

"Face it, Grant. You can deny it all you want, but we know you." Ben eyed him seriously for a moment. "When you make up your mind to go after something or, in this case, someone, you don't waste any time. You just make it happen. You did it with football, you did it when you wanted to leave town and you're going to do it with Bethany."

Grant clenched his jaw. He didn't like being the object of his brothers' scrutiny or the butt of their jokes. Andrew grinned at Grant's wilting glare. "Give me dirty looks all you want. We just call 'em like we see 'em."

"Speaking of calls—" Jackson passed Grant his cell phone from where he'd set it on the counter by the back door "—don't forget to call your agent back. It sounded important."

"You guys think you know me so well." Grant took the phone, scrolling through his texts to see if his agent had sent a message as well.

"Enough that I didn't barge into the barn," Jackson teased, waggling his brows at his brother.

Grant tucked his phone into his back pocket and crossed his arms. "Are you four finished acting like children?"

Ben snorted and elbowed Jefferson. "Hear that? The man who plays with balls for a living is calling us children."

"I'm done," Grant said, throwing up his hands before heading out the back door again.

He'd just go have dinner with his parents. At least over there he wouldn't have to hear the ridiculous jibes about how he was falling for a woman he had no business falling for. The trouble was, he knew his brothers were right.

"GRANT, IT'S ABOUT time you called back. What the hell is this on my desk?"

Bob Ribaldi had been Grant's agent since immediately after his final college game, just before he'd been drafted by the Mustangs. He'd negotiated one of the best contracts a running back had ever received and, thanks to Bob's savvy business sense, Grant had had the money set aside to invest in both the ranch and Jackson's breeding program. He just wasn't sure he'd done the right thing in not consulting Bob first and investing so heavily, far too certain that he could prove the doctors wrong and return to football. Now they would have to discuss the best option for his future.

"Wolf called me yesterday and told me he was sending over a buyout, regardless of what the doctors reported. Sounds like he wants to cut me loose."

"That's not what I'm talking about. I got that. I also have a couple of low-ball offers from a few other teams if you're cleared. Nowhere close to where they need to be to get me in the door for negotiations, but that's something to decide after your doctor appointment. I'm talking about this offer from the Fox Sports network to be their Sunday commentator."

"What?"

"I've got a contract here from them with a very lucrative offer. Far more than the Mustangs are offering you to babysit their rookies." The disparagement in Bob's voice echoed through Grant. He'd been afraid that was exactly what Wolf wanted him to do, regardless of the assurance that, in time, it would turn into a coaching position. "Who did you schmooze at Fox? And why didn't you tell me about it?"

Bob sounded as confused as Grant felt. He had no idea who could have even been aware of his precarious position with the Mustangs, to even consider making the offer. Networks didn't make offers like this based on nothing more than speculation.

"I'm at a loss. I don't know anyone." He wracked his brain trying to remember any connection he might have. "You know me. I keep to myself, keep my nose to the grindstone and just work. I don't do any *schmoozing*. I'm not that guy."

Bob chuckled. "Sometimes I wish you were. It'd make my job easier. I'll make some calls, see how legitimate this offer actually is. If it's as good as it looks on paper, you'd be crazy not to take it."

Grant ran a hand through his hair, pacing his bedroom. "What are we talking about here, Bob?"

"Nearly seven figures the first year and $1.5 million the second. That's far better than any of the other teams are offering too. Retirement might suddenly look a whole hell of a lot more appealing with that kind of time and money at your disposal."

"Where would I be?"

"I'm sure we could address that in the contract, but most likely you're looking at moving closer to New York. With that kind of cheese, would it really matter?"

Not to Bob, not to most players ready to retire. But when he thought of the hazel eyes that had burned with desire for him earlier tonight or the blue eyes of a boy that stared up at him with hero worship, it mattered. It mattered a hell of a lot.

Chapter Fifteen

BETHANY COULDN'T WAIT for her day to be finished. Not
just because she knew Grant was coming over, but because it had truly been the day from hell. It started off
with a bang when one of her students threw up on her as
she was helping him tie his shoelace. Luckily, Julie had
been able to watch the kids long enough for her to attempt to clean her blouse in the bathroom. At least as
much as soap and water could. The stain would probably
be a permanent reminder of why she needed to be more
careful about letting kids twirl the swings and let them
unwind by spinning.

If that, along with the sour smell she couldn't quite get
out of her hair, weren't bad enough, she'd dropped her coffee
in the teacher's lounge at first recess and now both thighs
of her jeans were tinged brown. She took a deep, cleansing breath and watched the children as they lined up after
lunch, trying to ignore the whiff she caught of her hair.

Only three hours left.

"I hear you've had a rough . . . whoa!" Stephen had been walking toward her and cringed, taking a large step backward as he came within smelling distance.

Bethany rolled her eyes at him. "Thanks."

"Sorry. I guess I didn't expect that." He tried to hide his smile while subtly plugging his nose. "Anything I can do to help?"

"You wouldn't happen to have a change of clothes and some dry shampoo, would you?"

He shrugged. "Can't say that I do. However, I'd love to take you out to dinner tonight to make up for your bad day."

She looked at him oddly. Their date a few days ago had been comfortable at best, but it certainly hadn't set off any seismic shock waves. She'd assumed he'd felt the same thing, especially after the way it had ended—with a hug at the door and a promise to see her at work. Granted, it had been a while since she'd dated, but she doubted that was the way *good* dates ended. In fact, she was pretty optimistic her date with Grant wouldn't end with anything so tame. Not if their last kiss was any indicator.

"Oh, I really appreciate that Stephen but, um . . ." She couldn't quite get her brain to function fast enough to figure out an excuse.

"Ms. Mills." Becky ran up and tugged at the side of her jeans. "Jeremiah pushed James because he had the football and James pushed him on the ground."

The child instantly had Bethany's full attention. "What? Where are they?"

Steven looked at the open field area where the boys tended to play ball. "Over there." He pointed toward a crowd of kids looking their direction helplessly. "Come on."

She ran beside him, the burn in her lungs reminding her that she needed to get back to her workout schedule since she could barely keep up with Steven's long stride. By the time she reached the boys, Steven was already kneeling on the ground beside Jeremiah, who was howling about his bleeding lip. Several other boys had surrounded them and began to try to slink away as both teachers looked around the group, expectantly.

"What happened?" Bethany asked, waiting for someone to answer. No one said a word. "I'm going to ask one more time," she warned.

"I was playing football and he grabbed it out of my hands and said he wanted to play." James stepped forward, his head hanging sheepishly. "I just tackled him like Grant and Ben showed me."

He chanced a glance at her. As his parent, she could see the sorrow in his eyes, but as his teacher, she couldn't let him get away with pushing or hitting another student.

"Mr. Carter, why don't you take Jeremiah to the nurse's office? I'll have Julie take the rest of the students into my room to play a game while I take care of this situation with Mr. Hunt."

She saw the fear in her son's eyes when he realized he was being escorted to the principal's office. Bethany was torn. She knew her son hadn't meant any harm to Jeremiah, but he had to learn that he couldn't go around tackling other kids. She tried to tamp down the anger rising up in her. She'd told Grant she didn't want him to play football, but not only had he played with him, he'd obviously shown him how to hit hard enough to give a boy twice his size a fat lip.

Mr. Hunt came into the main room of the office as Steven escorted Jeremiah in to see the nurse. James' steps faltered when he saw the principal.

"This way to my office, Mr. Mills." Mr. Hunt gave Bethany a nod.

She knew he was a fair man, but her mama-bear instincts rose to the surface. It wasn't entirely James' fault. If Jeremiah had been willing to share the ball instead of snatching it from James, something she'd scolded him for several times over the past week, this might not have happened.

If Grant hadn't taught him how to tackle...

"Mr. Hunt, I'd like to come in too, if that's okay."

Steven returned from the nurse's office. "I'll go help Julie with the other students until you're finished," he offered.

Bethany could have hugged him.

"Follow me," Mr. Hunt said as he led the way.

James moved like a prisoner on his way to execution but Bethany didn't miss the confusion on his face either. Tears welled in his blue eyes and it broke her heart, knowing that she couldn't rescue her child from a situation he hadn't meant to create. She knew she could bail him out, she'd seen plenty of parents who did it daily, but it wouldn't help James learn to accept the consequences of his decisions. She steeled herself and clenched her jaw as Mr. Hunt steepled his hands, pressing a finger to his lips.

"Why don't you tell me what happened, Mr. Mills?"

James looked at the principal, then to his mother, pleading with his eyes for her to rescue him. *Tell him*, she signed.

Her son looked so small, swallowed up by the large cheaply upholstered chair in front of the principal's desk, his shoulders slumped as he wrung his hands.

"I didn't mean to." His breath hitched as his tears began to spill onto his cheeks. "He said he wanted to play football."

Mr. Hunt shot Bethany a quick, knowing look and nodded, closing his eyes slowly. She knew he was a good man, a strong presence who demanded respect from the older students, but he was also fair and beloved by the younger kids.

"Did you have the ball first?" James nodded, staring down at his hands, unable to look Mr. Hunt in the face as tears fell onto his pants. "And did he ask for it?" James shook his head sideways. "So he came and just took it away from you?"

At her son's affirmative nod, Mr. Hunt stood up and moved around to the front of his desk before squatting down in front of James and laying a hand on his knee. "Why did you tackle him, James? Were you angry?"

"No, I thought we were going to play."

Bethany bit her lip, wishing this was over for her son already.

"You know we can't tackle people at school though,

right? Haven't you heard me tell the older boys not to roughhouse in the field before school?"

He nodded again. "But Grant told me that's how you play. He showed me how to hit with my shoulder and not my head." James twisted his lips to the side, trying to remember what else Grant had told him. "He said to wrap up."

"Ah, I see," Mr. Hunt said on a sigh. "I'm betting that Mr. McQuaid meant that you should tackle that way when you play Pop Warner football next year. But we don't do that on the playground at school, okay?" James nodded solemnly as Mr. Hunt turned back toward Bethany and rose. "James, I think that as long as you apologize to Jeremiah, we can assume that you won't tackle anyone again. Am I right?"

"Yes, sir," he mumbled, his lower lip still quivering as he swiped away his tears. "I will."

Mr. Hunt nodded to Bethany who held her hand out for James. He jumped down from the chair and grabbed for her fingers, practically dragging her from the principal's office.

"Thank you, Mr. Hunt," Bethany said as he walked them out of the office. "I'll be having a chat with Mr. McQuaid as well."

"I'll bet you will," he said with a chuckle. "I'd love to be a fly on the wall for that conversation."

GRANT TUGGED THE baseball cap lower on his forehead, reaching into the passenger seat to scoop up the deep-dish pizza and a paper bag with the two liters of soda. He pressed the button on the key fob, and the truck chirped, signaling that it was locked, and then he began the trek around the block to Bethany's house. He'd driven the area several times, making sure that he didn't see anyone who might have followed him or realized who he was under this asinine disguise. He looked ridiculous, but he was going to do whatever he could to make sure there weren't any more news articles about Bethany. Several times in town today, he'd heard whispers and rumors about their relationship. Luckily, years of publicity had taught him to evade direct questions and he was able to fend off the gossip mongers. For now.

He glanced up and down the sidewalk as he approached the house, knowing that the pizza was getting colder with each passing moment. Seeing no one outside, he jogged up the walkway and rang the bell.

It took a moment before Bethany answered the door, and when she did, she walked outside onto the porch, shutting it behind her and leaning against the door frame. Her hair was still wet from a recent shower and he could smell a fruity citrus that must have been either her shampoo or soap. Wearing yoga pants and a t-shirt, she looked as deliciously adorable as she had wearing a sundress and cowboy boots. Even barefaced, she was beautiful, but he was a bit surprised to see she wasn't ready for their date, considering how she'd dressed up for their park outing and when she'd gone out with Mr. Kindergarten Teacher. And then he looked into her eyes.

"This can't be good."

"You showed my son how to tackle someone?" She crossed her arms over her chest, not letting him past.

"I guess. Sort of?"

The tone of her voice spoke volumes. She was pissed. This was the protective woman he'd seen the first day, when she thought he was using James to get close to her. He glanced over his shoulder. If she raised her voice, the entire neighborhood would know he was there.

"Can I come inside and explain?"

"I told you I didn't want him to play football. You knew how I felt about it."

Her brows knit and she jabbed a finger into his chest, forcing him back a step. Even with him standing a step lower than she was, she was still looking up to meet his gaze. Not that it mattered to this woman. She was protecting her son, at least in her mind, and she'd take on someone ten times her size if she had to. It almost made him smile but, wanting to keep his head still attached, he kept his grin in check.

"It was one thing for him to play catch with you and your brothers, but you had to push the limits I set. I am his mother. If I don't want him playing, he won't. Do you realize how hard it is for him to fit in? How much harder he has to work at it than other kids his age?"

He narrowed his eyes, trying to guess at the real reason behind this sudden indignation. "Is this really about James playing football or you sharing him, Bethany?"

She stood even straighter, stretching her tiny frame a few inches taller as she inhaled a furious breath and clenched her jaw. "He tackled a boy at school today for taking the football from him. He had to go to the principal's office, Grant."

Grant pinched his lips, trying to hold back the proud grin that tugged at the corners of his lips. "I'm sorry."

He said it because he knew it was what she wanted to hear. In truth, he was proud of the kid for standing up for himself. He'd watched a few of the kids bullying James the day he'd gone to the school. Even his presence hadn't stopped them from trying to push James around. If he had played even a small part in shaping James' self-confidence, he was thrilled.

"You should go."

He sobered instantly. "What? Are you serious?"

"Completely." She turned back to open the door.

"Bethany? Look, you're right. I shouldn't have taught him how to tackle if you didn't want him playing football. But I have seen how hard he has to try to fit in. I've also heard him talk about being bullied. So have you," he reminded her.

She spun on her heel, ready to do battle again. "Teaching him to tackle people isn't how he needs to learn to handle it."

"No, it's not but, damn it, that kid needs to know how great he is. He shouldn't be getting kicked by girls or pushed around by other boys on the playground just because of . . . because he's different. He's the most incredible kid I've ever met, and I've met a lot of them in my career. I should have asked you before I showed him, but it just happened the other day. I'm sorry."

She took a deep breath, staring at him with an expression he couldn't quite read, a mixture of anger and awe. He decided he might as well push his luck a little further and pray she was leaning toward wonder. "Can I bring this in before it gets any colder?"

She pursed her lips and he caught himself before he smiled. It was a less exaggerated version of the face James made when he was thinking about something seriously.

"Fine." She opened the door for him and he eased through it carefully in case she changed her mind and slammed it shut in his face. "But, Grant?" He looked back at her over his shoulder. "Don't let it happen again."

He held up his pinkie finger. "Pinkie promise."

She turned away from him and walked toward the kitchen, but not before he caught a glimpse of the smile she was trying to hide.

Chapter Sixteen

GRANT HADN'T FELT this content in years. Bethany was tucked into his side, her hand resting over his stomach. He inhaled the scent of her, his fingers brushing the side of her arm lightly as he traced patterns on her smooth skin. James was sound asleep on the living room floor, wrapped up in the old quilt Bethany had informed him had once belonged to her Great-grandmother. Grant had laughed when James asked to be rolled up in it like a burrito from the waist down and Bethany obliged, turning him so that he faced the television. Now he snored softly as the end credits played on the television.

"I should probably get him upstairs," she mumbled, sounding sleepy.

"I'll help you," he offered, but neither of them moved and he smiled into her hair, more content than he could ever remember being.

His heart swelled with longing. As much as he loved

football and his career was his life, in this moment, he could honestly say that he didn't care if he played again. He finally understood what his mother had been wanting for him all along. If he closed his eyes, he could almost imagine each and every night like this with Bethany and James. He could visualize tucking James into bed, taking Bethany into his arms, into their bed . . .

She released a long sigh but instead of the relaxed sound he'd expected, it was a regretful exhale.

"What's wrong?"

Grant wasn't sure he really wanted to know. He didn't want to ruin this moment of domestic bliss. It was something he'd never considered worth letting go of his career for, at least not for many years to come, until he'd met her.

When she didn't answer right away, Grant tipped his head down to look at her. "Bethany?"

She bit her lower lip and he felt desire kick him in the chest before sliding straight to his groin. He closed his eyes for a moment to regain control of the yearning racing through his veins, touching off a wildfire of desire.

"When do you leave for camp?"

He laid his hand over hers, twining their fingers together, pressing his palm to hers. "Do you really want to talk about this now?"

"Do you *not* want to talk about it?" Her voice was tentative, hesitant and wary.

"Okay, you're right. We'll talk, but let's get James up to bed first." She nodded slightly and rose from the couch. Grant immediately felt a chill in the air as it replaced the warmth of her body against his. He followed her, wishing they could go back an hour in time, before he had to tell her the truth about his future, or lack thereof. He had to admit to her that he had no clue what would happen.

Bethany slid the battery packs from James's slim arms and pulled the magnetic pieces from over his ears. "If you lift him, I'll pull the blanket off."

Grant did what she asked, wrapping his arms around the limp warm body, still sound asleep. At least that was what he'd thought until James stirred, his arms going around Grant's neck and his legs, now untucked from the blanket, wrapping around Grant's waist, clinging to him like a monkey.

Parental love and devotion swelled inside him for the boy, taking Grant by surprise. He liked the kid, more than liked him, but the desire—no, the burning *need*—to protect him and keep him safe, to keep *both* of them safe, rushed over him like a tidal wave. He could understand the fierce protective instincts Bethany had shown because he felt the same way. It didn't matter that James wasn't his son by birth, or that he'd only known them a short time. These two had filled an emptiness in him that he had never realized existed.

He followed Bethany upstairs and tucked James into bed, feeling oddly bereft when she pulled the door nearly closed behind her, leaving it open a crack. He stood peering through the doorway at the sleeping child, unwilling to leave just yet, and she paused at the top of the stairs, just outside her bedroom doorway.

"Are you coming?"

He made his way to where she stood, uncertain he should move any farther. There would be no going back if he did. "Have you ever thought you wanted something badly enough that you'd give up everything for it, only to realize it would have been a mistake?" His hands found the indentation of her waist, splaying over the narrow curves.

She frowned up at him, her eyes worried and confused, unsure whether she wanted to answer. Then she nodded. "I thought I wanted my marriage to work. For years I'd have given up anything to bring Matthew back, to let him be a father to James."

Grant felt a stab of jealousy at the mention of the other man. He didn't know what had ended her marriage, wasn't sure if she'd even be willing to tell him, but he wanted to know her, to know everything about Bethany and James. "What happened?"

Her eyes widened, surprised by his question. She gave a sadly bitter laugh. "That's a story that deserves its own Lifetime movie. Let's just say, when the going gets tough, some guys would rather run out than face the difficulties."

"He left you?" Grant couldn't fathom anyone leaving Bethany. She was the kind of woman men dreamed of finding, the kind a guy would only find once. It was something that had plagued him the past few days when he'd worried he might be forced to make a choice between her and his career.

She lifted her shoulders in a slight shrug, twisting her mouth to one side. "A week after James' diagnosis. The morning after the appointment when the doctors told us what we could expect in the first few years." Bethany moved to the stairs, taking them quickly but not before Grant saw the hurt shadow her eyes. Either the rejection still stung or she wasn't yet over James' father.

"Do you still love him?" He steeled himself to face the truth she was about to hit him with. If she still loved her husband, he couldn't stand in the way.

"Matthew?" She turned at the bottom of the stairs and looked back at him incredulously. "No! The man ran out me and our son. He quit his job so he wouldn't have to pay child support and asked to terminate his parental rights during our divorce. He didn't even have the guts to show up in court. He left me to figure out how to raise our child alone."

"But you said—"

"I said, for years I thought that my marriage was what I wanted. But it would have been a mistake. Matthew didn't love James, he obviously didn't love me. Not the way we deserved to be loved, the way he *should have* loved us. I'm not sure he ever knew how. He wasn't evil, but he was just a bad husband and father. James and I have been better off without him, even through the struggles we've faced. It hasn't been easy, but James has only been surrounded by people who love him."

She slipped her hand into his and pulled him back into the living room, shutting off the television as they walked back to the couch. She folded her legs beneath her and patted the seat beside her, urging him to sit. "What are *you* thinking about? You're the one who seems troubled."

"I have an appointment with my doctors early next week. If all goes according to plan, I could be heading for spring training right after." He studied her face, watching for any reaction, any indication of her feelings about his revelation. He didn't mention that he probably wouldn't be playing in Memphis, that there was a possibility he'd be on another team, that he might not be playing at all.

"I see." She folded her hands in her lap, staring at his face but looking through him. She shrugged stiffly. "You have a job to do, a life there. I get that, Grant."

Grant reached for her hand. "But I'm not sure I want it. I mean, I do, but that's not *all* I want anymore. I thought it was but . . ." He ran a hand through his hair. Everything he said was coming out wrong.

"Hey, it's okay, Grant. I understand. You like me and you like James, but you have a job and responsibilities. Those things have to take precedence and—"

"No, they don't," he interrupted. He couldn't stand the idea that she might think he put anything above how he felt about her.

She gave him a patronizing look, tipping her chin down, and he could easily read the doubt in her eyes, even as her voice was quietly empathetic. "Grant, you barely know us."

Pain radiated through his chest as her words hit home. "Is that how you feel about me? Like you barely know me? Like this is just some fling? Some short-term experiment to jump back into the dating game?" He clenched his jaw, trying to stop the words that spilled out. He didn't want to hear her answer, didn't want to know that he was nothing more to her than a way to test the waters after a long dating drought.

She pinched her lips together, her eyes misting. "You know it's not."

Hope flared hot and bright in his chest. "Then why would you think that I feel that way?"

"Because." She started to rise from the couch, to run away from the conversation, but he wasn't about to let her and pulled her back to his lap. Bethany refused to look at him, her body rigid in his arms.

"Bethany?"

"Because you're Grant McQuaid." She said it as if it should be self-explanatory.

"So?" He breathed the word against her neck and felt her shiver in his arms.

She glanced backward, looking at him over her shoulder. "You could have you pick of women anywhere. Why would you give up everything to stay here?"

"You mean, with you?" She nodded, unwilling to speak. Her teeth clamped down on her lower lip. "Bethany, look at me." He ran his finger along her jawline, turning her to face him. "You are amazing. An incredible woman. Any man would be an idiot not to give his right arm for you."

Before he could finish what he wanted to say, she turned in his lap, her legs to one side, and captured his mouth. She didn't wait for him to finish telling her that he wanted to stay, that he wanted to be there for her in a way James' father had never been. She didn't hesitate or wait for him to guide her to him. For the first time since he'd met her, Bethany took what she wanted because *she* wanted it.

Her hands cupped his face, her fingers covering his ears as her tongue plunged between his lips. She tasted salty, like the popcorn they'd had during the movie. But sweet as well. The hand that had been at her jaw, plunged into her hair, dragging her closer, their breath mingling seamlessly. Her kiss was innocent and dangerous, seductive and sweet, every puzzling contradiction that made up the woman in his lap. The fingers of his free hand moved to her back, sliding her down his legs and pulling her upper body against his chest. It was an awkward position that didn't allow him the freedom to hold her, to touch her, but he was afraid that if he moved, she'd run away again.

"Grant," she whispered, her lips against his, "I might be out of practice but I think there are at least twenty other positions that would be more comfortable than this."

He smiled against her lips. Her practicality knew no bounds. Just one of the many things he adored about her. "I guess which position we choose depends on who wants to be in control."

She stood up and pressed her hand against his shoulder, urging him to lie back before lying down beside him on the couch, one of her legs between his. "My house, my rules."

She gave him a wicked grin that made him wonder how out of practice she could possibly be. The woman was a natural seductress, sweet innocence with just a hint of spice.

"Bethany," he warned as she leaned over him, pressing her lips against his.

"Shh, we'll figure out logistics later. Stop trying to ruin our first real date."

He was helpless against her allure and, yet, he found he didn't mind one bit.

BETHANY KNEW HOPE was a dangerous thing. She hadn't missed the regret in Grant's eyes when he talked about leaving. It would happen, regardless of what she'd hoped for. She accepted that his job was just a part of who Grant was. She would have to pick up the pieces, again. The way she had when Matthew left, the way she had when her mother had practically forced her to move out last year. At least this time, it was only her heart on the line. But, oh, how thoroughly it would break.

Oddly, it didn't make her pause now the way it should have. She'd been alone for a long time and Grant had made her face the loneliness, and what she'd kept both herself and James from experiencing over the past six years due to her fear.

James had missed having a man in his life. It was obvious from the way he practically worshiped the ground Grant walked on. While being his favorite football player might have initiated the devotion, the respectable man Grant had proved himself to be had only fueled James' adoration. Even when he ignored her rules, Bethany could see that Grant had done it out of genuine concern for James' well-being.

It was going to hurt when he left. Maybe even more than Matthew's betrayal. She'd known Matthew behaved like a spoiled child, that he had always expected her to be the responsible one. But Grant was a man, a gentleman through and through. He'd reached into her soul in a short time to find the aching places, the never-before-touched places that whispered words of future love.

She liked him, a lot. Not just as a person, but as a man. He stirred things in her. Not just desire. But a deep yearning for what should have been. Long buried images of white picket fences and more children running in the yard tried to surface, but Bethany couldn't let them rise up. Hope was one thing, but when it had no basis in reality, it was nothing more than a dream, and dreams were folly.

"You okay?" Grant's question drew her back to the present. With his hand at her waist, her t-shirt rode up over her stomach slightly and his thumb brushed over the sensitive flesh, making her insides quiver with dizzying delight.

"Yes."

He didn't look convinced and arched a brow in question. When she didn't say more, he sat up. "I should probably go."

Grant brushed his finger over her cheek and along the side of her neck. She wanted to cry at the tenderness in the touch and the burn he ignited within her for more—more than she was willing to ask for, more than he was willing to offer. She knew without a shadow of a doubt he would leave, knew it would break her heart into pieces when he did, but trying to bank this fire burning within her was just as painful.

Bethany slid from the couch and stood, taking his hand. He followed suit, forlorn and filled with remorse as he followed her into the hallway. Instead of leading him to the door, she took him to the stairs.

"Where are you going?" He stopped midstep and she could see the uncertainty in his face before desire flared.

"Come with me." She moved to the second step, so that she was almost eye-to-eye with him. "Spend tonight with me."

His jaw clenched and she could see the muscle working, ticking with the seconds before he finally answered, his voice strained. "You have no idea how much I want to, but we can't."

The heated wash of embarrassment swept over her and she was grateful for the dark hallway. She took a step back but he caught her.

"It's just that I didn't come—" he searched for the word he wanted to use "—prepared."

Her impression of Grant rose several notches, even as disappointment seeped into every crevice of her needy body. She wasn't the type of woman to sleep around. Hell, she hadn't even slept with Matthew until just before their wedding, but Grant had a way of making her forget more than just the list of dating rules she'd set for herself. He seemed to make her want to throw out the entire book. She'd assumed that men like Grant, those in his line of work, were always prepared. He was a celebrity, after all.

What was wrong with her? Instead of being so frustrated with what she couldn't have tonight, she knew she should have been thrilled that he hadn't simply assumed that sleeping with her was a given.

But she wanted him. For the first time in six years, she wanted to be intimate with someone, and taking that giant leap, only to find out it wasn't going to happen was like ice water to her face in a sound sleep and it stopped her in her tracks. The blush in her cheeks still burned, even when he brushed his thumb over her cheekbone and smiled down at her.

"Do you have any idea how beautiful you are when you get embarrassed?" He breathed slowly, deeply, and laid his cheek on the top of her head, pulling her into his embrace. Bethany wasn't about to waste the opportunity to hold him and wound her arms around his waist. The man was solid muscle, from head to toe. His back was long and lean, tense beneath her hands. Where her cheek pressed against his chest was a broad expanse of cotton, and she inhaled the scent of him. The spicy musk of his cologne mixed with soap and a scent that was all Grant, like warm summer afternoons at the park and crisp fall days. He smelled like home.

"You're going to kill me, Bethany," he mumbled into her hair.

His fingers trailed over the back of her neck, beneath her hair while the other slid down her spine to her lower back. Her body responded without her permission, arching into him and he released a quiet sigh of longing.

"Stay with me tonight, please?" The request fell quietly from her lips against his chest before she could stop it, almost as if she were whispering it to his heart.

She hated the pleading note in her voice, but she needed him the way she needed her heart to keep beating or air in her lungs.

"Okay, but only on one condition." His answer surprised her and she leaned back slightly, trying to look into his eyes. His hand slid over her rear, cupping it and pressing her against his groin, his arousal exciting and frightening. "It may be your house but we follow *my* rules tonight."

She had no idea what that meant but as the blood throbbed in her veins with renewed desire and every nerve ending in her body seemed to be on high alert, she didn't care.

Chapter Seventeen

THE QUIET PLEA in her voice was his undoing. Grant knew he couldn't give her everything he wanted to, couldn't come close to what she deserved, couldn't even promise her more than a few days but he could give her that much. If a few days was all they might have to hold on to, if circumstances came crashing down around them, he was going to make sure she would never regret those few days. He knew he would never forget them.

Taking her hand, Grant led her up the stairs to her room, closing the door behind her and turning the lock. Her gaze found his, hesitant.

"You sure you want this?" She chewed at the soft inner flesh of her lower lip and he felt himself swell with hunger as she made her decision. "Bethany, you can still change your mind about this."

He knew she would assume *this* was unprotected sex since he'd already told her he hadn't brought any condoms with him. He had. He never went anywhere without them, although most of the time he was slapping it into the inebriated hand of one of the other players bent on a one-night stand. He'd seen far too many players trust a groupie's word only to end up standing at the altar with a baby nearby.

But Bethany wasn't some one-night stand. She wasn't a woman to toy with. She was a forever kind of woman, the kind he'd always hoped to find, *after* his career had ended. So tonight, he would be the man she needed, not the one she thought she wanted.

"I want you."

Her voice was a whisper of sound in the silence, the only light in her room filtering in through the sheer curtains from the full moon hanging high over her yard. Her house, while small, stood out among the other older homes in the neighborhood since it was one of only three two-stories on the block, which meant no one could see into the room from nearby houses. It was a blessing for him because it meant he could admire her body bathed in moonlight.

"Come here."

He pulled her toward him, wrapping one arm around her waist as his mouth captured hers in a kiss that shook his very resolve. Her arms found his shoulders as she clung to him and he felt his body answer with raging hunger.

But this wasn't about him—it was about Bethany, reminding her of the love she deserved to find. His lips moved over her jaw, tipping her head backward with a sigh, and he pressed hot, open-mouthed kisses over her neck. One hand slid under the hem of her t-shirt, his fingers gliding over the indentations of her ribs, over the soft cotton padding of her bra, and Grant smiled against her skin. His sweet, innocent woman didn't have time for things like lace and lingerie, opting instead for something practical, and he'd be damned if it didn't make him want her even more.

Bethany had no idea how seductive she was without even trying. The scent of her hair, the sweet taste of her skin, her soft sighs and the way she dug her fingers into the muscles of his back when his lips found a spot on her neck that covered her arms in goose bumps. He brushed his thumb over the curve her breast, just above the top edge of the cup, and felt her shiver against him, arching into his hand. Grant tugged her t-shirt over her head, tossing it aside and looking down at her.

She was perfection. For a woman so petite, she had full breasts and a narrow waist that curved out into womanly hips. She wasn't at all like the stick-thin, straight-bodied women who chased so many of the players at camp. She had curves, soft edges, dips and valleys he couldn't wait to explore. His hands slid to her back and unclasped the bra, dragging it from her arms, exposing her perfection to his hungry gaze. He held his breath as he took in every inch of her, unable to tear his gaze away but even less able to keep from touching her. His fingertips grazed over the outer curve of her breast before his palm covered her. Bethany's body trembled, the nipple pebbling against his hand, begging for his attention. Grant smiled at her response to his caress and sat at the edge of her bed, drawing her between his legs, pressing light kisses to her cleavage before covering one taut peak with his mouth.

His name was torn from her lips on a ragged breath as her fingers gripped his shoulders, clinging to him. Grant slid his hands into the waistband of her pants, easing them down her legs and pulling her to straddle his lap. She cupped his jaw, staring into his eyes with reverence as he lifted her, still clutching him as if he was her only lifeline, and laid her on the bed. Grant hovered over her still fully clothed and Bethany snuck her hands under his shirt, letting her fingers trace the lines of his muscles, making him agonize for a release he knew he wouldn't allow himself.

Jerking his shirt over his head, Grant tossed it near hers on the floor, sliding up her body, relishing the feel of their bare skin heating one another to a volatile explosion of hungry desire. Her legs wrapped around his hips, pressing the two of them together and he couldn't help but imagine himself buried deep within her. Just the thought was almost enough to make him give in to his longing to possess her fully.

Grant held his breath, trying to slow himself, to restrain his desire, but Bethany had other plans and slid her hands to the front of his jeans, tugging at the button of his pants. He sucked in a hissing breath of sheer ecstasy as her fingers found him, straining to be free of the confining denim.

Grant pressed his forehead to her collarbone, his lips brushing over the sensitive flesh of her breasts. "Baby, you can't touch me."

"What?" Her gorgeous hazel eyes were slightly dazed, slumberous with desire. "But—"

"My rules, remember?"

He swirled his tongue over the peak and her back bowed, arching into him and pressing her fully against his erection. Grant growled low in his throat, fighting to rein in his passion. He moved her hands to his chest.

"Trust me."

Bethany nodded slightly and his heart soared. It was a huge step for her and he knew it. He also knew he couldn't betray her trust. His hand moved over the curves of her body, and he followed the path with his lips, whispering his praise over every inch of her skin. He wasn't a romantic man but her body was poetry, ethereal sweetness and seduction, practically glowing in the pale light with her dark hair spread over the pillow. His fingers traced the lines of her hips, over the plane of her stomach before dipping low to find the core of her desire and Bethany gasped in surprised ecstasy.

"Grant." She reached for his hand. "Wait."

He nipped at the point of her hip, his teeth barely grazing her flesh and she arched into his touch. Grant wrapped his arm around her, moving his shoulders between her thighs and she reached for him. His gaze crashed into hers and he could see the fire inside her blazing. The heat from her skin branded him. His own body was screaming at him, begging for release, but he ignored the demand in favor of her pleasure.

"Let me do this for you."

Grant brushed his thumb over the folds of her and

Bethany's body bucked against him as she closed her eyes in sweet surrender to her desire. He was greedy for more from her, tasting her, teasing her, letting his lips and tongue dance over her and Bethany let go of the control she'd clung to for far too long.

"Grant, please," she begged, unable to remain still as he found the secret places of her body that excited her even further, leaving her gasping and limp in his arms.

His hands worshiped her as her body quivered, waves of release washing over her one after another as he refused to let it end. Bethany lay unable to move with the most bewitching smile on her lips.

Moving over her, Grant let his denim-encased thigh brush against her hypersensitive flesh, congratulating himself as she gasped in awed pleasure again. He circled her nipple with his tongue, his own smile breaking against her skin as his fingers continued to toy with her.

"You have to stop," she pleaded.

"Stop? I don't remember that being one of my rules," he warned, his voice a low growl against her throat and she practically purred in pleasure.

Grant wasn't sure how much more of this torture he could take. He was feverish with need for her, wanted to plunge himself into her, to reach her soul and connect them as one. But this wasn't the right time and he was no stranger to self-denial. He'd beaten his body into submission for years in training. He wasn't going to do anything that Bethany might regret later.

Bethany sighed as he rolled onto his back, still clothed from the waist down, and she curled against his chest.

"Just let me rest for a minute," she murmured sleepily against his skin, each brush of her lips sending sharp jolts of desire straight to his groin.

Grant knew she would fall asleep and willed his body to resign itself to the fact that there would be no release for him tonight. He didn't care. He wouldn't have it any other way. His sweet Bethany had gifted him with her greatest treasure—her trust. She had come alive in his arms and that was more valuable than any trophy.

BETHANY WOKE THE next morning to voices in her kitchen. She jerked upright in her bed as the sound of James' giggles carried upstairs through her closed door.

"What the hell did I do?" she wondered aloud, her hand reaching for the pillow that still held the indentation of Grant's head. She drew her bare knees to her chest and buried her face in her hands. "No, no, no, no, no."

Images of her and Grant played through her mind as the blush crept over her shoulders and covered her cheeks. Even as she burned with embarrassment, other parts of her body—most of them, if she was being honest—tingled with hot, dark pleasure, begging for Grant's touch again. How could she have let herself get so carried away?

"Hang on, buddy." She heard the deep timbre of Grant's voice downstairs. "Why don't you start your breakfast and I'll make sure she's awake."

Bethany had barely tugged the sheet up under her arms, covering her breasts, when Grant slipped through the doorway and smiled at her, a cup of steaming coffee in his hand. "I see you're up."

He set the coffee on the nightstand and moved to her side of the bed, grabbing her clothing from the floor and passing the items to her as he sat down on the edge of the mattress.

"What time is it?" She glanced at the clock on her nightstand. *Six-thirty a.m.*

"I didn't want to wake you but I figured you'd prefer that to being late for work. James is downstairs eating a bowl of cereal."

"What did you tell him?" Dread grabbed a hold of her lungs and squeezed with a viselike grip.

"That I came over early this morning to surprise him."

Relief coursed through her. James was already too attached to Grant. She didn't want him to get the idea that he was going to become a permanent fixture in their lives. Now if only Bethany could convince herself to let go of that hope as well.

She reached for the cup of coffee, catching the sheet as it slipped slightly. Grant smiled wickedly and reached a finger out to tug it back down slightly, allowing him a better look at the swell of her breasts.

"Grant, about last night," she began.

"I know." He nodded slightly.

"I mean, I like you. I *really* like you, but I don't usually . . ." She closed her eyes, trying to gather her embarrassed thoughts into something that sounded coherent. "I just don't want you to think—"

"Bethany," he interrupted, giving her a lopsided grin that made her heart race. "Don't worry about what I'm thinking. I know what kind of woman you are, okay?"

He rose, leaning over her, and before she could put the cup to her lips, he captured her mouth in a kiss that stole her breath and made her want to call in sick to work just so she could stay in bed with him all day. Her entire body sizzled with longing and she could barely think straight, almost dropping the cup of hot coffee into her lap. Grant ended the kiss slowly.

"Go, take your shower. I'll help James get ready." She watched him walk toward the door, appreciating his backside even more now that her hands had memorized every dip and curve of muscle intimately. He paused with one hand on the side of the door, partway through the opening. "For the record, Bethany, next time I'll be prepared."

He closed the door behind him and she thought she might faint. Desire, hot and liquid, pooled low in her body and her heart raced erratically.

There was going to be a next time? There was going to be a next time.

"WELL, WELL, LOOK what the cat dragged in." His mother eyed him speculatively, disappointment creasing her brow. She slid a mug of lukewarm coffee across the table in his direction, shaking her head as she turned away from him.

"Mom, it's not what you think."

Not exactly *what you think.*

"Sure it's not." She looked him up and down before dropping the newspaper on the table beside him. "Grant, I like her. You treat her right and be careful."

"I know, Mom." He glanced at the paper.

Grant McQuaid's Undercover Hot Date. It was easy to make out the close-up of his face with the baseball cap. "Son of a bitch," he bit out.

"Grant," she scolded, the lines etching deeper into her forehead. "You want to tell me what's going on because you're not acting like yourself. It's not like you to sneak around."

"You'd sneak around too if you had some damn reporter following your every move."

"Maybe your *moves* wouldn't matter to this reporter so much if you'd just quit trying to be sneaky." She tapped the newspaper. "Be upfront with everyone and they'll go away. They only do this because they think they're getting something juicy that you don't want people to know about."

Grant ran a hand through his hair. "I can't. Not yet."

His mother pursed her lips and glared at him. "The boy I raised to be honest never had a problem with reporters before, and he never had to sneak in and out of the house."

"Yeah, well the boy you raised wasn't sidelined and about to get fired." Grant stared into the coffee, wishing he'd learned the art of divining because he could sure use something that might give him some solid direction now. He felt like a leaf in the midst of a tornado.

"What?"

He heard the concern in her voice and knew he should have just kept his damn mouth shut. He hadn't meant to let it drop like a bomb but, as usual, his mouth outran his brain. "Don't worry about it, Mom. I've got it under control."

She arched a doubtful brow at him. "Do you now? Because you don't sound like it's under control. This," she said, tapping the paper, "doesn't *look* like it's under control."

"The ranch is set for the next two years and Jackson should be in the black next year. By then, I'll have figured something out." He took a swallow of the brew, letting its bitterness wash away the foulness building in his chest.

"I'm not worried about the *ranch*. I'm worried about *you*." She laid her hand on his forearm and he met her deep brown gaze, filled with fierce devotion to her son. He gave her a half-smile, trying to set her mind at ease. "Grant, I know what football means to you, what this career has meant, but there is more to life than football. You're nearly thirty-three years old and you've been lucky to spend the last ten years playing a game you love. Maybe it's time to start living a *life* you love."

She rose from the table and ruffled his hair, the way she had when he was little, moping at this very same table. Grant ran his hands over the table's planks, taking in the grooves cut into the hardwood from daily wear and tear. Years of homework. Too many nightly meals to count, surrounded by his brothers and sister. Life happened here but, as much as he loved it, loved them, he'd gotten out as quickly as he could because he'd thought staying meant getting stuck working the ranch just like his father. If he was going to do something, he wanted it to be something he loved to do and football fit that bill.

It had taken him all over the nation, even out of the country at times. Sure, there'd been long hours practicing, lonely nights in hotels, events like his brother's graduation from the police academy that he'd missed out on at home, but he'd traded all of that for the ability to provide for his family by doing something he loved. Hell, he'd been able to put Andrew, Ben and Maddie through college without his parents ever having to worry about any of it. He'd kept the ranch afloat in hard times and been able to fund Jackson's dream of breeding premier cow horses.

Knowing his family was well-supported made it worth missing *life*, as his mother called it. He'd sacrificed a few years of his own to keep his family from going into debt for multiple loans. And, to be honest, he hadn't minded the sacrifice. He couldn't have asked for a better way to be able to do it.

Grant rose from the table and slid his cup into the dishwasher, rubbing one hand over the tight muscles at the back of his neck. "I'm going to go work out."

"I'll call Ben at the station and tell him you're on your way."

Grant shook his head. "No, I'm just going to go for a run."

He didn't need the angry testosterone pounding of pumping iron. What he needed was a long run to clear his head, to put a few things into proper perspective so that he could decide what he really wanted. Because for the first time, he wasn't thinking about the game or the fans. He wasn't even thinking about the money being thrown his way by the network in New York. He was thinking about the way Bethany looked last night, sleeping on his chest with her hand tucked under her chin. Or the way her eyes had gleamed like multifaceted jewels when she made the decision to trust him. Or a blue-eyed little boy who'd asked Grant if he could be his Dad over breakfast this morning while his mother slept upstairs.

Chapter Eighteen

"PLEASE TELL ME you were Grant McQuaid's hot date last night," Julie practically squealed as soon as Bethany entered the teacher's lounge.

"Shh!" She held a finger to her lips and shoved the other woman toward the coffeepot, trying to avoid several pairs of surprised eyes in the room. However, there was one set that didn't look shocked. Steven simply looked disappointed.

"Why are you shushing me? It's great!"

Bethany glared at her and shifted her eyes toward Steven across the room, where he was busy pretending that he wasn't listening to their conversation. Julie waved a hand. "Pfft, he was the one who showed me the paper. I'm pretty sure he's figured it out."

Bethany bit the inside of her lip, hard. This was just one of the reasons she didn't date guys she worked with. Now she had to say something, at least explain herself after blowing him off yesterday, and it was sure to be awkward between them. She poured a cup of coffee and took the pot to Steven. "Want a refill?"

"Bethany, it's fine. I kinda had a feeling when I picked you up."

"You did?" She slid into the chair, setting the pot on the table. "Why? I mean, when you and I went out, Grant and I were just friends."

One of the second grade teachers took the pot from where Bethany had set it and shot her a scathing glare before walking away. Bethany cast the woman a curious glance and Steven gave her a sympathetic grin.

"Better get used to that," he said. "I think you're going to get that a lot more from some of the single women in town. And, for the record, *friends* don't look at you the way he was, Bethany."

She wasn't sure what to say. Grant had been the one to suggest she go out with Steven in the first place. Why would he have done that if he'd been interested in her? But she couldn't deny that only a few days later he'd stayed the night, even if they didn't actually have sex. She cringed. What the hell was she thinking? This was moving far too quickly.

"Steven," she began.

"Like I said, it's fine. Maybe I shouldn't have waited so long to ask, or maybe I should have moved faster, I don't know."

"That wasn't it."

He nodded, shaking his head slightly with a look of self-deprecation. "Maybe I should have just been Grant McQuaid."

Guilt raced through her, choking her. Grant's celebrity wasn't what drew her to him. It hurt that Steven, someone who knew her, could think she'd been attracted to Grant for that reason. And if he believed that, what would the rest of the town, people who barely knew her, think? There was far more to her attraction to him than that. For starters, there was the way he treated her son.

Before she could say anything else, the bell rang. Bethany scooped up the construction paper she needed for their project this morning and, walking by the newspaper, she grabbed it and tucked it on top, pressing it against her breasts. The fewer people who suspected she was Grant McQuaid's "hot date," the better.

SITTING IN HIS car outside the small two-room office building on Main Street, Grant debated what he was about to do. Confronting the editor about the lack of professionalism on the part of his reporter probably wasn't going to go over well. He took a deep, cleansing breath, willing himself to let go of his anger, but it wasn't working. Frustration continued to build in him. His five-mile run hadn't done anything to clear the dissatisfaction he was battling and taking it out on an editor was likely going to cause more trouble instead of less.

The front door opened and a woman walked by his car. "Hey, Grant, what are you doing here?"

He recognized Gina Bradley, one of the girls who'd been on the cheerleading squad in high school. She'd been a few years younger and, while they'd hung with the same sports crowd in school, they'd never been more than acquaintances. He wasn't exactly in the mood to reminisce old times, but Grant wasn't about to be rude either.

Plastering the fake smile he usually reserved for the media on his face, he met her gaze in hopes this would be a quick conversation. "I'm good. What about you?"

"Good. I heard you were back in town for a while."

He rolled his eyes and jerked a thumb toward the newspaper office. "You'd have to be living under a rock *not* to know I'm here, thanks to these guys."

She laughed and brushed a lock of dark hair behind her ears, giving him a coy smile. "Yeah, you do seem to be quite the topic of conversation. If it's not your brother, it's you."

"Which brother?" She giggled and he felt the warning bells signal in his brain.

"Depends on who's conversation it is, but it's usually your name or Linc's I hear mentioned. I guess that's the price of fame, huh? Everyone wants a piece of you."

"Oddly, the shit I'm catching here has been worse than what I've gotten anywhere else. It's pretty ridiculous."

She shrugged. "I don't know. The paper's only trying to keep afloat. You and Linc sell papers."

He glanced back at the doorway she'd just exited. "You work here?" Maybe she could give him some help figuring out who the anonymous reporter was.

Gina laughed again and rolled her heavily made-up eyes. "I wish. Nope, I'm at the coffee shop down the street. My Mom bought it, so guess who gets to manage it." She jerked two thumbs at herself. "I was just dropping off the payment for an ad she wants to run next week."

"Between you and me, how receptive do you think the paper would be if I asked nicely for them to leave my family alone?" Grant jerked his chin at the office in front of his car.

She gave him a bright smile, one that used to dazzle most of the football team. "If you were the editor of a struggling media format, and you had a meal ticket like reporting on not one but *two* famous brothers in the same family, and could get exclusive photos, how would you respond?"

Grant's confidence in the idea plummeted. She was right but he had to do something to make this stop.

"Don't sweat it, Grant. You're leaving for camp soon anyway, aren't you?" She looked up as the door to the newspaper office opened. "Look, I gotta head back to the coffee shop. I'll see you around. Come by before you leave, okay?"

Grant nodded and agreed to try as he slid out of the car, prepared to go to battle for his reputation as well as his ability to walk around this small town with Bethany without worrying that their picture would be plastered on every doorstep in town the next morning.

"HEY." GRANT'S VOICE over the phone was husky and seductive.

How was it possible that one simple word could send her entire body spiraling into a quivering, heated ball of need?

Other than a few texts during the day to tell her that he couldn't wait to see her, she hadn't talked to him since he'd left her house yesterday morning. However, he hadn't mentioned when she might see him again or indicated that he wanted to make any solid plans, and it had led to some serious doubting on her part. Bethany was beginning to wonder if she'd hadn't been reading too much into their relationship and acting like a stupid girl with a crush. But hearing the warmth in his voice, she tried to cast her doubts aside, at least for the moment. She would deal with the heartache later.

"Hi. What have you been up to all day?" She settled back into the couch cushions as James glanced up from his homework at the kitchen table. She gave him a quick wink and he turned back to his handwriting.

"I ran a couple errands in town, made some phone calls, helped my brother check some fences and missed you like crazy."

She felt her anxiety slip a little further into the distance. "I missed you too." She glanced at James and saw his face light up. He must have guessed who she was talking to on the phone. "I think someone else is missing you too. And it doesn't look like he's going to finish his homework until he talks to you."

"Put him on." She could hear the smile in his tone, could visualize the way his dark eyes lit up when he was with James.

"Hang on." She waved James toward her and handed him the phone.

"Hello?"

Bethany would have laughed at the excitement in her son's voice if the reality of their situation didn't worry her so much. Watching James' face as he talked to Grant, she could feel her misgivings building again. She'd willingly opened herself up for heartache but, in doing so, James was going to be hurt too. The longer this relationship with Grant went on, the more devastated James would be.

James handed her back the phone, a wide smile gracing his face while his eyes shone with renewed excitement. *I get to ride Shorty this weekend if I do my homework,* he signed.

What? Bethany signed back. "Wait, what is this about Shorty this weekend, Grant?"

"I thought that you guys could come stay here for the weekend."

"Stay? As in spend the night?"

"Or two," he amended.

"Why didn't you ask me first?" She sighed, trying to balance the heady longing to agree with her need to protect James. "Grant, I don't know if that would be a good idea. I mean—" She looked up to see James watching her, his entire demeanor going from ecstatic to sullen in a matter of only a few words. Bethany sighed and pointed at the table where his homework was waiting. "Hang on."

You do your work and let me talk to Grant, okay? Bethany signed to her son and pulled his chair out.

He clenched his jaw angrily and plopped back into the chair, shooting her an angry glare. She arched a warning brow at him and he went back to his homework without argument. Bethany walked into the backyard and shut the sliding door behind her for privacy.

"I wish you'd talked to me before you made him any promises."

"I wanted to surprise you both with a weekend away. I want to see you, and for more than a movie night."

"I want to see you too," she admitted, swallowing the agony she could already feel her next words dredging up. But her first loyalty was to her son. "Grant, I'm not sure we can do this. I thought I could, and I've tried to ignore the newspaper articles, but people are putting two and two together. Steven even said something today."

"So?" His voice was tight as if she'd insulted him.

"People are talking, Grant. Pointing and making judgments about me, and James." He was quiet and she pressed on. "You're going to be leaving again and I'm the one who has to face everyone in town when they look at me like your latest conquest. James has enough to deal with without being the kid whose mom—"

"It's not like that, Bethany. You know that."

Did she? "That doesn't mean everyone else does."

"Which is part of the reason I wanted you guys to come here this weekend." Grant sighed into the receiver. "I can't take the two of you out of town somewhere, to Tahoe for the weekend maybe, the way I'd like to, but there are no reporters trying to get a story here on the ranch."

"Grant, do you have any idea what this is doing to James? It's going to wreck him when you leave." She felt the tears forming a lump in her throat. She tried to swallow and cleared her throat. James wasn't the only one who would be wrecked. "I can't do this to him."

Grant didn't respond immediately. This wasn't how she'd meant for this to happen. She hadn't wanted good-bye to come so soon, but after seeing James' face as he talked to Grant on the phone, she knew she had no choice.

"Bethany, you're assuming that I'm going to completely cut ties with him like your ex. That I'm going to walk away and never come back like he did."

Her heart stilled as she grasped what he was saying, what he was offering. She had never expected even this. "Grant, we've only known each other for a week."

"Okay?" He couldn't possibly be serious but his tone said nothing less. "I'll bet I've learned more about you and James in the past seven days than anyone else here has in six months."

He sighed again and she knew he was running a frustrated hand through his hair. She'd seen him do it several times over the past few days. She might not have known him long, but he was right. It felt like far more time had passed. It wasn't about the quantity; it was the quality of time they'd spent together.

Bethany had tried to convince herself that it was because he was in the public eye, and that she felt like she knew him because she'd seen him every Sunday over the years while she watched the game with James and her Dad, but it was a lie. They had a connection she'd never felt with anyone else. She'd opened up to him and, in doing that, opened herself up to being vulnerable again.

But he'd done the same with her. She knew things he'd never talked about to the media, things she only knew from spending time with him this past week. She knew how much he adored his mother and his sister. She'd seen his devotion to his family first-hand at their house. She knew he didn't want to be a cattle rancher, in spite of respecting his father and brothers' choice to do so. She knew there was a gentleness to his hands, in spite of his violent career choice. Just as she knew if she gave herself half a chance, completely let down the wall around her heart, she'd fall madly in love with Grant McQuaid.

"Bethany, do you really think I'd have introduced James to my family if I was going to bail on him? On either of you?"

Bethany felt her heart clench at the thought of what it sounded like he was promising. Her heart was pounding against her ribs, like it was trying to escape her chest.

"Please come." His voice was quiet and softly seductive.

How could she refuse?

SHUT UP! STOP talking! Grant's brain screamed.

He wasn't entirely sure where the words that fell from his lips came from, but he knew better than to make any sort of promises. He should have stayed away from Bethany and James from the first day in the park, but he hadn't and now he couldn't imagine not seeing them, not talking to her, not being with them.

Yet, it was possible that was exactly what was going to happen after Monday, he realized. He was flying out for an appointment on Monday with his own doctor before meeting with the team physicians on Tuesday. It was basically nothing more than a formality at this point, but this final assessment would give him a better sense of the direction his career would take.

If he was cleared to play, Wolf had already made it clear they were going to buy out his contract, which would allow Grant to be picked up as a free agent. However, if he wasn't cleared . . .

Grant wouldn't even entertain the idea. He'd worked too hard over the last few months, forging his body into a machine. He was more fit to play now than he'd been in years. At least, he had been until this past week.

Images of Bethany and James filled his mind. He'd actually thrown his workout schedule out the window in order to spend time with them. He'd never missed workouts before. Then again, he'd also never found a woman who made him rethink his desire to continue playing football. Physically, he was ready to go back to the game. Emotionally, he was torn between the future he'd spent his life working for, and his present—a woman he'd met a little more than a week ago who was forcing him to see a new vision of what he wanted for his life.

He didn't have much time left to make some sort of a decision, but he had no doubt that what time he had left in Hidden Falls, he wanted to spend with Bethany and James.

Chapter Nineteen

JAMES SAT IN the back seat of Bethany's run-down sedan practically bouncing in his booster seat as he recited what he and Grant had planned for their weekend. After she'd agreed to come for the weekend, Grant had asked to talk to James again and the two of them had schemed for over an hour, until she'd finally told him that if he didn't get his reading homework done, then they couldn't go.

She glanced in her rearview mirror to see his big blue eyes bright with excitement. He might look just like his father, but he reminded her of herself when she was younger—filled with optimism and zeal for adventure—before life had decided to kick her in the teeth. Not once but twice, leaving her divorced and trying to navigate motherhood with a special needs child as well as going to college full-time while maintaining a job.

Matthew had taken so much from her but she also realized now that, in leaving, he'd given her something she never would have had otherwise—strength. She'd let so much of her identity become wrapped up in Matthew and what he'd achieved in and after high school that she'd lost who she was deep inside. She'd allowed herself to become an extension of him and she realized now, he'd been weak. Not a bad person, but cowardly.

For years she had overlooked the signs—the conflict avoidance in the name of intellectual superiority, the hesitancy to step out of his comfort zone and the endless supply of excuses—but she'd seen the look in his eyes when the doctors gave them James' diagnosis. He might have been physically present for another week but he'd been planning his escape from that moment in the office. He'd run, first emotionally, then physically, and never looked back.

To his credit, James rarely asked about his father but she'd always been as honest as she could be without telling her son of his father's abandonment. She'd told him stories of their dates in high school and college, showed him the pictures of their wedding or of them together while she was pregnant. She let him see the happy times, the good memories she had of Matthew. As with everything, she didn't want to give James any more struggles to overcome, and knowing your father had abandoned you was a doozy to deal with.

"I asked Grant to be my dad."

James' nonchalantly spoken bit of information in the midst of his excitement over riding Shorty made her heart stop in her chest as she looked into the rearview mirror again. "You what?"

He wasn't even looking at her. He was too busy drawing a picture on the notepad she kept the in back seat for him. "I like him. He's my friend. I want him to be my dad."

Her mind raced with questions she couldn't ask James. When had James asked Grant? What did Grant say? What could Grant be thinking? She couldn't even imagine the sort of shock that must have been for him. Was that the reason for this impromptu weekend trip?

James glanced up at her reflection. "Then we could have guys' days all the time."

"Grant is a nice man, baby, but—"

"He's your friend too, right?" She nodded wondering how to best make it clear that he shouldn't ask questions like those of Grant.

"He is," she agreed with a nod.

"Then I could have a mom *and* a dad like Carlton."

She could see the simple hope in James' eyes and it broke her heart that she couldn't make his circumstances any easier. "Baby, it isn't always that easy for grownups. Before they become moms or dads, they have to be friends for a very long time."

He set his pencil in his lap and rolled his eyes at her, pursing his lips. "I know *that* but you've been friends forever already, since we played in the park together."

He shook his head like she was being ridiculous and a bubble of irrational laughter almost burst from between her lips. It was useless to argue the semantics of relationships with a six-year-old who couldn't possibly understand interpersonal dynamics, let alone the complex issues of sexual attraction. Nor was she about to start explaining them.

"Grown-ups like to be friends even longer than we have."

"But it's been like forty days, Mom."

She smiled at him as she turned off the exit leading to Grant's parents' cattle ranch, her mind still reeling with unanswered questions. "Not quite. Are you ready to see Shorty?" she asked, changing the subject. "We're almost there."

"Yes!" He held up the picture he'd been drawing, a crude stick figure sketch of him riding the pony. Standing beside him were two people she could only assume were her and Grant, holding hands. "There's Shorty, me, you and Grant. When he's my dad, will I still call him Grant?"

She should have known he wouldn't drop this subject that easily.

GRANT WATCHED THE car coming down the driveway and tried to still his nerves. He didn't even get this nervous before a game.

That's because you know what you're doing in a game.

True, in a game he was prepared, had practiced every scenario in his head days, sometimes weeks, in advance. With Bethany, he was flying blind. He had nothing to compare with how he felt when he was with her.

Not that he hadn't dated, but he'd never let anything move beyond a couple of dates, nothing serious. He'd never had the time or inclination. His life had revolved around football for as long as he could remember. There hadn't been room for anything else.

Even when he was younger, he was too focused on keeping his grades high enough to attract a Division I recruiter. College was spent trying to stand out enough to attract agents and scouts before the draft. Any spare time was either spent making sure he got his degree or in the gym. By the time he'd joined the Mustangs, he'd put in too much time to risk his position for something that wasn't the real deal. There were too many women willing to date any player who'd take them out. He'd seen enough of them, especially when he first started with the team, but he'd learned his lesson quickly. As long as he was in the public eye, he was vulnerable to lies, treachery and betrayal, even from people he thought he could trust.

"Grant!" James yelled at him through the window he'd rolled partway down. "Hi!"

"Hey, little man. Shorty's been asking when you were going to show up."

Bethany dropped the car into Park in front of the bunkhouse and helped James out, trying to hide a smile. As soon as she opened his door, James jumped out and ran to Grant, throwing his arms around his legs. Scooping him up, Grant tossed him into the air, catching him effortlessly and walking back toward Bethany.

"Mom made me do my reading before we could come," he complained.

"Ah, I see. Well, that was probably a good idea because I don't think you're going to do much reading while you're here. Jefferson and Jackson want you to help them with the cows tomorrow." He didn't miss the way Bethany's eyes widened in horror. "They need someone to count the cows as they bring them in."

"I get to help?" He bounced excitedly in Grant's arms, clapping his hands.

"Yep." Grant looked at him seriously. "But you can't play. I told them how good you are at counting and you'll have an important job. I'm trusting you, okay?"

Bethany frowned, no doubt concerned about the pressure she thought he was putting on her son, but James matched Grant's somber expression with one of his own.

"I promise." He held up a pinkie finger and Grant smiled, remembering the first time he'd done it with the boy at the park when they met. He curled his pinkie finger with James'.

Grant set him back on the ground. "Why don't you go find Maddie in the kitchen?" He patted James on the rear end as the boy took off for the house. Turning his attention back to Bethany, he said, "I'll take your things upstairs and show you the room Mom got ready for you."

She looked beautiful and he wanted to wrap his arms around her, to welcome her properly with a kiss, but she seemed unsure how to proceed. She bit her lip and he could see the apprehension in her eyes. He could tell she was chewing something over in her mind and knew she was probably overthinking this weekend.

Her eyes clouded and she turned away, opening the trunk. "That bag is mine and that one is James'."

"I'll grab his when I come back out."

"Why? We can just take both in one trip?"

"He didn't tell you?"

She looked confused and he was pleasantly surprised James had been able to keep the secret. It must have been even more important to James than Grant realized.

When she shook her head, Grant laughed. "Then you're actually in for a few surprises this weekend. James is pretty excited to stay in the bunkhouse with the guys." He stared at the boy running up the back porch steps. "Huh, I didn't think he'd be able to keep quiet. I guess I should have given him more credit."

"Grant, I don't like the idea of him sleeping in the bunkhouse. What if he needs something?"

He grinned at her. "He'll have five men at his beck and call all weekend."

His hands itched to pull her close but she seemed unusually tense right now and he didn't want to push his luck. He slid the strap of her overnight bag over his shoulder and closed the trunk of her car.

"Relax. We'll try it for tonight and if it doesn't work out, he can come back into the house and stay in your room, okay?" She twisted her lips to the side, debating his suggestion, and he laughed. "You know you look just like James when you do that."

"Do what?"

"That face he makes when he's thinking about something. It's adorable."

"Adorable?" Her eyes ignited in playful defiance and her brow quirked. "That's not exactly a term women find complimentary."

"No?" he asked, taking a step closer. He congratulated himself on the way she'd relaxed a bit, even as she pursed her lips, trying to hide her smile. This was the Bethany he'd come to know. "What about cute?" He slid his arm around her waist and pulled her closer. "Or bewitching?"

"Those two things are even cl—"

Grant didn't wait for her to answer and his lips slanted over hers, unable to keep himself from sipping from that well of temptation. She opened beneath him, like the morning glories his mother had planted around the house, as if she'd been waiting for him to release the woman she held hidden inside. Her hands slid to his chest and she fisted his shirt in her fingers, pulling him closer, demanding more from him.

He withdrew and glanced back at the bunkhouse where he suspected there were at least three sets of eyes on them. Grant saw the blinds snap closed, confirming his suspicions. "Bethany, you have no idea how much shit I'm going to catch tonight for that."

He couldn't help the shit-eating grin that spread across his face. It didn't matter how much crap his brothers wanted to give him about falling for her. It was more than worth it. He leaned his forehead against hers. "Do you have any clue how much I've missed you?

"Want to show me again? What's a little more harassment?"

He looked down at her, surprised by the playful fire in her hazel eyes and more than a little enticed by it. "Yes, I do, but I see James and Maddie heading out."

She jumped backward like she'd been burned and he

immediately regretted his warning. He hadn't expected her reaction to sting, especially since he knew she was trying to protect James. But he was praying that after this weekend, she wouldn't feel the need to hide their relationship any longer, especially after the surprise he had planned for her tomorrow morning.

BETHANY LAY AWAKE in bed, the silence of the night deafening. She felt on edge. She hadn't had a quiet night, one where she didn't check on her son, in six years. It was odd and disconcerting.

She'd been in the bunkhouse when James fell asleep and Grant carried him into Linc's empty bedroom. She'd shown Grant how to take off the implant microphones and instructed him on how to put them on in the morning, warning him about how it was a good thirty minutes before James was ready to put them on. Even though it was barely nine o'clock, Grant had walked her across the short distance between the bunkhouse and his parents' home, warning her that they would have a busy day ahead before giving her a disappointingly gentlemanly kiss on the cheek and opening the back door for her.

It wasn't what she'd wanted, or expected. She'd thought he would give her a kiss with a bit more substance. Hell, the kiss at the car had had been pretty chaste, even if it had nearly turned her bones molten. She'd been looking forward to some time alone with him.

Unless James' question had him second-guessing

their relationship and he wasn't sure how to deal with this limbo-style relationship.

She lay in the guest room, frustrated and unsatisfied, tossing and turning on the large bed. Thoughts of the night Grant had stayed at her place heated her blood and forced her to give up any hope of sleeping.

Bethany swung her legs over the side of the mattress, unsure where she was heading, but knowing she couldn't just lie here any longer, staring at the dark ceiling, waiting for dawn to break. It was still hours away, but Grant's mother had told her to make herself at home, and maybe a cup of tea would settle her mind. Grant's father had already explained how he got up early and planned to be rising at five. She glanced at her cell phone screen—only four a.m.

She would have to be quiet so as not to wake anyone. Creeping down the stairs and into the kitchen, Bethany reached for a glass in the cupboard. She nearly dropped it when the kitchen light flicked on and she spun to see Grant's father, Travis, sliding a chair out at the table.

"Couldn't sleep?"

"I . . . I just came down to get . . ." He didn't say anything but the way he continued to stare at her was disconcerting, and she found she couldn't even try to make an excuse. She shook her head. "No."

He chuckled as if that was the reaction he'd expected. "James is a good kid. He's got your smile."

She'd met Travis the last time she'd been to his house but they hadn't really had much of a conversation. He'd been working with the cattle and then had stayed by the fire with his sons most of the evening. He wasn't unfriendly, but he was definitely intimidating. "Thank you, sir."

"Sir?" He laughed. "Just Travis is fine." He ran a finger over a groove in the table. "I'm surprised to see a young woman like you with Grant."

That was cutting straight to the heart of things.

"Sir?" He shot her a playful warning look. "Sorry, Travis," she muttered.

"Better." He smiled warmly. "Grant's always been a serious boy, and an even more serious man. When he sets his mind to something, he gets it. Whatever that thing might be. There's no doubt that he will, it's just a matter of his making the decision that he wants it."

She wasn't sure what he was trying to tell her. It could be anything from a question to a warning and Bethany didn't know him well enough to read which this was, nor did she feel comfortable asking him directly.

"I always knew he wasn't cut out for ranching. He's too big a personality to fit into this small of a pond without trouble ensuing. Football has been the only thing he's ever really cared about." He scrutinized her carefully. "You know, he's never brought a girl home to meet his mother, not even when he was a kid."

Bethany felt as if she were on trial, as if he was only just getting to what he wanted to say. Her stomach twisted into knots waiting. Her fingers gripped the glass so tightly she thought she might shatter it. Bethany chewed at the inside of her lip, tasting blood, but unable to still the nervous dread welling up inside her as Grant's father worked his way around to his point.

"I like you and James, Bethany. And I can see that my son cares about you and that boy of yours, more than I've ever seen him care about anyone who isn't family, but I don't want to see anyone get hurt when it doesn't work out." His tapped his index finger on the table and sighed. "His mother would probably kill me for interfering but . . . I should probably mind my own business."

"Yeah, you should, Dad."

They both spun to see Grant standing in the doorway behind them. He shook his head and ran his fingers through his hair before turning and storming out.

"Well, shit," Travis muttered.

"Grant," Bethany called, jumping up to follow him, catching him as he hit the front porch. "Stop." She reached for his arm and he paused, not turning toward her. "It's not what you think."

"What?" He gave a bitter laugh. "That my Dad was trying to warn you to stay away from me because I'm going to hurt you?"

"Are you?"

Grant turned around, the wound evident in his eyes. "What do you think?"

He'd never been anything but tender with her, gentle in every touch, kind in every way, but she couldn't just dismiss the concerns she'd had about his leaving, the same concerns his own father had brought up. Grant might care about her and James, but the fact was, he was going back to his team in Memphis, and she would be here with her son, trying to pick up the broken pieces of their hearts.

"Yes, I think you're going to hurt me." She saw the sadness flicker in his eyes at her admission.

"Grant, I was devastated when Matthew left, broken for months when I received divorce papers by mail." She shook her head and dropped onto the porch swing, reaching for a throw pillow and tucking it into her lap, wrapping her arms around it. "He couldn't even tell me himself." She glanced up at him, still standing, watching her carefully. "But I got through it. I moved on and I came here to start a new chapter for James, for both of us. Then you showed up and threw a monkey wrench into everything."

She saw him clench his jaw, dejection written in his eyes, his hands tightening into fists at his sides. "Is that what I did?"

"Yes. I had a routine. My life was predictable. Go to work, take care of James, go to bed and get up to do it again. Everything in my life made sense, not like this roller-coaster ride I've been on with you."

"Are you sure it's me and not the fact that you're finally living in the real world again, instead of that bubble of perfection you try so hard to maintain?"

She scowled at him but he was right. She knew it. She'd been living in self-imposed isolation, thinking that it would protect her and James. It hadn't. Life had still happened all around her, without her. She'd simply wasted years of her life thinking about what-ifs and could-have-beens because of a man who chose to walk away. It was time she finally faced it and admitted that she didn't want that for either of them any longer.

"Am I really the first woman you've ever brought home?"

Grant stuffed his hands into his front pockets and shrugged, looking hopelessly like the young man he must have been when he left this ranch to find his future. "I never met anyone I *wanted* to bring home to meet my family. That was something I'd always reserved for when I found someone special."

Her heart pounded against her ribs. She tried to still the hope building in her heart. Was he suggesting that *she* might be that someone special?

"Bethany," he began, sliding onto the swing beside her and reaching for her hand. "I don't want to hurt you or James."

Bethany felt her heart plummet to her toes. They'd started this conversation several times—how to define their relationship, what would happen when it came time for him to leave—and she wished they'd come to some sort of resolution before now. But neither had wanted to face the crossroads where their feelings met with reality. Now the conversation with his father had forced it and she was scared to hear what he said next.

Chapter Twenty

GRANT KNEW HIS father hadn't meant any harm. It was who he was—brutally honest, to a fault—but he wondered how deep the doubts about him had been instilled in Bethany now. If his own father was warning her to leave, to walk away from whatever they wanted to call this relationship they had, what woman in her right mind would stay? And if she wanted to walk away, she might as well rip his heart from his chest now.

His thumb brushed over the back of her hand, sending a sizzle of heat up his arm and making his heart pound. Just touching this woman had the power to undo him. Fear swelled in his chest at what he was about to say.

"Bethany, if you decide that you need to walk away from this, from me, please, do it before I fall for you any harder than I already have."

Bethany's lips parted slightly in shock, her eyes

startled by his admission, but they brimmed with tears, liquid and warm.

"Honey, please, say something."

She pressed her lips together and looked down at their hands, still clasped. Without warning, she leaned into him, pressing her lips against his and cupping his whisker-roughened jaw with her fingers. Every part of his body lit with longing for her. His tongue swept against hers, caressing her even as his free hand slid up the column of her neck into the waves of her hair, losing himself in the taste of her, the scent of her, the feel of her soft curves under his hand. He wanted to escape with her, if only for a short time, to show her exactly how much he cared for her.

But there was no privacy here. At least not until later this morning when he could show her the surprise he'd arranged for her. Sighing, he withdrew from their kiss slowly, wishing it could last.

"I should get back and check on James."

She lifted her gaze to his, her dark lashes shadowing her eyes. "Is he okay?"

One corner of Grant's mouth lifted. "He's fine, sleeping soundly. I actually just came over because I saw the light go on in the kitchen."

She matched his grin with a wicked smile of her own. "Why, Mr. McQuaid, were you sneaking into the house to tuck me in?"

Hunger, white-hot and electric, shot to his groin making him ache and he couldn't stop the agonized groan that slipped from between his lips. "That was just cruel and unusual punishment."

And now that is the image that will be in your mind. So much for getting a few more hours' sleep.

Yes, he did want to tuck her in, and climb in with her, cradling himself within her body. She laughed quietly, her gaze innocent.

"You still could." Her eyes gleamed.

He knew she was teasing him. "Now you're just being mean."

Grant stood slowly, adjusting his jeans and reached for her hand. He pulled her up from the swing, tugging her into his arms, sliding his hand down her back to press her hips against his, even though it tortured him.

She gasped as he leaned his head down, his lips just a breath from hers. "I will definitely make you pay for that later."

"Promises, promises," she whispered.

"Oh, you better believe it. I am a man of my word, remember?"

His fingers dug into the flesh of her rear, pressing her fully against his erection. As much as he wanted to pick her up and take her back to his room, he didn't want either of his parents to question his motives, or hers. Besides, the surprise he had waiting for her would be that much more special for waiting.

"I need to get you inside or I'm not going to be able to behave."

"What if I don't want you to?" She brushed her lips

over his jaw and he could feel the pressure building within him making him want to cave.

He wanted her, more than he'd ever wanted a woman. But he also respected her more than any woman he'd ever met. They still had to make some decisions but he felt like they'd at least face his departure, and whatever happened with his career, together.

He wasn't going to ruin what could be for a quick romp, even if it was amazing—and he had no doubt it would be incredible—but he was also pretty certain that what they could have was the real deal. He wasn't willing to risk losing his family's respect for her.

Grant brushed his fingers over her jaw, lifting her face for a gentle kiss, one that he couldn't let deepen into more. "I'll see you in a few hours. I have a surprise for you."

"I thought we were helping your brothers with the cattle." She looked confused.

"*James* is helping them. Mom and Maddie are going to stay with him. *We* are doing something different. I'll be here about seven." He couldn't help but have one last taste of the sweetness of her lips. "Sweet dreams, Bethany," he whispered against her lips.

Grant forced himself to walk down the porch steps and head back to the bunkhouse without looking backward.

BETHANY WAS SITTING in the kitchen with Grant's mother at five minutes to seven when he and the rest of his brothers showed up.

"Sounds like the army is coming," Sarah said with a laugh as she rose from the table, opening the back door. "Well, good morning!" Bethany's eyes misted when Sarah signed *good morning* to James. "I was beginning to wonder if you guys were ever coming in."

"Mom, I got to help feed horses this morning. The hay was this big!" He held his arms open as wide as they would stretch.

"You did?" Her gaze immediately sought out Grant and she felt her insides heat when he returned James' grin. The man had a way of getting her to let down every barrier she had around her heart. "I bet you're hungry then. You should sit down and try some of the pancakes that Mrs. McQuaid made."

James frowned for a moment as he sat, twisting his lips to one side. *I only like yours*, he signed.

She tipped her chin down at him with a warning look, but before she could answer, Grant moved behind her and she saw his hands moving from the corner of her eye. She was just about to ask what he was signing when James' eyes grew wide and a grin split his face.

"Really?"

Bethany turned in her chair. "What did you tell him?"

"That Mom usually keeps whipped cream in the refrigerator for boys and that she probably didn't tell you about it." He opened the door. "Yep, here it is." He set the can in front of James. "And you're going to work up quite an appetite today, so you'd better eat up." He winked at her son who began bouncing slightly in his chair.

"More sugar. Just what he needs," she scolded Grant.

"Don't worry, Mom and Maddie can handle a boy on a sugar high. They're pros." He cocked his head to one side and jerked his chin toward the twins. "Trust me, those two were a handful."

"Speaking of that, are you sure we should leave him with them? What if something happens?"

"Like what?"

She could see he realized she was trying to wiggle her way out of leaving James behind. It was one thing for her to be comfortable leaving him with Maddie when she was nearby, but she had no idea what Grant had planned. They could be leaving town for all she knew.

"We won't be far. I'll have my cell and you'll have yours. Plus we'll have this." He held up a walkie-talkie. "Just in case the cells don't work for some reason."

"Where exactly *are* we going?"

"I know," James chimed in.

"Don't tell, James. Remember, it's a secret."

"I 'member," he replied through a mouthful of pancake and whipped cream.

"We should probably head out. Jackson saddled Ginger for you again."

She eyed him distrustfully. "I have to ride again."

"Riding is something you might want to get used to sooner than later if you plan on spending much time around here," Sarah warned. Bethany didn't miss the hopeful note to her voice. "I wasn't too fond of horses either when I first married Travis. They'll grow on you."

"Kinda like this guy." Maddie jabbed Grant in the ribs

with an elbow. "Go, we'll manage to keep this little man out of trouble today."

Grant pinched his sister lightly in the ribs, making her squeal as she scooted out of his reach and eliciting a giggle from James. Grant wiggled his fingers at James. "Careful, buddy, or you'll be next," he warned playfully. "You ready?"

"When you're all done with breakfast, James, one of the cats had kittens in the barn. We can go see them," Maddie offered.

His smile could have lit up a city block. "I'm done," he said, pushing his full plate away.

Maddie laughed. "They're too little to go anywhere. Go ahead and finished those, then we'll go out." She jerked her head to one side, indicating to Bethany that they should leave. "Say bye to your mom."

Bethany squatted down in front of her son as he wrapped his arms around her neck. "Bye, Mom." He pressed a sticky kiss to her cheek. "I love you."

"Love you too, baby. I'll see you when I get back." She looked to Grant for confirmation as to when that might be, but he simply nodded.

Well, that wasn't very informative.

"You be sure to count those cows for Jackson, okay? Otherwise he's going to want to arm wrestle me again and I don't want to hear him cry when he loses." Grant scooped up whipped cream on his finger and plopped it on James' nose.

"Hey!" he yelled before giggling. Grant reached out a hand and ruffled his blond hair. James held up his hand with his thumb, index and pinkie fingers extended.

I love you.

Her heart stopped beating. Grant lifted his hand, repeating the gesture to James. Bethany felt her heart swell two sizes, making room for the football player who'd just filled it with so much tenderness, she thought she might explode.

BETHANY COULDN'T BELIEVE her eyes as they rode over the hill, entering a small valley. The area was dotted with pines and spruce and the sweet scent of the coming spring hung in the chilled air. In spite of the warmer than usual weather, there were still a few puddles left from melted snowfall. The chatter of squirrels and the warbling chirp of several birds in the trees as they awakened to the coming season greeted their arrival. In the center of the meadow, surrounded by trees to the rear, was a large canvas tent.

"What's this?"

"Privacy." Grant smiled at her. "An entire afternoon away from everyone. We can stay as long or short a time as you decide."

She bit the inside of her lip as they rode closer and she tried to see inside the tent. It seemed far too elaborate to set up for one occasion but it was far too immaculate to have been out here long.

He'd done all this for her? And he was willing to go through this much effort for only a few hours if that's what she decided? He couldn't possibly be for real.

"This is a chance for us to get to know one another."

He dismounted and reached for her mount's reins to hold the animal so she could climb off. He led both horses to a rope tied between two tree branches and tethered them. When he turned back toward her, she moved closer to him, sliding her arms around his slim waist.

"Mr. McQuaid, if I didn't know any better, I'd think you were trying to seduce me."

She was rewarded with one of his playboy grins that made her heart skip. "You haven't even gone inside yet."

Her brows lifted in question as he slipped his hand into hers and pulled her toward the opening. As soon as she stepped inside, she realized this was no regular tent. This was a portable hotel room, complete with a screened patio with wicker furniture. Moving farther inside, a large bed—a *real* mattress with a comforter—filled much of the room and in the back was a small portable bathroom, complete with shower and generator.

"How did you even manage this?" She couldn't keep the awe from seeping into her voice. How in the world had he arranged this on such short notice?

He shrugged. "Would it surprise you if I told you this was one of the business interests I had outside of football? I invested in some property not too far from here where I offer glamping facilities."

"Glamping?"

"Camping for people who don't want to rough it."

She leaned backward to look up at him. "You're serious?"

He laughed. "You'd be surprised at what people will

pay for these. At my place, we even deliver breakfast. I had my staff bring up one of the tents yesterday and set it up while we were at the house."

Bethany ran her hand over the rough canvas as she peeked out of one of the six windows lining the walls of the tent. She turned back to face him and clasped her hands behind her back. "You continue to amaze me. You're a real jack-of-all-trades. Rancher, plumber, football star, businessman . . . Is there anything you can't do?"

"I'm sure there's something." His eyes were mischievous and she knew he was up to no good. His hands circled her waist and pulled her close to him. "For the record, I'm no rancher. That is *definitely* something that's not in my wheelhouse."

"Your Dad mentioned that you don't like it." He frowned and Bethany cursed herself for bringing up the early morning conversation. She looked up at him and spotted another window on either side of the ceiling of the tent. "Is that a skylight?"

He smiled down at her, his eyes heated with yearning. "It is."

"Were you hoping we could discuss astronomy tonight?"

"Not exactly."

His head dipped to her throat as he pressed kisses to the pulse that kicked into warp speed. Bethany sighed and dropped her head backward, her fingers sliding to the nape of his neck, holding him to her. His hand slid down her spine to grip her hips and she pressed herself into his body, feeling his arousal through their clothing.

Grant groaned deep in his chest, the rumble vibrating against her own chest deliciously as he pressed kisses to her collarbone. She splayed her hands over his back, feeling the muscles rippling against her palms. He lifted her and she wound her legs around his hips as he carried her to the bed. Laying her down gently on one side, he moved to lie beside her.

Grant ran a finger over the thin strip of her skin bared as her shirt rode up slightly and she shivered in response.

"You're so beautiful, Bethany."

She wasn't sure what to say, or if a response was even necessary. What she wanted to do was straddle his body and strip him naked but she held back, sensing him doing the same. His palm slid under her shirt but simply lay against her skin, warming it and sending butterflies racing through her limbs.

"So," he began, pausing a beat. "I want you to ask me anything."

"You want to *talk*?"

Grant nodded and Bethany was confused. Other than the one night he'd stayed over, whenever she felt any sexual tension building between them, he pulled away and shut it down. He was obviously attracted to her but unwilling to act on it. She knew he was a gentleman, but this was taking it a bit further than necessary. Her confusion must have been evident in her expression.

"On the phone, the other day, you said that we barely knew each other. I don't want you to feel that way. What do you want to know about me? For you, I'm an open book."

He was willing to go to this kind of effort to make her feel more at ease with pursuing a relationship? Her heart crashed through what was left of the protective wall around it. No man had ever cared for her, about how she felt, her worries and concerns, the way Grant did. He'd more than earned her trust. He'd won her over completely.

She lay her hand over his, wanting to ask a thousand questions but unsure where to begin. "Why did you choose football?"

"You mean instead of another sport or as a career?"

"Both."

"I enjoyed the game as a kid and we had plenty of practice wrestling with the cattle, just screwing around. But I figured if I could toss a calf for junior rodeo, getting hit on the field wasn't much different. I did track in high school too but football was where my heart was."

"You were a rodeo cowboy? I thought you didn't like ranching."

"They are two very different things. I rodeoed when I was younger. I started around James' age riding sheep and stopped in high school." She smiled at the thought of him as a young cowboy. He must have driven the girls wild. "Getting beat up in football was bad enough, I didn't need it in the arena with rough stock too."

His fingers traced the line of her hip and she could feel the hunger coiling in her, begging to be released. She could see it in his eyes but he didn't seem inclined to act on it. Either that or he was in far better control of himself than she was.

"What about you? Did you always want to be a teacher?"

His hand moved to play along hers, his long, tapered fingers gliding over her skin. Bethany couldn't help but remember the way his fingers had played her body just a few nights ago, like a musical instrument made especially for him.

She and Matthew's sex life had been okay, but she'd loved her husband and never wondered how it might have been better. However, with Grant she had no self-control. Her body reacted apart from her will, wildly, leaving her breathless, calling out his name. And that was before they had even actually—

"Are you listening?"

Her gaze leapt up to his face and she realized he'd been talking to her but she'd been too busy fantasizing about him to listen. Grant's eyes darkened, turning nearly black, and she could see the desire pooling in them.

"No, I'm not," she admitted on a whisper.

Grant brushed a lock of hair back from the side of her face. "You're off somewhere else. Tell me."

She swallowed as he braced himself on an elbow, his cheek in his hand, and let his fingers trail over her arm, falling to a halt at her ribs. Desire smoldered in her, like a flame barely banked, ready to blaze out of control if he wasn't careful. He'd sparked it in her and now she wanted to be burned. She wanted to let it rage.

"I was thinking about the other night."

A blush crept to her cheeks and Bethany wondered where she'd ever found the courage to admit her wanton thoughts to him aloud. A week ago she wouldn't have admitted having them at all, let alone confess them to the man inspiring them. How had she changed so much in the last week and a half?

Grant smiled as his thumb brushed the curve of her breast. "I haven't stopped thinking about it."

"Grant," she pleaded, closing her eyes with a sigh.

"Sorry." He pulled his hand back from her and Bethany reached for it, catching it before he could move.

"Why are you sorry?"

She could see the concern in his eyes, a tender mix of worry and desire. "I don't want you to feel like I'm pressuring you, Bethany."

"Grant, you're not pressuring me. I told you the other night, I want this. I still do." She rolled over, pressing him onto his back and hovering over him, prepared to show him exactly what she was asking for. A slow smile curved her lips. "Please, tell me you came prepared this time."

Grant hesitated. "Bethany—"

Dread welled up. Had she been misreading his signals? Maybe this was his version of *friendship* and she was the one pushing him for more than he was prepared to give. But that's not what he'd said this morning. She sat up and scooted backward, putting some space between them as his rejection loomed like a dark cloud over them. "I know it's been a while since I did this, but am I misreading things? I thought we were on the same page."

Bethany saw the emotions run the gamut in his eyes. He'd never make a good poker player because his eyes showed everything. She could easily read indecision, fear and anger. But there was more—desire, sorrow, regret.

"What aren't you telling me?" He didn't answer for a moment, looking lost. Whatever he had going on in his mind was visibly tearing him up. "Grant?"

"Bethany, you're not misreading anything. It's killing me keeping my hands off you, but I also know you deserve the dream."

"What dream?"

He tipped his head to one side and rolled his eyes. "*The* dream. You know, marriage, house, kids, a couple dogs." He threw his hand up. "I don't know if I can give you that."

"I had that, remember? Well, minus the dogs, and it all fell apart. The problem with a dream is that it fades in the face of reality." She lay on his chest, her body molding to his, and moved her lips over his. "This is the only reality I need."

Chapter Twenty-One

GRANT KNEW THE moment to tell her the truth had passed. He'd been ready to confess everything—his appointment with the doctors, the likely outcome, the fact that unless he took one of the two positions offered—neither of which was appealing and both took him far from her and James—he'd be officially retired, unemployed and, for the time being, broke. What kind of irresponsible man would he be to take on a family without a job, just sitting around *her* house, waiting for next year's payout? Or the next opportunity, *if* Bob could even scrounge one up? He was raised to work hard, protect and provide for a family. That was what a *man* did.

She deserved the truth and a man brave enough to admit it.

Guilt ate at him, her words like stakes driving into his heart. His feelings for her were real but until he told her everything, this *wasn't* reality. Being with her, in his arms, this was his fantasy, a dream come true, if only for a short time. Because, like Bethany said, dreams would disappear when faced with reality. He couldn't come to her empty-handed and ask her to wait for him. But if he could settle the question of his future in the next couple days . . .

His hands slid to her waist as she covered his mouth with hers, swinging one leg over his hips to straddle him. He wanted their first time to be perfect. He'd brought her here to tell her everything because regardless of which job he ended up with, if any, he wanted her beside him. But watching her with his family, seeing them with James, he realized he could never ask her to leave Hidden Falls. She fit in here, far more than he ever had. Maybe he could be a rancher, like his father and brothers. Maybe he could learn to tolerate it with Bethany at his side. Settling was far better than losing her.

Wrapping her hands around the hem of her shirt, she pulled it over her head. Her long, dark hair cascaded around her shoulders, falling forward to tickle his face and chest. His entire body responded to the sight of her, longing spiraling through him, igniting every bit of the desire he'd been holding back since the first time he'd seen her in the park with James. His impatience fueled her own and she slid her hands under his shirt. Every muscle she touched tensed with anticipation and he took the collar of his shirt, yanking it off before wrapping his arms around her waist and rolling her onto her back. Staring down at her, Grant knew without a doubt, he couldn't let go of this woman. He would have to find a way to make his future work *with* her.

His thoughts about his career vanished as Bethany moved her hands over him. They were everywhere and he was desperate to touch her, to taste her again, but he didn't want them to rush this. He took her hands in his, lacing their fingers, and brought her hands to either side of her head, bending to sip from her lips. Her hips bowed into him and, as much as could understand the hunger driving her, he wasn't letting anything, not even desire, steal this precious moment from either of them.

He let go of her hands, letting his fingertips graze over her arms and to her breasts swelling over the top of her bra. Grant flipped the clasp in the front, releasing them to his gaze. She was as close to perfection as was possible. His hands covered her, feeling the tight buds pressing into his palms as she arched into his touch. He watched as she closed her eyes, her breath ragged as she gave herself to every caress, sending his senses reeling. Grant bent forward, his mouth replacing one hand and she cried out.

The sounds of the outdoors stilled, as if even nature understood the reverence of this moment between the two of them. Unbuttoning her jeans, Grant hooked his fingers into the material at her hips and slid the denim down her thighs, catching her underwear and following with his mouth, pressing hot, wet kisses over her flesh. He covered every inch of her, from her hips to the delicate curve of her ankles, and back up again, searching for and finding every caress that would make her gasp with hungry desire.

His thumb found the center of her pleasure as his lips caressed her inner thigh, moving higher. Covering her with his mouth, Grant worshiped her with his lips, tongue and hands. Bethany's hands fisted the covers of the bed, her body writhing beneath him.

"Grant," she managed through clenched teeth. "Please."

He slid a finger into her, slowly, watching her eyes fly open in wonder as her entire body quaked, her release gripping them both and she cried out his name. Grant took her to new heights, lifting her to crest the waves of her rapture until she came back down, lying satiated and weak beneath him. Pressing gentle kisses over her stomach, he slid up her body, smiling as she sighed with gratification. He swirled his tongue around a tight nipple, sucking gently, and she laughed quietly as her body trembled in sensual response.

"I can't move," she whispered, her fingers knotting in his hair, pulling him toward her for a kiss he was happy to provide.

He couldn't get enough of her, the scent of her surrounding him, the taste of her still on his lips, the feel of her hands on his feverish skin. It was intoxicating.

Her fingers moved over the button of his jeans, sliding the zipper down and lingering over the evidence of his desire beneath. Sliding out of them quickly, Grant plucked the package from his pocket before kicking the pants aside. As he moved to lie beside her, she reached for him, her fingers wrapping around his length, and he thought he'd explode. Gritting his teeth, Grant stilled her hand.

"Not this time. I want you too much. I can't." The words were barely coherent but they were the best he could manage. "I need you, Bethany."

Her smile, the dazzling joy in her eyes, could light up an entire room. "Good, then I'm not the only one who feels this way." She sat up, taking the package from his fingers, and tore it open.

Grant thought he would die before she sheathed him. The mere act nearly driving him over the edge of sanity as she slowly ran her hands over him, touching him, stroking him as he throbbed in her hand. He groaned as she gave him what he needed, pressing her body against his, cradling him in her curves. His body begged for release as it nudged the entrance to her heat.

"Bethany," he whispered on a pained sigh. She moved her hands to his shoulders, then let one hand glide over his hip to press him closer.

"Please, Grant."

He couldn't wait any longer. Grant clenched his jaw, holding back the desire to plunge into her as he moved with devastatingly torturous slowness. Bethany arched her hips as he filled her, inching forward to create the rhythm that would ignite them both.

Her nails dug into his back, biting into the flesh, and he fought to maintain control as her body wrapped around his, urging him to join her. She wrapped her legs around his hips as her body trembled around him and he could feel his body answering, tightening, coiling, before letting go. He buried himself into her, carrying them both to the pinnacle. Grant lost his ability to think as her body urged his, riding the throes of their desire, taking him to the edge before he leapt over with her.

Bethany wrapped her hands around his face and

dragged him down to her, pressing her lips against his, seeking his heat as their mouths fused. Still buried within her, he rolled onto his back, taking her with him, breaking their kiss. She tucked her head between his neck and shoulder. Grant trailed his fingers down her spine, unable to deny himself the pleasure of touching her, and felt himself grow hard again. This woman was going to be the slow, very pleasurable death of him.

"Grant?" She said his name on a sweet sigh of breath, heating his chest, her hands curling against him.

"Hmm?" He wasn't ready for this moment to end, wasn't ready to return to reality, where she had a little boy waiting for her return and he had decisions waiting to be made.

"Do we really have to go back?"

"Not until you decide you want to." His fingers trailed over her shoulder. "We can stay as long as you like."

She curled into him. "Then I want to lie here and watch the stars come out with you."

He tipped his head down, inhaling the scent of her, letting his arms tighten around her. He didn't want to let go, wanted to stay like this with her all night. Hell, he'd stay like this with her forever if he could.

He couldn't help but feel as if he'd just stepped into new territory, as if Bethany and James had permanently marked him as theirs, rather than the other way around. James' big blue eyes filled his mind and he couldn't help but smile at the way the boy had so matter-of-factly asked if Grant would be his new dad.

He sighed with pleasure. "I'd love to, and we certainly

The frown was back on James' face as he searched Grant's eyes for some sort of explanation. *When are you coming back?* he signed.

Grant wanted to promise the boy he'd return soon, that he'd see him next week, that he wasn't leaving for good, but it could all be lies and would only hurt James more than the simple truth.

I don't know, he signed back. "As soon as I can, but it might be a while."

James took several deep breaths. Grant saw his little chest hitch and he caught the way his mouth turned down as James tried not to cry. A knot lodged in his throat, choking him from saying anything more, and he tugged the little boy into his arms. James buried his face into Grant's neck, wrapping his arms around it and squeezing tightly, as if he feared letting go would mean that Grant would disappear. Bethany took a step forward and laid her hand on James' back before circling her arms around them both. The three of them remained like that, clinging to one another as James' tears burned Grant's skin, scalding him, scarring him, the same way Bethany's had the day before.

Grant pressed a quick kiss to Bethany's temple. "What do you say we play a little catch before you have to go home, James?" The boy hesitated a moment, as if unsure he could even let go of Grant long enough to play.

James nodded but looked to his mother, his eyes begging her to change Grant's mind. It was almost enough to make Grant cancel his doctor appointment and meetings altogether. Almost.

can, but I think there's a little boy who'd be jealous."
Grant felt her tense against him and regretted his words.

"You're right." She lifted her chin to meet his gaze.

"I didn't mean we should leave now."

She pressed her hand against his chest and sat up. "I know you didn't, but we shouldn't stay too long."

Grant could feel her withdrawing from him, pulling away and trying to hide. He could feel her retreating but he wasn't sure how to stop it. Rather than fight her instincts, he decided it would be better to let her have some space, a moment to gather herself.

"I'll be right back."

Grant went into the bathroom and cleaned himself up before coming back out. She'd pulled the sheet around her but she hadn't left the bed. At least she wasn't running that far away. Grant slid in beside her and pulled her close, curling his body around her back. She let him but he could feel the tension in her, as if there was a wall between them again. Somehow, he had to break it down once and for all.

"Bethany, we need to talk."

"No, Grant. We don't."

That wasn't what he'd expected her to say. He needed her to understand how he felt about her. They still needed to talk about what might come next, where he hoped this relationship would lead from this point forward. "Yes, we do," he said against the back of her shoulder, his lips grazing the side of her neck. "I'm not letting you out of this bed until we do."

She didn't face him but he felt some of the rigidity

leave her spine and she laid her fingers over his forearm around her waist. Her touch ignited the deep yearning in him again. Grant's hand found the curve of her breast, his thumb brushing over a taut peak.

"I have an appointment with my doctor on Monday."

"That's what you said before." She sounded uncertain, as if unsure why he was telling her his plans.

"I'll be flying out to Memphis tomorrow night after you and James leave the ranch."

She stiffened. "For how long?"

His lips found the hollow at the base of her ear. "I'm not sure. It depends on what they say. If they clear me, I hope to be back playing as soon as possible." Grant felt her entire body coil with apprehension. "It probably won't be with Mustangs though." Time stopped while he waited for her response.

"And if they don't clear you?" she whispered.

He shrugged. "I don't know. I've been offered a great position as a commentator with a network." She didn't ask where and he wasn't sure how to tell her it was most likely going to be in New York. "I'll come back, Bethany."

"But you don't know when or how often or for how long," she supplied. "In the meantime, I'll just be Grant McQuaid's part-time fling?"

He moved so she could lie on her back. He wanted to see her face, to look into her eyes. "It's not like that, Bethany. Not for me."

"Are you sure?"

She was trying to sound confident, as if it didn't matter what people thought but he could hear the hesitancy in her voice, the hurt in her tone. He didn't miss the way her eyes misted over, or the way she bit the corner of her lower lip. As much as he wanted to convince her of how special she was to him, he wasn't sure anything he said would be enough.

Grant brushed his lips over hers. "I'm sure. I have never felt like this for a woman before. You and James are everything to me."

"Would you stay if I asked?"

Grant felt his entire body tense as he processed her question, trying to run through every scenario in a split second. It all came down to one simple fact—he loved her. The rest of it was just semantics.

"Yes."

Bethany rolled over, their legs intertwining. Their bodies pressed together and she laid her palm over his cheek. Tears shimmered in her eyes. "Grant, I would never ask you to. I've always known deep down that you would have to leave. It's your career and it's not in you to give up without seeing it through entirely. It's okay."

She sought his mouth, silencing the protests that would have been excuses.

"I'm just grateful for what we've already had, what you've already reminded me of."

"What's that?"

"That the gift of having is far more beautiful than the pain of losing."

There was nothing he could say to deny what he knew in his heart, what even Bethany realized. He *had* to leave, if only for closure. For the first time, he hoped that the doctors *wouldn't* clear him. He loved Bethany too much to ask her to wait, to face the life of a football "widow" and until he knew what came next, his life was too uncertain for him to promise her any more. But he'd always faced his career with a single-minded focus. Now that focus would mean coming up with some sort of plan before he returned. In the meantime, he would show her how he felt about her.

Grant lifted Bethany over him, burying his hands into her hair and stealing her gasp of surprise with his kiss. He might not be able to admit that he loved her yet but he would make sure she felt his love before he left.

GRANT DOZED WITH her head on his chest, his heart beating steadily in her ear as her fingertips brushed over the flawless perfection of him. As much as she wanted him to stay, for them to stay this way, she should wake him so they could get back to James waiting at the house. Back to the reality that would crush this euphoria. Back to the real world that was going to snatch him away from her.

Her heart ached but Bethany didn't feel any regret in spite of the pain she knew would come. Grant had taught her to trust again, both in herself as a mother and as a woman. He'd taught her to love again, and that, even when it hurt, the loving was worth it.

And she loved him.

There was no doubt about that fact. He'd somehow wiggled past her every defense and stolen her heart completely. Maybe it had been when he showed up at the school to see James, or the way he'd helped James learn to stand up for himself, or the simple fact that he saw beyond the surface of both of them. She'd fallen in love with a man who'd cared for her *and* her son.

But she would keep that information to herself because that would cross the line. Telling him would force Grant to make a decision she couldn't ask him to make. She wouldn't ask him to stay. If Grant decided to stay with a team, or to take this job he was offered, she didn't want to hold him back, even if it meant losing him. That wasn't fair to any of them. He would only end up resenting her and James in the end.

However, if they could part on good terms, they could still be friends and maybe, she prayed, James wouldn't be as hurt. If they were still on good terms, Grant would stay in touch and call or visit James whenever he came through town. It would have to be enough.

Who's using James now?

She wasn't, not really, but she couldn't deny that she wanted to remain connected to Grant, somehow, no matter how bittersweet it would be. The reality of their situation was that he was leaving and was likely to be so busy soon that he would forget about both her and James in the bustle of his busy career, whichever path he chose. She didn't doubt his feelings for either of them, but he'd laid out his two options for his future and he'd never suggested they join him.

She pictured the face of her beautiful, wide-eyed son. She'd poured every waking moment of the last six years of her life into him, adored him beyond belief, but Grant had come along and poked a hole in the bubble she'd created around them both. She thought she'd been enough for him and he'd been enough to complete her, but they were both missing a vital part. Grant had filled that void without really trying and now she wasn't sure how she was going to go back.

How was she going to explain to James that Grant was leaving and she didn't know when or if he was coming back because she didn't even have an answer?

Hot tears burned in her eyes, sliding over the bridge of her nose to fall on his chest.

"Honey, don't." Grant's thumb brushed the trail her tears had created.

"I'm sorry." She didn't want him to see her cry, not after her confident words. Not after the tender way he'd made love to her a second time. She swiped at the tears, blinking them back. "I'm just going to miss you."

"You don't have to." She lifted her gaze, praying he couldn't see the hope that his words caused to flare in her. "What if you and James came with me?"

"What? He has school."

"We'll get him a tutor, or you could teach him." His fingers played over her shoulders sending tingles of longing down her spine as he brushed her hair away from her neck. "We could travel and he could come to games. We'd be together."

She let herself bask in his offer for a moment, to relish the idea of being with Grant, for just a little longer. As much as she hated to admit it, Bethany knew it wouldn't work. James needed stability, *she* needed stability, and traveling across the country to games, watching him play, being an accessory, wasn't a life she could manage for her or her son. She'd had enough difficulties facing the newspaper articles here in town, she couldn't imagine dealing with the national news media. As much as she wanted to accept Grant's offer, she knew it would never work.

Grant sighed, as if he'd come to the same realization. He pressed a kiss to her forehead. "Will you let me tell him?"

She'd spent so many years protecting James from being hurt that her natural instinct was to say no, but James needed to hear the truth from Grant. They'd built a relationship apart from her and she had to trust that Grant wouldn't hurt her son.

"But don't do it until tomorrow. Let him enjoy tonight with you."

Grant's face was grim as he nodded and she was sorry that she'd broken the spell he'd woven around them with her pathetic tears. "We should head back."

She barely managed the words without crying because the sooner they returned to the ranch, the closer she was to Monday and Grant's departure.

"In a second," he said, winding his arms around her tightly, pressing their bodies together so closely they were practically one. "I want to hold you just a little longer."

Chapter Twenty-Two

GRANT AWOKE WITH a sense of dread building in the pit of his stomach. It had begun yesterday when he'd asked Bethany to come with him. He hadn't even meant to make the request. He had no business asking her to follow him when he had no idea where he was even going. What kind of life was that to offer her? But once the words had slipped from his lips, he knew he wanted her to say yes more than he wanted his next breath.

She'd made the right decision, both for James and herself. He knew that, so he hadn't brought it up again, but the hollow ache had started building immediately. The same hollow ache he'd once felt at the thought of losing football.

When he'd taken that last hit, he'd known something was wrong. When he couldn't jump back up the way he usually did, when the dizziness wouldn't quite clear and the ringing in his ears wouldn't go away, he'd known. The thing with football was that even when you got hurt, you played through it. Every player knew that. The same way they knew that there were only so many hits you could take before you're through—you just don't know that number until it arrives.

In spite of what he'd tried to convince everyone else of over the past three months, and what he'd tried to convince himself of, he had a suspicion that he'd taken the last hit he was going to be able to physically take without permanently damaging his body. Later tonight, he was boarding a plane to find out just how true that suspicion might be.

But it wasn't just the possible end of his career that had him on edge, it was what that end might signify. Regardless of what the doctor said, he was standing on the precipice of a new beginning—he could start over, either with one of a few options for his career or with a woman who made him feel more alive than did a game that had been his life for almost twenty-five years. But he still hadn't figured out a way to have both.

Grant had to either cut himself off from football or from Bethany and James. As he watched them walking toward him, he felt the emptiness spread through him at the thought of telling them both goodbye, even temporarily.

"Grant!" Little legs pumped quickly as James ran to him, throwing his arms around Grant's legs. He scooped James into his arms and tossed him into the air, catching him easily before holding him in one arm and wrapping the other around Bethany.

He knew he probably shouldn't pull her close, knew it might make James question their relationship, but he needed to touch her, needed her presence to ground him and give him the strength for what he was about to say. He tried to paste a bright smile on his face.

"You ready to go for a walk before you head home?"

"Aw." James pouted slightly. *I don't want to go*, he signed, as if saying the words were too difficult.

"Not just yet, but soon," Bethany promised. "We'll go for a walk and you guys can play catch for a few minutes." Bethany's voice seemed too controlled and Grant couldn't bear the finality in her tone. "But first we should go say goodbye to Shorty."

The three of them walked to the pen where the pony lazily grazed. As soon as he saw the three of them approach, he nickered quietly and walked to the fence for attention.

"He's going to miss me," James stated confidently. "We need to come visit him a lot more, Mom."

Bethany gave Grant a watery smile at James' childish simplicity.

"You can come visit Shorty whenever you want. You and your mom are always welcome to drop in here."

"Mrs. Sarah and Ms. Maddie told me that too." James beamed up at him.

Grant glanced at Bethany and could see the tears misting her eyes. He wasn't sure whether they were tears of sorrow or joy but, assuming she felt even close to the way he did, they were both. She nodded at him slightly and he knew the moment had come for him to tell James about his departure.

"Hey, James." Grant squatted onto the balls of his feet so that he was nearly eye level with the boy he'd come to care so deeply about in a very short time. "You know it's almost time for spring training to start."

"I don't know what that is," he informed Grant, not even looking away from Shorty as he pet him through the fence. "But Grandpa asked me if you were going."

"When did Grandpa ask you that?" Bethany sounded concerned.

"The last time I talked to him, before we came here. He said spring training was starting soon and Grant would have to go unless he was too hurt." He turned to face Grant and laid a hand on his shoulder, a look of concern far too wise for a six-year-old boy on his face. "I hope you're not hurt."

"That's actually what I wanted to talk to you about." A frown marred the boy's brow and Grant knew he'd do almost anything to wipe it away. "I have to go on a plane later today to see what the doctors say, to see if I'm too hurt to play football anymore. I might be gone for a while."

"My doctor appointments take a long time too." James sighed and rolled his eyes as Grant looked to Bethany for confirmation.

"He means his audiologist and the surgeon," she explained. "Baby, Grant has to go all the way back to Memphis, where Grandma and Grandpa are, to see his doctors and hopefully, if he's not hurt, then he'll start playing football again."

BETHANY STARED BACK at Grant through the windshield of her car as she backed out of the driveway of his parents' ranch. With his hand raised, James had waved goodbye but Bethany hadn't been able to do anything except think back over the past weekend, wishing that she could have done something differently, something that might have made Grant want to stay. Driving her sleeping son to their empty house, Bethany was greeted by nothing but silence and it was deafening.

This is who he is.

She'd known it from the first time she'd met him but that didn't stop her heart from coming up with what-if scenarios to torture her. Nothing had shredded her heart the way James' silent tears had during the ride home. She'd never been so grateful as she was when her son had finally fallen asleep in the back seat. Even then, the trail of silver tears lining his cheeks and the little hiccups as his heart continued to break, even in slumber, shattered hers. She tried to stop the regrets from choking her, threatening to drown her.

She'd meant what she'd said when she told Grant that their time together was worth every bit of the pain losing him would cause, but that didn't lessen the hurt. And it didn't make her feel less guilty about James' suffering now.

She pressed the heel of her palm against the left side of her chest, where her heart used to reside. What she hadn't expected was that this didn't just hurt—it was agonizing.

Pulling the car into the garage, she pressed the button to close the door and unclipped James from his car seat.

Scooping his little body into her arms, she carried him into the house and slid him into his bed, removing the microphones and batteries. She brushed her fingers over the hair hanging into his face. At least he was peaceful for now, but tomorrow would bring new difficulties for him as he tried to return to life without Grant. She slid the sheets over his shoulders.

"Who are you kidding?" she whispered in the darkness. "You're going to miss him even more than James will."

Bethany heard the faint sound of her ring tone from the phone still in her car and hurried back to get it out of her purse, hoping it was Grant. She reached for the phone in the cup holder in time to see that it was only her mother.

She'd call her back. She couldn't talk to anyone right now.

Wandering into the kitchen, she dropped her purse on the counter as the cell phone vibrated in her hand, notifying her of a text message.

Just got to the airport. I'll call when I get to Memphis.

She stared at the screen for a few moments, waiting to see if he was going to text more. When he didn't, she typed her reply. *Have a safe trip. I'll talk to you soon.*

There was so much more she wanted to add to the message. A heart and an *I love you*, but she was afraid to say more. She didn't want to lay any more expectation in his lap when he had enough to worry about. She carried her phone into her room and sat on the edge of her bed, hoping he would text again but not surprised when he didn't. He had an important appointment tomorrow and needed to mentally prepare.

Minutes ticked by and she looked around her room. It was funny how it hadn't reminded her of Grant until now, when he was no longer there and the likelihood of his coming back was slim. She tossed the phone aside and curled up on the bed, pulling her knees to her chest, clinging to a pillow. She barely felt the tears as they started to slide down her cheeks. All she knew was that the pillow she clung to still smelled like the lingering scent of Grant's cologne, haunting her, reminding her of how close she'd come to having the man of her dreams.

And how she'd just lost him.

GRANT GLANCED AT his watch as he hailed a taxi outside the terminal doors. What should have been a seven-hour trip had turned into a nightmarish twelve hours, most of it stuck up in the air, thanks to a storm in Chicago. He'd be lucky to check into the hotel and get a shower before he had to leave for his ten a.m. physical with his doctors. He was tired, hungry and the only place he really wanted to be right now was lying in a bed with Bethany in his arms.

Loading his suitcase into the trunk of the cab, he gave the driver the address of the hotel he'd booked for the night. He'd subleased his condo when he'd left and the lease wasn't up for another two weeks, when spring training was set to begin. He probably should have just canceled the hotel room since he didn't have time to use the bed he was dying to crawl into. He'd tried to sleep on the plane but images of Bethany and James kept him awake cursing his decision, making him wonder what was keeping him from just turning his back on this ridiculous fantasy of playing ball again.

Tearful blue eyes filled his mind. The sorrow he'd caused James and Bethany ate at him and Grant knew this misery he was feeling was only a portion of the punishment he deserved.

Arriving late had its benefits, and Grant was able to check into his room quickly, tossing his bag onto the bed and turning on the shower. He rubbed his eyes, exhausted, but knew he didn't have time to give in to the weariness that threatened to overtake him. Instead, he prepared coffee in the small pot provided by the hotel. It wasn't the most appealing option but perhaps a little caffeine would give him enough of a jolt to keep his system functioning long enough to fake his way through this appointment. He stripped his clothing off, tossing it on the foot of the bed before opening the bathroom door, letting the steam pour from the room, invading his lungs. He stood under the scalding water, praying it would burn away the memories of stubborn hazel eyes that refused to ask him to stay.

Grant ran his hands through his hair, lathering it with shampoo and scrubbing roughly, trying anything that might rid his mind of the vision of Bethany lying in his arms. He'd been a fool to believe he could hold her, make love to her and leave. With the way he'd grown closer to her each day, he should have known that one time with her would never be enough. Even now, he would give anything to walk away—from the doctors, the game and his future in football—get back on a plane and return to her.

The sound of the alarm on his phone jerked him from reliving the fantasy of his afternoon with Bethany. He'd set the alarm early this morning when he'd been stranded in Chicago waiting out the storm and he realized there was going to be little opportunity for sleep. He'd wanted to make sure he didn't miss his appointment. The more he thought about it, the more he didn't really care if he made it, other than the fact that missing it meant he'd given up.

And that one fact was what was holding him back. He'd never been a quitter. Bethany had basically said the same and he'd loved her even more for recognizing the reality of the man he was. In his eyes, quitting was more than just weakness, it was something he knew he could never do and maintain any respect for himself. If he couldn't respect himself, he couldn't ask Bethany to respect him.

Rinsing quickly, he wrapped a towel around his hips and dug a pair of exercise pants and a t-shirt from his bag, not even bothering to shave. He quickly brushed his teeth and tossed a change of clothing into a small bag. Pouring a coffee into the to-go cup in the room, he grabbed it, his wallet and room key before rushing down to the lobby.

As soon as he reached the ground floor, Grant realized he'd left his phone charging on the nightstand. The clock over the concierge's desk reminded him that he only had twenty minutes to get across town for his physical. He didn't have time to wait for the elevator to head back to the room.

Damn it.

He was going to have to wait to call Bethany after his meeting. Grant prayed she was too busy with the kids at work today to even notice. "Excuse me, can you call a cab to pick me up?"

"Right away, Mr. McQuaid."

"Thank you," he muttered, heading out to the sidewalk in front of the hotel.

It wasn't unusual for people in Memphis to recognize him and, normally Grant was flattered, but today it was just a reminder of what was at stake with this doctor's appointment, as well as everything he was placing at risk if he didn't give it everything he had. Grant rubbed a hand at the back of his neck, unsure why he wasn't feeling more optimistic about today's outcome. He'd worked, sweated and literally bled for this moment for the last three months.

Maybe it was because, regardless of the outcome, he was going to lose something he loved.

Chapter Twenty-Three

BETHANY WOKE SLOWLY, dragging herself from sleep, rubbing at her eyes. They felt heavy, gritty, and it took her a moment to remember why. Before her grief could take root too deeply, James appeared at her doorway, rubbing his eyes.

"Mom?" His voice was thick with sleep and still groggy.

Crap! It's Monday.

Bethany reached for her cell phone to see the battery dead after she'd dropped it on her bed, waiting for a text from Grant. She bolted down the stairs to look at the clock on the stove. Sure enough, the clock made it clear they were running late. Insanely late.

She ran back up the stairs and into James' room, pulling clothes from his drawer and shuffling him into the bathroom. Bethany washed his face quickly, tugging his t-shirt over his head and signing to him to finish dressing because they were late. As he dressed, she grabbed his earpieces and slid the battery packs onto his arms. She hated having to rush him out of his world of silence but they weren't just a little late, they were an hour late.

"Baby, I'm going to have to make you peanut butter and you can eat it in the car, okay? We're really, really late."

I don't want to go to school, he signed.

"What's wrong? Is it your stomach?" Bethany automatically pressed the back of her fingers against his forehead, testing for a temperature.

James ducked his head. "No," he mumbled. When he looked up, she could see the tears welling in his eyes.

"Oh, baby, come here."

Bethany held out her arms and he threw himself into them. It didn't take much for her to know that this had far more to do with Grant's leaving than it did a virus. She held him as his tears slid over his cheeks, pooling on the shoulder of the t-shirt she'd fallen asleep in. She leaned back to look him in the eye.

"What do you think about taking a mental health day today?" His forehead knitted as he frowned. "It's where you forget about all the things that are making you feel sick or sad, and you watch movies and eat ice cream all day," she explained.

James gave her a single shoulder shrug. She'd hoped for a more enthusiastic reaction but it would have to do.

"Why don't you go take a bath and I'll bring in the bubbles after I call the school to let them know we aren't going to be there today, okay?"

His lower lip stuck out but he nodded.

It was a start and that was what they both needed. To simply keep putting one foot in front of the other until it became natural again, even if it meant moving forward without Grant.

"GRANT, HAVE A SEAT."

After all the testing they'd put him through, he should be glad they'd even allowed him time to shower afterward. Not that he'd had much of an opportunity to stop since he'd arrived almost five hours ago. Between the blood work and the fitness testing, this was the first time he wasn't being poked, prodded or attached to some kind of machine. Oddly enough, even with his lack of sleep, the realization that the time had come to finally get some answers had him wired and unable to sit still.

"You okay?"

"I'm good. I *feel* good." Grant didn't want to sound overeager but he felt like he was in the best physical shape he'd been in for more than three years. "So what's the verdict?"

Dr. Grady glanced in the folder in front of him, flipping through a few pages before he folded his hands over it and sighed. "Grant, I know you feel like you could climb a mountain. In fact, *that* you could probably do. But I just don't feel that your body can take the strain of another season. You've had several concussions in the past year, too many. The brain can only take so many hits before it begins to show signs of chronic traumatic encephalopathy. Even if you don't have signs of CTE now, who knows what will show up in the future? Not to mention that the C5 and C6 vertebrae are showing some deterioration of the disc. You probably remember that these are the two vertebrae we were most concerned with during your last injury."

Grant knew what was coming. He'd known it before he'd flown to Memphis. He should have saved them all the time and just stayed home with Bethany, not put everyone through the torment. "So what are you saying, Doc?"

"In a nutshell, you're finished with football, Grant. It's time to retire and move on to the next chapter of your life."

Grant's jaw jutted slightly as he tried not to clench it. The doctor tried to make the future sound great, and it might have worked if he had a next chapter to begin but, in reality, Grant had nothing to build a life on save a few side investments and an offer from a network.

You have Bethany. Go home.

The image of his beautiful Bethany filled his mind, his arms aching to hold her. But what good was he to her or James now? Unemployed and, other than the job in New York, unemployable unless he wanted to mentor rookies on his old team in hopes it might turn into a coaching job one day. He had his business degree but he'd never planned on doing anything with it because there had only been one profession on his mind, and now that was being stripped away from him. Bethany and James needed a man who could provide for them, a man who could take care of them, not a has-been with nothing to offer. He didn't even have his own place to stay unless it was a canvas tent in the foothills.

Grant ran a hand through his hair. "So you won't clear me to play?"

He knew there was no real point in asking but the words slipped out anyway. He wasn't sure what else to say, which way to turn, as his world seemed to crash in on itself.

"As your doctor, I can't recommend that you play. I doubt the team doctors will see it any differently, but you're welcome to see them instead and try. But, Grant, as your friend, I'm telling you not to do this. You take many more hits like you did last season and I don't see those vertebrae holding up. It would only take getting hit once, or landing the wrong way, and you could be paralyzed. It's too risky."

Grant rubbed his fingers and thumb over his chin. "Life is risky," he pointed out. "The same thing could happen on a horse at my parents' ranch."

"True, but how often have you fallen off a horse and taken a hard hit to the head the way you do in football, day in and day out? Is it something you do every single day?"

Grant knew there was no arguing, cajoling or begging that was going to change this situation. He'd suspected this was going to be the outcome but to hear the words finally spoken, to know with absolute certainty that his career was over when he still felt in his prime, was devastating.

"Grant, you've got a lot ahead of you." Dr. Grady

cocked his head to one side, as if trying to read Grant's expression. "This is a setback, but you are the most tenacious man I've ever met. Take some time and think about what you really want to do with the rest of your life. Then go do it."

This coming from a man who didn't have the same statistics at his disposal that Grant did. He knew most retired football players ended up bankrupt, that most ended up with broken bodies and empty pocketbooks. For all the media hype about million-dollar contracts, most players never saw the pot of gold at the end of the rainbow, either because of injury, poor money management or corruption within the system. He'd taken a few steps to make sure that didn't happen to him but, unfortunately, those few investments weren't enough to create the future he wanted with Bethany and James now and he was at a loss as to which way to turn now.

BETHANY SLID HER phone out of her desk drawer as Julie led twenty-five Kindergarten students out to recess. It had been two days since she'd gotten the initial message from Grant telling her he'd call. Tapping the screen, she searched for a text message that she knew wasn't there. She checked her voice mail again, even though her phone didn't show any missed calls. He hadn't called, nor had he send a message by text, email or carrier pigeon.

Face it, Bethany, you've been blown off.

It was just as likely he was busy. She was trying to stay positive, to trust the man she had met here in Hidden

Falls and ignore the speculations being thrown around in Memphis on television. But it wasn't easy when her father called demanding to know the latest information about Grant McQuaid's rumored retirement. It hadn't gone over well when she told him that she honestly had no idea about what he had planned, nor did it keep her father from asking if he needed to hunt the man down while he was in town. Obviously both of her parents could see the writing on the wall faster than she had—if she didn't know about his retirement decision, she wasn't as close to Grant as she'd thought she was.

If he loved you, he'd have told you his plans, talked them over with you.

She scrolled through the text messages on her phone again.

"Nothing yet?"

Bethany nearly dropped the phone when she saw Steven standing in the doorway. She slid her cell back into her desk and rose, smoothing her maxi skirt over her thighs. "Sorry, I should have gone out there with you guys and not stuck you with all the kids."

Steven raised a hand. "It's fine, Bethany. I'm not completely heartless. I could see you were upset when you got here this morning. It didn't take a brain surgeon to put that together with the fact that neither you nor James was here yesterday, the same day that McQuaid left town. Are you okay?"

Bethany took a deep breath, willing the lump in her throat to go away as she bit the corner of her lower lip to make it happen. "Yeah."

A one-word answer was the best she could manage.

He sat on the corner of the kids' table in front of her desk. She followed suit and leaned back against the edge of her desk with her hands behind her, needing something solid to cling to right now since everything else in her life seemed to have been turned on its head. She wasn't sure Steven was the best person to confide in right now, especially considering she'd turned down a second date with him to be with Grant, but she really needed a friend right now.

"You don't sound sure. What about James?"

"We'll both be fine. I mean, it's stupid really." She let go of the table and crossed her arms over her chest. "It's not like we were dating for months, right?"

Steven shrugged slightly. "Rejection always stings a little."

Guilt circled her, the way a storm comes in, rolling in waves. "Steven, I never meant to—"

"Bethany, don't. It's okay. That's not what I meant. This isn't about us—this is about you and James." He stood up and reached for her arm. "I just want you to know that if you need a friend, or if James wants a guy to hang out with, I'm happy to be there for both of you." His lips quirked to one side. "I mean, I'm no Grant McQuaid, but I might be able to teach James a few things besides football. I do play a pretty mean guitar."

Steven really was a kind man and he adored his students, treating them with a patient but firm hand. And the kids loved him for it. That and the comedic voices he was prone to ad lib for them. They might not have had the explosive attraction she felt with Grant, but Steven was here and Grant appeared to have forgotten her and James, walking away for something better.

Just like Matthew.

She forced her lips to smile, reminding herself that it wouldn't hurt to have a few friends she could count on, people who wouldn't leave.

"I'm sure he'd love that."

He let his hand slide down to meet hers and squeezed slightly when Bethany heard a knock at her open classroom door. She looked up to see Maddie and her heart tripped.

"We'll talk later," Steven murmured before turning to head out. "Hey, Maddie. How are you?"

"Good, you?" She smiled at him, but Bethany noticed it didn't quite reach her eyes and she wondered at the tension between them. Maddie walked up to Bethany and arched a brow as Steven headed out the door. "So the wolves are already circling, huh?"

"What?"

"Steven heard that Grant was gone and decided to see if he could move in." She jerked her chin back toward the door. "It was the same thing he did with me when I broke up with my ex. Steven's a nice guy, but he needs to stop trying to pick up the pieces for women unless he's satisfied with being the rebound guy."

"I don't think that's what he was trying to do." Bethany didn't mean for it to come out sounding bitchy, but Steven had called when he promised, unlike Maddie's brother. She moved around to the other side of her desk. "Is everything okay with James?"

Maddie nodded. "And I think we both know James isn't the reason I came." She crossed her arms over her chest, giving Bethany a pointed look.

Bethany sighed. "I'm not sure I can help you with anything else, Maddie. I don't *know* anything."

Maddie shook her head. "I'm coming by to help *you*, not the other way around. I wanted to let you know that we haven't heard from Grant either, Bethany. That means he's busy. Too busy to call."

Bethany frowned, clenching her teeth together so tightly she thought her jaw might break. Looking down, she saw she'd fisted her hands in her skirt and opened her fingers, releasing the tortured garment.

"What makes you think he hasn't called, or that I care?"

Maddie tipped her chin down and gave Bethany a dubious grin. "Because I saw the two of you together. The lovesick glances between the two of you were pretty hard to miss." Maddie stood up as the bell rang, signaling the end of recess. "Look, if it was me and the guy I was in love with was gone, I'd be worried. But I know my brother and he has a reason for not calling." Bethany opened her mouth to respond but Maddie held up a hand. "I don't know what his reason is but I know it's got to be good. He'll call as soon as he can. Just trust me. Please?"

Bitterness sliced into her, squeezing the air from her lungs and making it difficult to feel anything else, choking out the joy she'd felt with Grant. She almost wished he'd just said goodbye and been done with it. He'd said he didn't make promises he couldn't keep when that's all he'd done. He'd told her he'd call, promised he wouldn't hurt her. Why had she ever allowed herself to fall for a man she'd been certain would break her heart?

"I wish I could, Maddie, but unlike some people, I really don't make promises I can't keep."

GRANT SAT OUTSIDE the studio with his agent while the sports show looped on the television screens surrounding the room. How in the world had he ended up here even contemplating accepting this position on a trial basis? He glanced at Bob, seated next to him, fiddling with the diamond studded ring around his finger while they waited to meet with the executives to sign the short-term contract. Bob was the only reason he was here and that his retirement hadn't officially been announced yet. So far, the man had never steered him wrong in his career, and Grant was trusting him now more than ever.

But Bob didn't know about Bethany. Not that he'd have cared if he did.

Grant leaned over toward his agent. "You're sure about this? That this is the right direction for me to go."

Bob sighed and dropped his hands into his lap, glancing at the gold Rolex gracing his wrist. "For the fifth time in the last twenty minutes, yes. Will you relax?"

"I'm just not sure I'm 'on-air talent,' if you know what I mean."

Bob rolled his eyes. "Which is probably why they want you. You have this boyish, down-home-charm thing going for you. Guys all want to hang out with you and have a beer, but women want to be with you, period. It'll be good for their ratings and better for your career than being a babysitter for Wolf at some piddly bullshit salary. You're worth more than that, Grant, and these guys are willing to cough up."

"But what do I really know about being a commentator? You know I avoid the press as often as possible." Grant lifted his hand to run it through his hair and caught himself, letting it fall back into his lap.

"News flash, Grant, they aren't hiring you for your brains as much as they are for your looks. They want you to be yourself, that's what people like about you. When are you going to stop overthinking everything and realize that? I knew you were a good guy the first time I saw you play and you've only continued to prove it. People like you. Now's the time to capitalize on that charm instead of your athletic abilities."

The diamonds on Bob's watch glittered in the overhead lights. His ring practically winked at Grant as he sat, uncomfortable in his slacks and dress shirt. He tugged at the tie, wishing he could just take it off and hop back on a plane for Sacramento.

He knew he'd made Bob a lot of money. He wasn't even sure how much, but with this deal, according to Bob, they'd both be sitting pretty for a long time to come. And it was only a three-month trial. Surely he and Bethany could figure out how to manage a relationship, or come to a compromise, in that time. It wasn't perfect but it was the best option for them to make it work, somehow.

Grant would be one of four football commentators, spending several hours each weekend discussing game play and outcomes. He was the rookie of the group, the newly retired youngster, and likely the least qualified, but they'd handpicked him, certain he was the perfect man for the job. Grant wasn't nearly as sure. The only thing he was positive about was that he needed one hour to himself to get in touch with Bethany. The last few days had been nonstop flights, meetings and appointments. If Bob didn't have him schmoozing one person, they were in negotiations with another. He'd barely had eight hours' sleep in the last three days combined. He was exhausted, but he wasn't about to let another evening go by without calling Bethany. He needed to hear her voice.

She must be worried sick. He pulled out his phone to send her a quick text, to at least let her know he was still alive.

"Mr. Ribaldi, Mr. McQuaid, they're ready for you now." The secretary waited at the door to escort them inside.

Grant tucked his phone back into the pocket of his slacks as he rose. As soon as this meeting was finished, he was getting on the phone with her, he vowed.

Chapter Twenty-Four

GRANT STARED AT the three men seated across from him in awe. It wasn't often that he was starstruck, but two of the men across from him were Hall of Famers, his own idols. These weren't just men he looked up to but legends. Diondre Brown had been one of the best wide receivers to ever play the game of football and quarterback Michael Harvest had played in three Pro Bowls. Dale Scott had been heading up the show since its inception nearly six years ago. But all three insisted they needed new blood, someone who had a fresh take on the game and they were sure Grant was their guy.

Bob sat beside Grant, nodding his approval, reminding them of all of Grant's accomplishments, on and off the field. They looked impressed by his numerous records and accolades, but Grant couldn't help but wonder if any of it really mattered. These three men, along with the producer seated nearby in the shadows watching their chemistry quietly, were deciding his fate, and he was letting them. At any other time in his career, this might have been a dream come true, working with men he'd esteemed for years. But now, he was facing a catch–22.

He couldn't be the man he wanted to be, the man Bethany and James deserved, if he couldn't provide some sort of stability for them, but he couldn't be with them if he was here in New York permanently. Listening to the conversation around him, it wouldn't matter that he had a three-month trial contract. Once they had his signature, they weren't letting him go unless *they* decided it was best.

"So, Grant, how does it feel to be a free man again?" Diondre asked with a chuckle.

"To be honest, sir, I feel a bit at odds and lost. I keep thinking I need to hit the gym for a workout." The men around him laughed, with the exception of Bob who shot him a hard glare warning him to be more charismatic and less honest. "But I'm looking forward to facing the new challenge that television would offer."

Diondre glanced at Michael and laughed. "Yeah, I remember lying and saying the same thing."

"Oh, I know Grant pretty well," Bob said, interrupting, "and he's ready for this new experience."

Grant saw Dale glance at the producer in the shadows before giving a quick jerk of his head to one side. The producer, a tall man wearing ripped designer jeans and a polo shirt, rose and walked up to Bob.

"Why don't we go into my office and discuss the numbers while these four get to know one another?" he suggested.

Bob's grin spread and his brown eyes practically sparkled, making him look like an overgrown, slightly overweight child on Christmas morning. He squeezed his hand on Grant's shoulder, one last warning not to screw this up. "I think that's a great idea."

As the pair headed out, a door at the other end of the studio closed with a solid *clunk* and Dale rose, making his way to a table filled with catered food nearby. "I'm starving and we have a couple spots to film when we finish here. You don't mind if we eat, do you?" he asked Grant.

Grant shrugged and the other two rose, obviously relieved. "Here." Diondre held out a plate for him. "You too. We'll talk while we eat."

"Like you ever stop eating," Michael teased, smacking Diondre's flat stomach.

"Gotta keep my girlish figure."

They laughed together good-naturedly and Grant wondered if he was ever going to fit in. These three had been working together for five years, and Diondre and Michael had played together before that.

"So what's the real story, Grant?" Dale asked as he sat back down. "Because we all know you wouldn't be here if you could be on that field."

"Even if it does pay better and hurt a lot less." Michael grabbed a bottle of water from a cooler. He sat down with a faraway look in his eyes and a sigh of regret. "I'd give my right nut to be on that field for one more game."

"That's because you're single again," Diondre pointed out. "I don't think I'd go quite that far. My lady likes having me home every night."

They all turned to Grant expectantly, waiting for him to fill them in on the details of his departure. He wasn't sure how much he should tell them. Although the buyout of his contract had been finalized with the Mustangs yesterday, along with him turning down the position Wolf had offered, the news wasn't going public until their press conference tomorrow morning. It was also when he was supposed to announce his new position as a commentator.

What the hell? They'd know in a few hours anyway.

"Neck injury sidelined me and they bought out my contract at a fraction. They also wanted me to work with the rookies."

"Damn."

"That sucks," Michael sympathized.

"The same one that took you out last season? And then they offered you a pity position?" Dale asked. At Grant's nod, he sucked in a breath through clenched teeth. "So, that's how they ended up getting someone as young as you?" He shrugged. "Well, you're bound to help our ratings, that's for sure."

"Make way for the female viewers," Diondre predicted.

Grant didn't feel young. They were making him feel like he was a rookie out of college again instead of a grown man. And, honestly, he didn't like the idea of being thought of as nothing more than eye candy for women viewers.

"Not for this one," Dale said. "From what I hear, you're off the market now, right? Or was that just media hype?"

"What?" Grant frowned and wondered where Dale had gotten his information.

"Good, that means more ladies for me," Michael joked with a blast of laughter. The other men joined in, but Grant felt like he was missing the punchline. "So it's about the money for you?"

"No." Grant didn't want them to think he was only doing this for a paycheck.

Are they wrong?

If he was going to be completely honest with himself, he *was* simply entertaining this idea for the money it would provide. It was enough that he could not only replace the money he'd invested in his family but he'd be able to offer Bethany a future together, only in New York instead of Hidden Falls. Especially when she'd already said she wouldn't move. The idea wasn't setting well.

In fact, he felt sick to his stomach at the thought of sitting in the studio several days a week while Bethany and James were across the country. Even now, he was dying to get a message to her. How would it be for him not to see them for the next three months? Maybe longer.

"You don't want to be here, do you?" Dale eyed him speculatively. "Your agent told you to take this."

He wasn't asking and Grant felt the overwhelming urge to be completely honest with them. "Was this what you guys planned on doing afterward?"

Michael laughed, coughing as he tried to catch his breath. "Hell, no. I got lucky with this. After I blew out my knee, no one wanted to talk to me. It was like I'd just disappeared. It was tough for a while, living off what I'd saved up, and I'd been smart with my money. But people still wanted to get paid and the bills add up fast. When no one wants to hire you and there are no endorsement deals . . . well, the sharks come out when they smell blood in the water. But this guy," he said, jerking his thumb at Dale, "saw me at a charity event and hooked me up."

"He pulled me in too," Diondre said, throwing a head bob at Dale. "But I've heard it's not like that now. How many endorsements have you got lined up?"

"There are a few but they're pretty small. Everyone wants a QB," Grant admitted. "Bob thought this was a better path, more exposure and marketability."

Dale rolled his eyes toward Diondre and Michael, who nodded in agreement. "He would. Look, if this isn't where you *want* to be, at least four days a week for twelve to eighteen hours a day, don't take this gig. There are much easier ways for a guy like you to make a buck, Grant. You're going to get the endorsements and commercials coming in; you've got the look they want." He clapped a hand on Grant's shoulder. "I like you, so I'm going to be honest with you. I don't think this is the right fit for you. For us, sure. Your being on the show would help us out, but I'm don't think it would be mutual. You seem . . . I don't know. Torn, I guess."

Grant ran his index finger and thumb over his chin, waiting for Dale to say more. "Look, I'm a journalist first. I've read the papers and the gossip columns, but I've also been around this business a long time. If you've got some place better to be, where you want to be, go. The money will come to you. You're a smart guy. You'll figure it out, just like you did with the game."

Grant tipped his head at the man, curious. "I'm a fan," Dale admitted with a grin.

"Without a doubt," Michael agreed. "Besides, are you sure you want to hang around here talking nothing but football 24/7? These two get a bit trying." He jerked a thumb at Dale and Diondre.

"Only because we have to listen to you," Diondre said with a chuckle. "Seriously though, if you're unsure this is where you want to be, don't sign the contract. Negotiate it down for weekly guest spots or something. Then you're still in the limelight and good for our ratings. Besides, we'd love to hang with you."

"Guest spots." Grant hadn't even considered that option to be on the table. Hell, according to Bob, there hadn't really been *any* other options at all. Guest appearances would only mean a flight to New York and back. A weekend at most. He could bring Bethany and James with him.

"Now that's something we could manage." Dale grew excited, slapping his hand on his thigh. "Especially if you'd give us the first shot at talking with you after your retirement announcement." His voice grew more excited as he waved a hand in the air. "We could have the exclusive interview and air it right after the press conference."

"I think that's the kind of deal I've been looking for." It might not be seven figures but it was a plan he could work with.

"Good." He thrust his hand out toward Grant. "Then let's go get this contract rewritten and signed."

EXITING THE TERMINAL doors, Grant saw his sister standing alongside his Camaro. "I don't recall telling you to pick me up, and I know I didn't tell you to drive Betty." She unlocked the trunk, lifting it for him before she slapped the keys into his hand.

"Yeah? Well, I don't remember telling you to break the heart of one of my favorite kids, but you did that anyway, so what the hell?"

Grant frowned. He didn't have to ask who she was talking about, but it couldn't be anything that serious or deserving this kind of animosity from his baby sister. "Overdramatic much?"

Maddie shook her head and climbed into the car. "You think so? Maybe you should have called while you were gone."

"What are you talking about?"

He twisted the key in the ignition, feeling himself relax as the rumbling purr of the engine soothed his aggravated nerves. The flight had been jam-packed and, as his luck would have it, he was seated next to his "biggest fan" who talked nonstop and followed him through the terminal to their connecting flight. He'd caught a break when the man had received a phone call from his wife and Grant was able to sneak away. Now that he was back, he was looking forward to heading to Bethany's after a shower and some food to tell her the news.

"I'm talking about James and Bethany."

"I know that much." He rolled his eyes and pulled out of the airport, easing onto the highway. "I mean the calling part. I texted you guys."

"Did you call her? Or send her a text?"

"Before the press conference. I told her I had a surprise and I'd be home soon."

"Nice and vague." Maddie glared at him. "Did you tell her when 'soon' would be or that you were coming home for good? Because Steven Carter is already trying to move in on her."

Grant felt the jealousy rise up in his gut, squeezing at his chest. He'd deliberately avoided telling Bethany anything, avoiding calling once he'd made the deal with the show, and had texted her instead so that he could surprise her when he returned. They had so much to talk about, to figure out together, including how they could make their relationship work because he was determined to make sure it did. He might not have a traditional fulltime career at this point, but he had a direction and a contract and he was excited about starting.

Right after his press conference with the network, Grant received a phone call from the Hidden Falls high school principal and the sports director informing him that they were in dire need of a new varsity football coach. The pay was minimal but with his buyout, the guest spots on the show during football season and the two endorsement deals he'd signed, the salary didn't even deter Grant. It was the first time since he'd left his doctor's office that he felt excited about his future. He would be earning enough to support the ranch and still have plenty left to start a life with Bethany and James.

Plus the coaching position offered him a measure of satisfaction he'd been lacking. He would not only have free rein to hire his own coaching staff, but he'd be shaping the entire Hidden Falls football program for years to come and motivating the players of tomorrow to find the same love of the game he still carried.

And he could be near Bethany and James.

Every decision he'd made this past week had been with her and James in the forefront of his mind, to find a way that they could stay together. Now his sister informed him that she was already going out with someone else. Someone she'd hadn't even noticed until he'd opened his big mouth

"You need to talk to her. Just drop me off at home and go to her place."

He rubbed a hand over his weary eyes. "I've hardly slept in a week, Maddie. I need a shower and something to eat."

"Holy crap, Grant." She slapped his bicep. "Nut up and just go see her. I guarantee you'll be sorry if you don't."

"You kiss your mother with that mouth?" He arched a brow at her.

"Fine." She heaved an exasperated sigh. "If you want to make jokes, then fine. Lose the best thing that's come your way since your scholarship, but I'm not going to ride along while you do it. Just drop me off at the coffee shop and I'll get a ride from someone else."

"You're serious?"

"As a heart attack." She crossed her arms over her chest.

Grant wasn't in a mood to toy with her and play childish games. He pulled off the highway where it slowed through town and into the parking lot of the town's newest coffee shop. "There you go."

She opened the door and got out of the car. "You're an idiot, Grant."

"And you're a busybody just like the rest of the people in this town. Maybe you should just mind your own—"

Grant didn't want to believe it. Seated in the window on the coffee shop, he could see James bouncing happily on a stool beside his mother while Bethany laughed at something the person with her was saying. Seated across from her was Steven Carter. Maddie followed the direction of his gaze and planted her hands on her hips.

"Should I say 'I told you so' now or save it for later?"

Grant didn't think. He simply reacted, the way he'd done during every football game, letting instinct take over. Dropping the car into Park, he climbed out and stalked into the coffee shop, barely noticing that Maddie ran in behind him. Several sets of eyes turned in his direction, but the only person he saw was Bethany as he quickly closed the distance between them.

"Grant!" James slid down from the stool and ran to him, wrapping his little arms around Grant's legs. "Hi, Ms. Maddie. Are you going to have hot chocolate with us?" He waved excitedly.

Grant scooped James up in one arm and carried him back to the table, but he had his sights set on only one person, and she looked so shocked by his presence that she couldn't speak.

"Hello, Bethany." The icy tone in his voice matched

the frigidness of his heart as he nodded slightly to the other man. "Carter."

"McQuaid."

"Grant, what are you doing here? I didn't expect you to come back this soon." She gave him a hesitant smile and rose from the stool.

"I can see that."

"What does that mean?" Bethany took a step backward and Grant settled James on his stool again.

Carter chuckled from across the table. "I think what Grant's alluding to is that we are out together and he's interrupted us."

Grant glanced at James, still smiling, but the excitement in his face had dulled slightly and Grant could see the concern in the boy's eyes, as if he realized there was more to this situation than what he could understand. He didn't want to upset him, especially if he'd already been as upset as Maddie claimed he'd been.

"Something like that."

"Can we talk for a second?" Bethany reached a hand to his forearm, her fingers barely grazing his skin. He instantly felt his body respond to her touch, to the memory of the last time they were together and he cursed his weakness, jerking back.

"I don't know that we have anything to talk about."

She looked hurt by his reaction and, in reality, this was his own fault. He should have talked to her about their relationship and where he wanted it to go already, should have done more than just text her, but after the roller-coaster ride he'd been on the past week, he didn't have it in him to argue about semantics. He certainly didn't want to do it in front of an audience. Grant ran a hand through his hair.

"You know what, Bethany? Why don't you guys finish your . . . whatever this is," he said, waving his hand at their table, "and give me a call when you're done. We can talk then."

He turned and stormed past his sister through the coffee shop and headed for the door. He'd no more put his hand on it when Bethany's voice stopped him.

"I'll call you the way you called me."

Grant hung his head. Maddie was right; he should have called, and now he may have just lost the only chance he had because he'd let himself get too wrapped up in planning a future he wanted that he hadn't taken the time to stop and do the one thing that might have solidified it.

GRANT'S MAD? JAMES signed, his brow furrowed and his lips twisted to one side.

"No, sweetie. He's just . . . tired. It's been a long trip."

Bethany wasn't sure how to explain the situation to James, how to make him understand that this was nothing more than a complicated relationship between two adults, something he wouldn't understand until he was older.

In truth, she wasn't sure she understood why Grant was angry. He'd been the one to walk away, the one to not call and only text once, simply to tell her that he'd be in touch soon. She certainly hadn't expected "soon" to mean arriving home the next day, especially when every reporter speculating that his guest spot on the sports talk show was a trial run for a permanent position. She could only assume he'd made his decision and she and James weren't included in Grant's future plans.

"You want me to take you home?" Steven watched Maddie run after Grant, barely making it to the car in time to jump inside before he sped away, his tires spinning in the parking lot, kicking up gravel. "This wasn't exactly what I had in mind when I suggested coffee."

Bethany glanced at James. "I should probably get him home." She gave Steven an apologetic smile. "I'm sure there will be some questions." She glanced back at the window where they'd watched Grant's departure. "I'm sorry, Steven."

"Don't worry about it." He waved her off. "You ready to head home, James?"

"Can we go see Grant?"

Bethany scowled at her son, willing him not to bring up Grant again. "Maybe in a few days, after he's been able to get settled and rest up from his trip, okay?"

"Okay."

He sounded disappointed but he couldn't feel any more disillusioned than she did. The past week had been a hard lesson in getting her hopes up only to have them crushed like the gravel under the tread of Grant's spinning tires.

BETHANY HEADED BACK downstairs after almost an hour of *Where the Sidewalk Ends* in an attempt to make James laugh. Even that hadn't made him giggle the way it usually did, but they'd both been off this week. As much as she wanted to pretend that everything was fine, she didn't feel fine. Seeing Grant today had sent her senses skyward then plummeting, like they were free-falling. It was exactly what had happened when they'd been together. Their entire relationship was one exciting free fall, glorious in the highs and painful upon the crash-landing lows.

A quiet knock at the door had her pausing at the foot of the stairs. Butterflies took flight in her stomach as she moved closer to the door. Bethany knew exactly who it was without looking through the peephole. No one else would feel entitled enough to show up this late. She opened the door to find Grant leaning with both arms outstretched overhead, against the top of the door frame.

"What do you want, Grant? I don't have the energy to fight with you tonight." She turned away from the door. He could follow or not but she wasn't about to play games.

"I'm sorry." His voice was tight, hoarse, as if even uttering the words was painful.

She turned back toward him and crossed her arms over her chest to keep herself from reaching out to brush back the hair that had fallen over his forehead. He needed it cut and she desperately wanted to run her fingers through it, but the look on his face made it clear he wasn't hers to do that to any longer.

"Please, stop saying things you don't mean."

She left him standing in the entry and walked into the kitchen, wishing she'd bought the bottle of wine she'd been contemplating purchasing after she'd left the coffee shop, wanting something that might dull the ache in her chest that had taken up residence for the past week.

"Like how you're going to call or how much you care. I

don't need any more false promises. I'd much prefer your honesty to your flattery."

Grant's hands landed lightly on her hips, drawing her back toward him, against the hard wall of muscle, causing desire to ripple through her, making her shiver with want.

"Bethany," he whispered as he brushed her long hair to one side and pressed a kiss behind her ear.

She willed her body to remain rigid against him, to not give in to the yearning coursing through her veins, telling her to turn toward him and wrap her arms around his neck. That would only lead her back down the road she'd fought hard to move away from this past week, every day a battle to try to forget her feelings for Grant. Every ring of her phone agonizing when she realized it wasn't him.

"Don't," she pleaded. "I can't do this."

"I should have called you. I wanted to, but I barely found time to get the text to you as it was. And this is something we needed to discuss in person." His voice was raw, gritty and anguished. "I need you, Bethany."

She shook her head, letting it drop forward, away from the magic of his lips. "Needing, wanting . . . I have to think about what James needs, as well as what he wants. He needs a stable man in his life. You said so yourself."

"Someone like Steven Carter?" Bitter jealousy tinged his voice, making her wonder about the man in front of her, a man she suddenly didn't recognize.

"Steven and I are friends, nothing more." She turned to face him, pressing her palm against his chest to keep him at a distance. "But even if we were, *you* were the one who pushed that. You were the one who suggested I go out with him."

Grant backed up a step but she wasn't about to stop now that she'd begun letting the vulnerability of her emotions spill out. "You were the one who left, who walked away with vague promises. I was the one who had to face James' tears all week, to be the one to help heal his heartbreak at losing his hero."

"I went to find out what my future was going to hold, what I could manage to do if I couldn't go back to football."

"And now you know. Congratulations, you'll make a great commentator."

"I'm only doing that once a week, even less after football season."

Grant circled his fingers around her wrist and slid her hand off his chest, pulling her closer. Her heart leapt into her throat and she couldn't take a breath. As much as she didn't want to admit it, even to herself, Bethany wanted him to kiss her.

"Every decision I had to make, I made for you and James, with our future in mind."

"Why?" It was barely a whisper of sound. She couldn't manage anything more.

"Because I can't stand to not have you with me, to have you both with me."

She bit her lower lip, looking into his eyes earnestly, searching for honesty. She had no idea what his intentions were, she never had because he'd never opened up and shared that part of his life with her. He claimed to want them to be together, that she and James were important, but he was making decisions without even consulting her.

"I don't know if I can believe you." She backed out of his arms, away from his touch, and wrapped her arms around her waist. He blinked, as if her calling his integrity into question hadn't even been a consideration.

"I've never given you a reason to doubt my word." She arched a brow in disbelief and Grant threw his hands in the air. "Is this really because I was too busy to call?"

"Too busy to call, too closed off to explain." She shook her head. "You can say that you made decisions with us in mind, Grant, but the reality is that you made decisions alone without even including me in any discussion."

"What?" He ran a hand through his hair. "What was I supposed to say, Bethany? That I might be going back to Memphis or to another team. Or that I might have a job in New York City, but I also might not have any job and that either way I still want you and James to go with me wherever I end up?"

She opened her mouth to speak but he didn't give her the opportunity.

"Because that would make perfect sense, right? You want me to open up? How about if I admit that I can't stop thinking about you or that I can't sleep because I'm dreaming about you? What about the fact that I was torn between a career I've spent my entire life cultivating and being willing to give it all up just to stay here where I might have a shot with you, even if it meant working the ranch with my parents?"

He closed the distance between them, his hand moving to the curve of her jaw. "Don't you get it, Bethany? You and James mean more to me than anything else, anything."

She searched his eyes, and this time she could see his heart there, open and vulnerable. "Grant."

"Bethany, I'm falling in love with you, with both of you. I didn't expect it and, damn it, I certainly didn't plan it this way, but I also can't help it. I wouldn't if I could."

Grant didn't wait for her to respond before he covered her mouth with his, seeking her answer in the passion that had always burned brightly between them. She clung to him, her arms circling his neck, her body pressed against his, their breaths and heartbeats becoming one. Bethany knew there was far more that they needed to discuss but, for this moment, his confession was enough. Grant's strong arms held her against him as his mouth plundered hers, the way his heart had stolen her will to resist him.

He was the first to regain control of himself and pressed his forehead against hers, his breath hitching in ragged gasps. "I love you, Bethany."

"Why didn't you say something before you left?" Her hand covered his cheek, the rough hair rasping deliciously against her palm.

"Because you deserved more than an out-of-work has-been. Until this week, I had nothing. I'd sunk everything into the ranch and had no future. I couldn't tell you unless I knew I had something to offer you."

"Grant," she scolded. "Is that really how you see yourself? You were injured, you're retired. That doesn't make you a has-been. If you were a has-been, they wouldn't have put you on the show."

"I didn't want to leave you and James. Not for that long. I'm doing guest spots once a week and they've agreed that most of those will be filmed at the L.A. station." She shook her head, but he curled his arm around her waist, drawing her back to him. "You said it yourself. James needs stability." He brushed his fingers through the hair at her temple. "Bethany, everything I want in my life is right here, in Hidden Falls, in this house. I guess the question is, do you want me?"

GRANT'S HEART DIDN'T beat as he waited for Bethany's answer. After what felt like forever, she met his gaze.

"Grant, when my ex-husband left me, I had no idea what was going to happen to me or James. I was able to finish school and was determined to give James a good life, but I knew it wasn't going to be the life I'd envisioned when I first married Matthew. I was bound and determined that I would protect James, both of us really, from ever being in a position to have someone hurt us again or to strip away everything we thought our future held." Her hands fell to his waist and she looked up at him with eyes filled with awed wonder. "And then we met you that day in the park.

"I wasn't ready for you, to feel the things I've felt since James ran out in front of you that day. But it hasn't stopped any of it from happening and, seeing how much knowing you has changed him for the better, how much it's changed me, I wouldn't do anything differently. You've taught me that I can trust my heart again, feel alive again. I'm falling so deeply in love with you, Grant McQuaid, that I would have followed you to the ends of the earth."

Grant wasn't sure that his heart could be any more full of emotion. Bethany loved him.

Before he could respond, she turned her attention to the footsteps at the top of the stairs. "James is up."

He heard the instant concern in her tone. In spite of the bomb she'd just dropped on him, she didn't give it a thought before she rushed to her primary role as a mother.

Grant followed her up the stairs and saw the blur of James' little body as he ran into the bathroom and they heard him retching. She hurried in behind him, holding his body as he vomited, his face pale and frightened.

"Shh," she murmured, even though he didn't have his implant microphones on. She glanced back at Grant. "Can you wet a washcloth for me?"

Grant pulled a cloth from the drawer and dampened it, passing it to her.

"Are you sure you are ready to sign up for this?"

Grant smiled at the woman on the bathroom floor, her arms wrapped around the little boy who'd held his heart captive from the first moment. *I've been ready for a long time*, he signed. He held up his hand. *I love you*.

She held her hand up in the same sign toward him. "What do you say we get this little guy back to bed?"

"I'll take him," he offered. Grant didn't hesitate in

scooping James from her arms, tucking the boy's feverish head under his chin.

"I'll get the thermometer and medicine." Bethany scooted between him and the door, hurrying downstairs.

Grant reached for the cool washcloth before carrying James into his room. The heat from his little body burned through Grant's shirt and the smell of sweat was heavy on the child as he slipped him between the sheets. As he tried to stand, James whimpered, clinging to him, and Grant's heart fractured. With memories of his mother in the forefront of his mind, Grant lay on the blankets next to James and let the boy curl into his chest for comfort, running the washcloth over his temple, quietly whispering soothing words to a boy who couldn't hear them. James laid one hand over Grant's chest, just above his heart. Grant ached, his mind searching for something he could do to make James feel better, but he felt helpless, unable to do anything but hold him and try to comfort him.

Bethany moved behind him, her eyes tearing slightly and looking tender. She laid her hand over James' on his chest. "He's feeling your words."

Grant wasn't sure he understood.

"He can't hear you but he can feel the vibrations on his hand when you talk. When he's sick, I sing to him a lot and he does the same thing to me. Wearing his implant microphones is sensory overload at times and this helps." She ran the temporal thermometer over James' forehead as the child fixed his glassy gaze on her face.

Tummy hurt? She signed. James simply nodded weakly,

curling closer into Grant's chest. Bethany glanced at the thermometer. "One-oh-two." She poured the medicine into a small cup and Grant helped James into a seated position to drink it. "This flu has been going around. I guess it was just his turn."

James turned in Grant's lap to face him. *Will you stay with me?* Even the movement of his fingers seemed weak.

The pleading Grant could see in his blue eyes made it impossible for him to even contemplate leaving. *I'll be right here*, he signed back.

Bethany's fingers moved quickly as she explained to James that the medicine would help his stomach and that he should go back to sleep but the boy looked at Grant warily, as if afraid he wouldn't do as he promised and stay. Grant knew he was the only one to blame for James' distrust, just as he knew there was only one way to remedy the situation.

"Lie beside him," he instructed Bethany, waiting for her to curl up against her son. Climbing into the bed, with the wall at his back and Bethany against his chest, he spooned behind her with his arm around both of them. "There."

Bethany leaned on one elbow and smiled down at her son. *See? Now close your eyes. Sleep*, she signed.

James did as he was told and it was only minutes before sleep claimed the child. His lashes fanned over his rosy cheeks as he curled into his mother, tucking his hand under his chin. Grant pressed his lips to the hollow at Bethany's ear, his arm curling around her waist.

"Is this what it's like?"

She tipped her head back slightly, sighing quietly. "Sometimes. He doesn't get sick very often though."

"You're a great mom." He'd already told her several times but she continually astounded him.

She brushed the hair back from James' forehead. "So you've said but you've been pretty amazing yourself. Next to my Dad, you've had more influence on him than any other man."

Grant felt the weight of her statement settle over his shoulders. He hadn't understood the full impact he'd had on James until this moment.

"Maddie said he was upset when I left." Bethany tensed and he didn't need her to confirm it. "I'm sorry. I should have talked to you sooner, should have explained what was going on. I've made such a mess out of this."

"No, you haven't. He's resilient. Obviously he doesn't hold anything against you or he wouldn't have let you tuck him into bed or asked you to stay. He loves you, Grant, probably as much as I do." She glanced backward at him over her shoulder. "Maybe even more."

Leaning over her, Grant brushed his lips against hers, but only for a brief caress. He pulled her and James closer against him, knowing without a doubt he was the luckiest man on earth.

Chapter Twenty-Six

BETHANY STARED AT the headline on the newspaper: *Hometown Hero Saves Hidden Falls Bobcats.*

The article went on to detail how Grant had decided to return to Hidden Falls following his retirement from the NFL to coach the local high school varsity team and the high hopes they had for him to drag the team from the mire of several losing seasons. So far he'd done exactly that with an undefeated team and the league championship to be settled at the homecoming game tonight.

She didn't miss the fact that she and James had been cropped out of the photograph of Grant standing at a podium and knew it had been at his request. He'd been extremely sensitive to her desire to keep their relationship as private as possible. It wasn't that people didn't know they were a couple. As a matter of fact, it seemed to be the main topic of conversation in the small town, right up there with what sort of wild animal was killing local livestock recently, but it wasn't mean-spirited or based on rumors. Instead, most people were extremely supportive, especially Grant's mother and sister, who had doted on James over the past six months. Sarah claimed James had given her a new lease on life and hadn't stopped hinting how much she'd like another grandchild running around the house to keep James company. Grant's brothers were ready to choke him for getting their mother started on the "grandmother train" again, but Grant didn't seem to care.

In fact, he'd recently mentioned to Bethany that they needed to start looking for a bigger house, one with several more rooms for the football team he wanted them to have someday. However, other than talking about their future like a far-off idea, they'd never discussed any concrete plans about anything. Things like when he should move in instead of staying over secretly, whether James should start calling him something other than Grant and the topic of marriage were brushed under the rug.

"What do you have there?" Strong arms circled her waist and she felt his lips brush the side of her neck, scattering all thoughts.

She held up the paper for Grant to see. "Another article about the incredible Grant McQuaid and how he's going to save the day by leading his team to victory." She turned in his arms and pressed a kiss to his waiting mouth, not caring who might see them on her front stoop. "Hopefully, you'll at least stay long enough this morning to have coffee."

"I can. As a matter of fact, I'll even make pancakes."

He lifted her off the ground and walked with her back into the house, settling her in the entry and shutting the world out behind him. "You're still bringing James by the field after practice today, right? I promised the team he'd be there to help."

She arched a brow. "I still don't see why you want him down there so early. He's the water boy. Won't he get in the way?"

He shrugged as if that was enough explanation. "The team likes having him in the locker room when they are getting pumped up. Besides, I think the cheerleaders want to put him on their float for the trip around the field tonight."

Bethany frowned slightly. She wasn't sure she was ready to have her little boy riding on the back of a flat-bed trailer with cheerleaders and God-only-knows-who for a driver. Grant leaned forward with a chuckle, as if he could read her mind. "It's fine. Jackson will be the one driving. Relax. I wouldn't do anything that might hurt him."

That much she knew was true. Grant had become the father figure she'd always wanted in James' life but had been too afraid to hope for, and his brothers were terrific role models for her son as well. They had taught him how to stand up to bullies without throwing a punch, and how to back it up when push came to shove as well as how to tell the difference. The same men who were teaching him how to fix ranch machinery were the same ones willing to spend hours listening to James practice reading and working on his speech. The McQuaid men were teaching her son the value of being manly but keeping a vulnerable soft side, ways to give and earn respect as well as how to fish, hunt and pee standing up.

And she'd seen Grant learn a few things along the way as well. Not only was he now practically fluent in ASL, but James was teaching him to slow down and enjoy each moment in the present instead of trying to predict a future that could change in an instant. They were bringing out the best in one another and she couldn't be happier.

Are you sure about that?

Bethany tried to cast the thought aside. She didn't want to feel ungrateful for the gift she'd been given, but she couldn't stop the discontentment from churning in her belly. She'd begun to wonder if they weren't stuck in a holding pattern, if they hadn't become too comfortable with one another and whether Grant was getting bored with the familiarity of it.

He'd been staying at his parents' ranch more often this past week, claiming it was to help his father before leaving for his job at the high school in the mornings, but she could see the hesitation in his eyes. She wanted them to find a time to talk about it, but he was too busy with coaching, not even stopping by her house until James was heading to bed most nights. He'd insisted that the two of them stay home this weekend with no interruptions. Maybe this would be the best opportunity for her to bring up her concerns.

"Sit," he instructed. "James is getting dressed and the batter is almost ready."

Grant slid a pat of butter onto the skillet before pouring the golden liquid over it. James' feet pounded down the staircase and she turned in her chair to see him sliding into the room in his socks.

"Hey, slow down, ace. No running in the house."

Grant looked up from the sizzling griddle and gave James a conspiratorial wink. "Mind your Mom."

James wrapped his arms around her neck from behind and she wondered where the time was going. He was losing his "little boy" look and starting to look more like the man he would someday become. "Sorry, I'm just excited."

"What's got you so happy this morning?"

James slid into his chair and Grant laid a plate of steaming pancakes in front of him. The pair exchanged an odd look before James turned his attention back to her again. "It's homecoming, Mom. It's the biggest game of the season and if we win—"

Bethany held her hands in the air. "I'm sorry for asking. Silly me," she teased.

How was it possible that in only six months, her son had become more like Grant than he'd ever been like her? She wasn't going to complain, she thought, watching the pair discuss the game tonight over pancakes dripping with maple syrup and powdered sugar—Grant's sugar-bomb concoction.

This was the life she'd always dreamed of for herself and her son—well, almost—but she was happy. She wasn't about to let her knack for overthinking the situation ruin what they had.

GRANT COULDN'T LET anything distract him from the game tonight, and his years of practice tuning out the world and focusing on the task at hand should have made it easy enough, but the box in his pocket was jabbing into his leg and he couldn't think of anything but what it contained—a vintage-style diamond ring that he would be placing on Bethany's hand during half-time. He'd been planning the spectacle for her over the last two months with the help of the coaching staff, his team and the head cheerleading coach. He could only pray that it was still a surprise.

Glancing over at James seated on the bench, the container of water bottles sitting on his lap, he gave the boy a thumbs-up as the clock wound down the last few seconds of the half. James scrunched his shoulders toward his ears, excitement written plainly on his face. He'd known for over a week that Grant wanted to ask Bethany to marry him. In fact, he'd asked James' permission before they called her father together. He'd even taken James with him to select the ring. How the boy had managed to keep the secret, Grant would never know.

A buzzer sounded loudly. "And that ladies and gentlemen is the first half with your Bobcats leading twenty-one to three."

As the eleven players from the field jogged back to the sidelines, Grant's stomach plummeted to his toes and his heartrate sped up to triple time. The cheerleaders ran out onto the field and the trucks pulling the flatbed trailers moved onto the track inside the stadium, circling in front of the standing-room-only crowd, blocking the players from view. He quickly pointed at James to follow Jackson onto the field and off to one side of the cheerleaders as Grant jogged behind the bleachers where he wouldn't be seen.

The band moved onto the field and the quick drumbeats and xylophone notes of Bruno Mars' "Marry You" began to play. The floats moved past the crowd, splitting on the track so that people could see the band and cheerleaders perform between them in the center of the football field. Several people started clapping as his brother country music star Linc McQuaid walked out onto the field with a wireless mic in his hand and began singing the song.

While everyone's attention was focused on the field, Grant jogged into the stands to find Bethany in her usual seat near the fifty-yard line. The look of surprise on her face made every bit of the secrecy over the past few weeks worth it.

"Grant? What are you doing here? Why aren't you in the locker room?"

Reaching down, he took her hand and lifted her to her feet. Before she could protest, he scooped the woman he'd come to adore in his arms and carried her down the stairs toward the center of the field. As the cheerleaders danced around them, Linc and the band finished the song.

As the last notes sounded, Grant settled Bethany on her feet again and reached behind him to turn on the headset mic he'd been fitted with before the game began. Suspicion colored Bethany's eyes and she bit her lip nervously, looking around at the crowd as if that might give her an indication of what he had in mind.

"Bethany Mills, I thought I had it all, and then I met you and James." Grant signed as he spoke. "The two of you changed my life and made me want more. I know you don't like big productions and being the center of attention, but the past six months have been the most incredible days of my life and I want the world to know it. I want to spend every moment of every day I have left in this life with you."

He saw Jackson nudge James from behind Bethany and the boy ran forward to reach one of his little hands into theirs. Grant reached into his pocket with his free hand and let James open the ring box as Grant dropped to one knee and the crowd around the stadium erupted in applause. Bethany lifted her free hand to her mouth, tears glistening in her eyes under the stadium lights with her hair blowing loose from under her team beanie cap.

"Bethany, will you do me the honor of becoming my wife? I'll do everything in my power to make you and James happy." James pulled his hand from Grant's and stood between him and Bethany, signing quickly.

You do.

Grant felt his heart fill with wonder for this little boy whose impulsiveness had changed his life so drastically, and he ruffled his blond hair in desperate need of a trim. "I love you, little man."

"I love you too, Dad." James threw his arms around Grant's neck and hugged him tightly.

Grant looked up at Bethany, tears now flowing freely

down her cheeks, rosy from the crisp October night. "What about you, sweetheart?"

She pulled him to his feet and pressed a kiss to his waiting lips. "I thought you'd never ask."

BEN TOSSED THE newspaper onto the kitchen table where it landed in front of Grant. "It really doesn't matter what you do, does it? You always seem to make headlines."

Grant chuckled into his coffee mug. "Jealous?"

"Hardly." He rolled his eyes and slumped into the chair. "This town has far bigger issues to deal with and all we keep reading about is the latest details of your love life."

Grant felt his heart quicken at this morning's headline: *She Said Yes.*

He still couldn't believe his luck. Bethany had not only agreed to marry him but to do it before Christmas at the ranch. As if he'd conjured them up by thinking about them, James' footsteps tromped into the kitchen, followed closely by Grant's bride-to-be. He rose and greeted her with a kiss, trying to keep a tight rein on the desire still smoldering after their private celebration last night.

"Ugh," Ben scoffed, rising from the table. "If I wanted to see this I'd go watch a chick flick. Bethany, you've ruined my brother."

"Jealous?" she asked with a laugh. Grant joined her.

"I asked him the same thing. He's in denial." Grant turned his attention to James. "Jackson's got Shorty ready for you in the corral and said he needs your help today. Your mom and I have wedding plans to arrange."

"Are you sure you want it before Christmas? That's an awfully small window to plan this."

"I'm not waiting a single second longer than I have to for you to become Mrs. McQuaid." Grant pulled Bethany into his arms, his heart pounding so loudly he was sure everyone for miles could hear it.

She smiled up at him, her eyes glimmering with hope. She'd endured hurt before him, undeserved rejection. He'd been cast aside and fought his self-doubt. But together, they were more than the heart-wrenching circumstances they faced. Grant didn't have to be a fortune teller to see the bright future ahead of them. He only had to look into her face, reflecting every emotion she felt for him, to know their marriage would withstand any obstacle that arose because their love was everlasting, and together, they'd healed one another.

Don't miss the next Hidden Falls novel!

Coming January 2017!

Acknowledgments

THIS BOOK WAS such an incredible challenge for me and I loved every moment of it. But I never worked on this alone, not for one solitary second.

First, thank you so much to Tessa Woodward! For all of the cutting, polishing and shining you do to make me look good. You are a magician. And, for the rest of the HarperCollins crew who treat us like diamonds, even if we are in the rough. I adore you, Nicole, Jessie, Caro and Pam.

I can't let another second pass without thanking my agent, Suzie Townsend, and the New Leaf Family (that's you, Sara!) for always being ready for anything from me, no matter what time of the day, or what day of the week. I couldn't do this without you!

For my Country Crew and the Avon Addicts! You ladies are indispensable and far too much fun. For my local girls—Kristin and Deb, we are definitely doing that again but this time, we bring a calculator! Rebecca and Codi—you two are the best cheerleaders a girl could ever ask for. I love you both!

For my nephew, Cody. We didn't realize just how much you would change our lives, Little Man. Thank you for letting me be a part of your journey!

For my kids, it was so fun for me to remember back to the days when you were little while writing about James. He is a little part of each of you, and all three of you are precious to me. I can't believe how fast you've grown up and I cherish every day as your mother.

Bryun, you are the light of my life, my own personal hero and I thank God every day for bringing you into my life when we were fifteen (even if you swear it wasn't for another year!) I can't believe we get to live this amazing life together but I'm so very grateful that we do.

Finally, thank you, my dear readers! Every one of you is what keeps me going each and every day when the words don't want to come, or the characters don't cooperate. I picture you waiting and get to work.

About the Author

T. J. KLINE was raised since the age of 14 to compete in rodeos and Rodeo Queen competitions, and she has a thorough knowledge of the sport as well as the culture involved. She writes contemporary western romance for Avon Romance, including the Rodeo series and the Healing Harts series. She has published a nonfiction health book and two inspirational fiction titles under the name Tina Klinesmith. In her very limited spare time, T. J. can be found laughing hysterically with her husband, children and their menagerie of pets in Northern California.

Discover great authors, exclusive offers, and more at hc.com.

Give in to your Impulses . . .
Continue reading for excerpts from
our newest Avon Impulse books.
Available now wherever ebooks are sold.

THIS EARL IS ON FIRE
THE SEASON'S ORIGINAL SERIES
by Vivienne Lorret

TORCH
THE WILDWOOD SERIES
by Karen Erickson

HERO OF MINE
THE MEN IN UNIFORM SERIES
by Codi Gary

An Excerpt from

THIS EARL IS ON FIRE
The Season's Original Series
By *Vivienne Lorret*

Vivienne Lorret's Season's Original series
continues with an earl whose friends are
determined to turn him into a respectable
member of society ... and the one
woman who could finally tame him.

Liam Cavanaugh grinned at the corrugated lines marking his cousin's lifted brows. It wasn't often that Northcliff Bromley, the Duke of Vale and renowned genius, showed astonishment.

Bending his dark head, Vale peered closer at the marble heads within the crates. "Remarkable. Even seeing them side by side, I hardly notice a difference. The *fellows* will be fascinated when you present this to the Royal Society at month's end."

"It was pure luck that I had the original as well." Liam shrugged as if he'd merely stumbled upon the differences between a genuine article and an imposter.

Vale turned, and his obsidian eyes sharpened on Liam. "No need to play the simpleton with me. You forget that I know your secret."

Liam cast a hasty glance around the sconce-lit, cluttered ballroom of Wolford House, ensuring they were alone. Fortunately, the vast space was empty aside from the two of them and a dozen or more large crates filled with artifacts. "By definition, a secret is that of which we do not speak. So lower your voice, if you please."

No one needed to know that he actually studied each piece of his collection in detail—enough that he'd learned how to spot a forgery in an instant.

"Afraid the servants will tell the *ton* your collection isn't merely a frivolous venture? Or that your housekeeper's complaints of dusty urns and statues crowding each room would suddenly fall silent?" Vale flashed a smile that bracketed his mouth with deep creases.

Liam pretended to consider his answer, pursing his lips. "It would be cruel of me to render Mrs. Brasher mute when she finds such enjoyment in haranguing me."

"She may have a point," Vale said, skirting in between two crates when a wayward nail snagged his coat, issuing a sharp *rip* of rending fabric. He stopped to examine the hole and shook his head. "Your collection has grown by leaps and bounds in the past few months. So much so that you were forced to purchase another property to house it all."

"The curse of immense wealth and boredom, I'm afraid."

His cousin's quick glower revealed that he was not amused by Liam's insouciant guise. Then, as if to punish him for it, he issued the foulest epithet known to man. "You should marry."

Not wanting to reveal the discomfort slowly clawing up his spine, Liam chuckled. "As a cure for boredom?"

Vale said nothing. He merely crossed his arms over his chest and waited.

It was a standoff now. They were nearly equal in regard to observation skills, but apparently Vale thought he had the upper hand.

Liam knew differently. He crossed his arms as well and smirked.

If anyone were to peer into the room at this moment, they might wonder if they were staring at matching wax figures. The two of them looked enough alike in build and coloring to be brothers, but with subtle differences. Vale's features were blunter, while Liam's were angular. And Vale's dark eyes were full of intellect, while Liam's green eyes tended to reveal the streak of mischief within.

"Marriage would do you good," Vale said.

Liam disagreed. "You're starting to sound like Thayne, always hinting of ways to improve my social standing."

The Marquess of Thayne was determined to reform Liam into the *ton*'s favorite pet—the Season's *Original*. In fact, Thayne had been so confident in success that he'd wagered on the outcome. *What a fool.*

"I never hint," Vale said.

Liam offered his cousin a nod. "True. You are a forthright, scientific gentleman, and I appreciate that about you. Therefore, I will give you the courtesy of answering in kind: No. I should *not* marry. I like my life just as it is." He lifted his hands in a gesture to encompass his collection within this room. "Besides, I could never respect a woman who would have me."

Vale scoffed. "Respect?"

"Very well. I could never *trust* a woman who desired to marry me. Not with my reputation. Such a woman would either be mad or conniving, and I want neither for a wife."

He'd nearly succumbed once, falling for the worst of all deceptions. After that narrow escape, he'd vowed never to be tricked again.

"Come now. There are many who care nothing for your reputation."

That statement only served to cement his belief. If his despoiled reputation were the only thing keeping him far afield of the *ton*'s conniving matchmakers, then he would make the most of it. And the perfect place to add the crème de la crème to his list of scandalous exploits would be at Lady Forester's masquerade tonight.

After all, he had a carefully crafted reputation of unrepentant debauchery to uphold.

Liam squared his shoulders and walked with his cousin to the door. "If the Fates have it in mind to see me married before I turn sixty, then they will have to knock me over the head and drag me to the altar."

An Excerpt from

TORCH
The Wildwood Series
By Karen Erickson

**USA Today bestselling author Karen
Erickson continues her Wildwood series
with a hot firefighter who knows that
enemies make the best lovers . . .**

Wren Gallagher wasn't the type to drown her sorrows in alcohol, but tonight seemed as good a time as any to start.

"Another Malibu and pineapple, Russ," she said to the bartender, who gave her a look before nodding reluctantly.

"That's your third drink," Russ said gruffly as he plunked the fresh glass in front of her.

She grabbed it and took a long sip from the skinny red straw. It was her third drink because the first two weren't potent enough. She didn't even feel that drunk. But how could she tell Russ that when he was the one mixing her drinks? "And they're equally delicious," she replied with a sweet smile.

He scowled at her, his bushy eyebrows threaded with gray hairs seeming to hang low over his eyes. "You all right, Wren?"

"I'm fine." She smiled but it felt incredibly false, so she let it fade before taking another sip of her drink.

Sighing, she pushed the wimpy straw out of the way and brought the glass to her lips, chugging the drink in a few long swallows. Polishing it off like a pro, she wiped her damp lips with the back of her hand as she set the glass down on the bar.

A low whistle sounded behind her and she went still, her breath trapped in her lungs.

"Trying to get drunk, Dove?"

That too-amused, too-arrogant voice was disappointingly familiar. Her shoulders slumping, she glanced to her right to watch as Tate Warren settled his too-perfect butt onto the barstool next to hers, a giant smile curving his too-sexy mouth as he looked her up and down. Her body heated everywhere his eyes landed and she frowned.

Ugh. She hated him. His new favorite thing was to call her every other bird name besides her own. It drove her crazy and he knew it. It didn't help that they ran into each other all the time. The town was too small, and their circle of mutual friends—and family members—even smaller.

Tate worked at Cal Fire with her brothers Weston and Holden. He was good friends with West and her oldest brother, Lane, so they all spent a lot of time together when they could. But fire season was in full swing and Tate had been at the station the last time they all got together.

She hadn't missed him either. Not one bit.

At least, that's what she told herself.

"What are you doing here?" Her tone was snottier than she intended and he noticed. His brows rose, surprise etching his very fine, very handsome features.

He was seriously too good-looking for words. Like Abercrombie & Fitch type good looking. With that pretty, pretty face and shock of dark hair and the finely muscled body and *oh shit*, that smile. Although, he wasn't flashing it at her right now like he usually did. Nope, not at all.

"I'm assuming you're looking to get drunk alone tonight?

I don't want to get in your way." He started to stand and she reached out, resting her hand on his forearm to stop him.

And *oh wow*, his skin was hot. And firm. As in, the boy's got muscles. Erm, the man. Tate could never be mistaken for a boy. He was all man. One hundred percent, delicious, sexy man . . .

"Don't go," she said, her eyes meeting his. His brows went up until they looked like they could reach his hairline and she snatched her hand away, her fingers still tingling where she touched him.

Whoo boy, that wasn't good. Could she blame it on the alcohol?

Tate settled his big body back on the barstool, ordering a Heineken when Russ asked what he wanted. "You all right, bird?" His voice was low and full of concern and her heart ached to say something. Admit her faults, her fears, and hope for some sympathy.

But she couldn't do that. Couldn't make a fool of herself in front of Tate. She'd never hear the end of it.

So she'd let the bird remark go. At least he hadn't called her Cuckoo or Woodpecker. "Having a bad day," she offered with a weak smile, lifting her ice-filled glass in a toasting gesture. At that precise moment, Russ delivered Tate's beer, and he raised it as well, clinking the green bottle against her glass.

"Me too," Tate murmured before he took a drink, his gaze never leaving hers.

Wren stared at him in a daze. How come she never noticed how green his eyes were before? They matched the beer bottle, which proved he didn't have the best taste in beer, but she'd forgive him for that.

But, yes. They were pretty eyes. Kind eyes. Amused eyes. Laughing eyes. Sexy eyes.

She tore her gaze away from his, mentally beating herself up. He chuckled under his breath and she wanted to beat him up too. Just before she ripped off his clothes and had her way with him . . .

Oh, jeez. Clearly she was drunker than she thought.

An Excerpt from

HERO OF MINE
The Men in Uniform Series
By Codi Gary

The men of Codi Gary's Men in Uniform
series work hard and play hard . . . but
when it comes to protecting the women
they love, nothing stands in their way.

Tyler Best didn't believe in fate.

Fate was an excuse people who'd experienced really bad shit or really astounding luck used in order to explain how their lives tended to twist and turn. Fate was a fantasy.

Tyler was a realist. He didn't rely on some imaginary force to direct him. He'd taken chances and gotten knocked on his ass a few times, but he kept going because that's what life was. You didn't give up when it got hard.

Even in the face of devastating loss.

Tyler stared at the picture of Rex, his military dog, and the ache in his heart was raw, even eight months later. Rex had been his for three years before getting killed in combat. While Tyler was overseas, away from his family and friends, the dog had been his best friend, bringing him great comfort. When he'd lost Rex, he'd almost quit working with dogs. It had been difficult to be around them.

Yet, here he was, waiting to be led back to the "last day" dogs at the Paws and Causes Shelter. It was his first time here, as it was relatively new. Most of the time he visited Front Street Animal Shelter or the one off of Bradshaw, but new rescues and shelters were being added to the program every day.

Ever since he'd become the head trainer for the Alpha Dog Training Program, a nonprofit created to help strengthen the connection between military personnel and their community, he'd become the last hope for a lot of dogs. If they passed their temperament test, they'd join the program. Not all of them did, and on those days it was hard to remember all the lives the program saved. It was hard to walk away from a dog's big soulful eyes when Tyler knew the only outcome was a needle filled with pink liquid death, but he couldn't save them all.

Just like he couldn't save Rex.

"Sergeant Best?" a woman called from behind the reception desk.

Tyler stood up and slipped his phone back into his pocket. "Yes, ma'am."

"You can go on through. Our tech, Dani, is waiting in the back to show you around. Just straight back; you'll see the double doors."

"Thank you." Tyler opened the door, assaulted by high-pitched barks of excitement and fear. As he passed by the kennels, he looked through, studying the dogs of all shapes and sizes. He wasn't sure why he was so melancholy today, but it had been coming on strong.

He pushed through the double doors and immediately realized the man and woman inside were arguing. Loudly.

"No, he has more time. I talked to Dr. Lynch, and he promised to give him until the end of the day in case his owners claim him." This was shouted by the woman with her back to him, her blonde ponytail swinging with every hand gesture.

"Don't be naïve. You've been here long enough to know

that he won't be claimed." This was said by the thin, balding man in the lab coat, who was pushing sixty and had the cold, cynical look of someone who'd been doing his job too long. Tyler had seen it on the faces of veterans who had found a way to steel themselves against the horrors that haunted them. But once you shut that part off, it was hard to find it again. "Even if they come looking, they'll just tell you to put him down anyway. If they had the money to pay for his care, then they could afford a proper fence. All you're doing is putting off the inevitable and wasting valuable pain meds."

He tried to sidestep the blonde, who was a good head shorter, but she planted herself right in his path. When she spoke, her voice was a low, deadly whisper. "If you make one more move toward that cage, I will body check you so hard you'll forget your own name."

Tyler's eyebrows shot up, and he crossed his arms, hoping like hell the guy tested her. He really wanted to see her Hulk out.